New Wings

New Wings

Donna Stanley

CREATION
HOUSE

NEW WINGS by Donna Stanley
Published by Creation House
A Charisma Media Company
600 Rinehart Road
Lake Mary, Florida 32746
www.charismamedia.com

Unless otherwise noted all Scripture quotations in this publication are from *The Message: The Bible in Contemporary English*, copyright © 1993, 1994, 1995, 1996, 2000, 2001, 2002. Used by permission of NavPress Publishing Group.

Design Director: Bill Johnson
Cover design by Lindy Packard and Nathan Morgan

Visit the author's websites: www.donnastanley.com and www.facebook.com/newwingsbook

Library of Congress Cataloging-in-Publication Data: 2012955787
International Standard Book Number: 978-1-62136-336-1
E-book International Standard Book Number: 978-1-62136-337-8

Although this is a work of fiction, the supernatural encounters portrayed in this book are based on true events that have happened to real people.

While the author has made every effort to provide accurate telephone numbers and Internet addresses at the time of publication, neither the publisher nor the author assumes any responsibility for errors or for changes that occur after publication.

First edition

13 14 15 16 17 — 9 8 7 6 5 4 3 2 1
Printed in Canada

DEDICATION

For those who "see" in silence.

ACKNOWLEDGMENTS

FIRST AND FOREMOST I want to thank my heavenly Father, the originator of all that is creative. Without Him, none of this story could have seen the printed page.

Thank you to Lindy Packard, who read the first couple of pages and began to cry. That moment launched this work into the book form that I knew had to be written. You kept me biblically accurate. I'll always appreciate your support and vulnerability in sharing your story. You are a wonderful friend and a gifted seer.

Without the support of my husband, Jonathan, and my daughter, Olivia, I would not have felt the freedom to put the countless hours into this project. Thank you for the hours you gave up so that I could bring this story to life.

I also wish to thank Gordon Cooper and Tim Duzik for the "umph" they added to some of my scenes, and for their input and support.

Thank you, Kristin Minotti, for the author photography.

Thanks to many others (you know why you are listed here): Elaine Miller, Elise and Dave Cosgrove, Sylvia Stansfield, Jason Oksa, Brenda Vogel, Bev Wales, Mom, and my big sis, Debbie.

For all of those out there who see themselves within these pages, thank you for your faithfulness to your gift. And no, you are not crazy. You are chosen.

Many thanks to Kathy Ide for meticulous editing, never-ending patience, prayer, mentoring, and friendship. I literally could not have finished this project without you.

Thank you, Frank Peretti and C. S. Lewis, for kicking open the doors that many of us Christian novelists are walking through now. We all owe you a debt of gratitude.

Last of all, thank you, Gideon. You know why.

PREFACE

I KNEW I WAS in trouble when I saw the menacing shadow lurking in a corner of my dark bedroom. An invisible fist twisted my heart until it felt like it would explode. Unseen hands gripped my mind, paralyzing me with fear.

The shadow emerged, and I saw a grotesque face with hollowed-out eyes and skeletal features framed by a black cloak. I sensed a fire of hate in its crimson eyes as they flashed at me. I knew it intended to kill me. But I couldn't move. I was pinned to my bed.

Its rage enveloped me as it choked me with its bony fingers. My head swam as I gasped for oxygen. Was this the end?

My eyes rolled back in my head. As I attempted to draw one final breath, I saw a flash of light. I was sure my spirit had departed from my body.

But as I gave in to inevitable death, the brilliant light lingered. When I focused on it, I recognized him. The one who was sent to fight for me. The one who had promised to battle beside me.

That's when I realized that I was not in this alone. And that the struggle was far from over.

This is not a love story. No. This is war.

Chapter 1

MY BREATH BECAME shallow as I left the school gym after volley-ball practice, wondering if I'd see *him* again.

Would Mr. Super-Hot be waiting for me? He'd been in the parking lot for two days now, leaning against his shiny red Camaro with tinted windows and chrome wheels. As I walked toward my rusty brown Honda, he stared right at me. Part of me hoped he was a new transfer student who didn't know I was probably the only seventeen-year-old girl in our class who'd never had a boyfriend. Part of me wondered if he was a stalker. At least I wasn't alone in the parking lot. Other students were with me.

I looked away, acting like I hadn't noticed him. But I had my ignition key poking out from between my fingers like a small blade just in case.

Yesterday I saw him again. Same time, same place. Same hot-looking guy standing next to his red Camaro, staring at me. I dared to take a few glances at him. His eyes followed me all the way to my vehicle. I felt both nervous and excited.

Today, as I rounded the corner of the gym, there he was, looking my way again as if he knew I'd be in this exact spot at this very moment.

This was getting bizarre. A little bit frightening, yet at the same time thrilling.

I hurried to my car and jammed the key into the lock. As soon as I felt the click, I jerked the door open, tossed my gym bag and purse onto the front passenger seat, and started the engine. Stretching the seat belt across my shoulder gave me a slight sense of security, but that feeling left when I looked in the rearview mirror and saw Hot Guy get in his car.

My tires screeched a little on the blacktop as I sped toward the exit, my blonde ponytail banging off the headrest as the car bounced over the speed bumps. I was probably overreacting. Most likely he was harmless. But I'd seen too many movies about girls being abducted and heard too many warnings from my parents about strangers.

Hoping to lose him, I raced along several side streets, making numerous right and left turns, hardly slowing down for stop signs, constantly checking the rearview mirror for any trace of that red Camaro.

When I finally figured I'd evaded him—or he'd given up chasing me or maybe never started in the first place—I realized I had no idea where I was.

Dense forest surrounded me, with thick greenery on both sides. The sun, already dipping close to the horizon, barely made it through the mass of huge, gnarly trees with overlapping leaves.

The paved road turned to crunchy gravel. Just then I noticed the yellow low-fuel light on my gas gauge. How long had that been on?

Sweat tickled my upper lip.

The engine sputtered and coughed. I wrestled the steering wheel to get my Honda to the side of the road.

I had to call my dad. Hopefully he'd be able to find me. I tried to recall the last street sign I'd seen. Was it Old Johnson Road? Something like that.

I grabbed the cell phone out of my purse. No battery bars. Stupid technology! I tossed the phone back into my purse. Now what?

The ticking of the car's engine as it cooled felt like the second hand of a clock counting down to my demise. Sweat drenched my forehead and armpits.

God, what should I do?

Seeing no alternative but to try to find a main road, I opened the door, gathered my gym bag and purse, and got out of the car. I looked up the road ahead of me, wondering where it led.

The sound of tires on gravel made me whirl around. I squinted at the headlights coming my way.

Had God sent someone to rescue me? Or was this the part of the suspense movie where the girl alone in the woods is attacked, chopped up in little pieces, and buried somewhere in the mud?

Jumping back in the car, I threw my things on the passenger seat and snapped the locks on both doors. *God, please let it be someone who can help me—at least let me use their cell phone to call somebody!*

In the rearview mirror I watched the car pull to a stop behind mine. When the headlights turned off, I saw the bright red hood of a Camaro.

The door opened and closed. The driver got out and ambled toward me.

My good-looking stalker rapped on the glass. "Having trouble, ma'am?" The muffled voice sounded friendly and polite. But then, weren't all serial killers friendly and polite at first?

"Um...I...I think I'm out of gas."

He made a spinning motion with one finger, pointing at the window, and cupped his ear with the other hand. Apparently he couldn't understand what I was saying. Did I dare open the window? Maybe just a crack. But a crack was all it took to slip in a gun. Or tear gas. Or flesh-eating acid.

I definitely had to stop watching those movies.

He reached for the door handle. Taking that move as a threat, I jerked toward the passenger seat. He backed away, his hands up and palms out.

His features were so perfect he could have been a model in a magazine. His wavy blond hair and light complexion reminded me of an ivory statue I'd seen in an art gallery once. Surely someone this gorgeous couldn't be all bad.

I hit the button for the window and opened it an inch. "I ran out of gas." I felt embarrassed but also a little excited that this great-looking guy had come to my rescue. I marveled at his perfect timing yet panicked a bit at how uncanny it was that he had found me.

"I can run home and get some gas out of the garage. I live just down the road, on Sullivan Street. It'll only take about fifteen minutes to get there and back."

I recognized the address. It was in one of the super-classy neighborhoods nestled in the rolling hills of Maryland horse country. Still, I didn't dare get out of the car. "That sounds great. Thanks."

"Are you going to be OK?"

"I'll be fine."

"I'm Mike." He looked directly into my eyes, causing knots to form in my stomach.

"Olivia," I said, averting my gaze from his.

When I didn't roll down the window any more, Mike returned to his car and took off down the road.

I felt foolish for being so cautious. I should have gotten out of the car to thank him instead of treating him like a creep who was going to attack me at the side of the road. But how could I know for sure?

For what seemed like an eternity, I waited to spot his headlights coming over the hill. I opened the window farther to let in more air. The familiar sound of chirping cicadas made me feel as if I had some company out here in the middle of nowhere.

With nothing to do but wait, my mind rehearsed what I would say when Mike returned. Each scenario made me groan at how horrible I was at striking up conversations with guys.

I tapped my index finger on the steering wheel. If he didn't come back, I'd have to find a pay phone, call my dad, and ask him to come get me.

He'd be irritated that I ran out of gas again. How many times had he told me to keep a close eye on the gauge? And to keep my cell phone's battery fully charged in case of emergency?

Headlights came over the hill in front of me.

I waited until the car pulled in behind mine, then I gathered my wits and got out, shutting the door.

As Mike approached carrying a red plastic container, I said, "I feel ridiculous for hiding in my car when you pulled up earlier." I stuffed my hands into my jacket pockets and peered up at his face. His kaleido-scope-like blue eyes were almost translucent.

"No problem, ma'am. I'm not offended." His soothing voice matched his genteel words. I almost giggled at him calling me *ma'am*.

As he emptied the contents of the container into my gas tank, I tried to think of something to say. Nothing intelligent came to mind.

"How far do you live from here?" he asked.

"Just a few miles."

"This should get you home then."

"Can I pay you for the gas?"

"No. I'm glad to help."

I don't want you to leave, said the voice in my head, which had turned strangely bold all of a sudden.

Mike cast a knowing gaze at me, as if he'd heard my thoughts. Looking slightly flustered, he cleared his throat and returned to the task of filling my gas tank.

I twirled my long blonde hair as I watched him pull the nozzle of the red container out of the tank. "Thanks again."

"My pleasure." Crinkles formed at the sides of his eyes when he smiled. "Maybe I'll see you around?"

"Maybe." Since he'd been watching me from across the school parking lot for the past three days, seeing him again seemed pretty likely.

Strangers usually terrified me, but I felt as if I'd known Mike for years. Why did my fears suddenly subside?

"I should get home before my parents start to worry."

Mike nodded and returned to his Camaro. Before getting in, he waved. I waved back, then got in my Honda and closed the door.

I turned the key and the engine started. When I glanced in the rear-view mirror, Mike and his car were gone. I stretched around to look out the back window. There was nothing but the road and the shadows of trees.

How could he have disappeared so fast? I hadn't heard his engine or seen his car pull out.

Goose bumps prickled my arms and rose all the way to my face.

I remembered something I'd heard in church last Sunday. The preacher had talked about people entertaining angels unaware, like when Abraham served dinner to some angels in the Bible. I wondered if I had just entertained an angel. I never thought that one might come to my rescue, perform some menial task, and then suddenly disappear. But I didn't have a better explanation.

During the sermon I had prayed that God would somehow let me know if I had a guardian angel. It seemed like a good idea at the time. High school can be pretty difficult to navigate. I figured a girl could use someone to look after her. Had God actually answered my prayer?

I rolled my eyes. *What a stupid idea. A guardian angel wouldn't look like a hot guy, nor would he drive a red Camaro.* My imagination always did get the best of me.

Arriving home, I parked the car in the garage and sat there a few minutes, waiting for my pulse to settle. Finally, I grabbed my books and headed into the house.

When I entered the kitchen I smelled meatloaf. Since I arrived an hour after dinner whenever I had volleyball practice after school, Mom usually put a plate of leftovers in the refrigerator for me. I wasn't at all hungry, especially not for meatloaf, so I headed straight for my room.

"Hey, Goldilocks," my dad hollered from the living room. "Can't you even say hello?"

"You're late," Mom called out. She always worried when I didn't get home on time. She'd lost her sister in an automobile crash when they were both in high school, so I understood the reason for her overprotectiveness. But it still grated on my nerves.

I went into the living room, where my mom's favorite candle burned in its usual place on the mantel, filling the room with the aroma of sweet cinnamon spice. Dad sat in his wingbacked leather chair to the right of the fireplace, a hardback novel in one hand and his reading glasses in the other. Mom lowered the magazine she'd been reading and looked up at me.

"Everything all right?" Dad leaned forward in his recliner.

Mom tilted her head, her eyes squinting as if she were trying to figure out why I was late without my saying a word.

"I ran out of gas. But some nice man stopped and brought me some." I left out the details that my rescuer was young and attractive.

Dad shut his book and sank back into his chair. "How many times have I told you to keep a close eye on the gas gauge?"

"I know, Dad. I'm sorry."

One corner of my mom's mouth twisted up in disapproval. "You could have called. Your father would have been—"

"Battery was dead." I raised my cell phone with the blank screen. "And I know, I should always keep it charged. I'm going to go do that right now." I nodded toward the stairs.

"I'm just glad you're all right." Dad put his glasses back on and opened his book to where he had left off.

Mom went back to her magazine. I took that as a clue that it was safe to escape.

"Night, guys."

"Good night," they said in unison without looking up from their reading.

I clamored up the stairs to my room. All I wanted was a warm shower to clear my thoughts. But I couldn't stop thinking about Mike.

As the warm water rinsed the sweat off my body, I replayed the strange scene in my mind. I'd been too nervous to think about asking him what he'd been doing in the parking lot staring at me after practice for three days. Or how he found me on the side of the road.

If I saw him again tomorrow I would walk right up to him and ask him. At least I hoped I'd be brave enough to do that, and that I could say it without sounding ungrateful for his help.

I forced myself out of my stupor long enough to soap up and shampoo, then got out of the shower and dried off.

If I did manage to talk to him tomorrow, I'd also ask him how he disappeared so fast. After all, people don't just vanish into thin air.

What if he really were an angel—maybe even the guardian angel I prayed God would somehow show me? Would he be offended that I questioned him coming to my rescue? Had he already told God about my lack of appreciation or my skepticism? Would lightning strike me dead while I slept?

After changing into clean shorts and a T-shirt, I collapsed into bed and pulled the covers up to my chin. Lying there in the darkness I listened to the silence. I felt like a toddler wondering if the boogeyman might be under the bed.

God, I don't know what happened tonight. Or who that guy was. Please help me understand and know how to respond. Thanks for sending someone to rescue me—whoever or whatever he was.

As my eyes fluttered closed as I drifted off to sleep, I felt someone brush the hair off my forehead. My dad hadn't done that in years. It felt comforting.

A few moments later, peace fell over me.

As his charge finally fell asleep, Mike brushed his hand over Olivia's hair as he'd done a thousand times before. This time she moved when he touched her. She felt his presence!

Oh, how he hoped she would open her spiritual eyes. Few humans did. But that prayer she prayed last Sunday in church had activated his duty to a level that was seldom allowed. As a result, he'd been able to appear to her in human form.

He didn't want to scare her, so he'd chosen to look like an attractive young man—or at least what she perceived as attractive. He'd thought the red Camaro was a nice touch, but she still seemed afraid.

Mike recalled the day she was born. He'd pressed his forehead against the glass of the hospital ward alongside her father. They'd both beamed with pride, peering in at the little bundle wriggling in her tiny plastic bed.

Earlier that day her mother had prayed for angels to protect her. Mike was there before she even prayed. He'd been with her ever since—and would be with her till she took her final breath on Earth.

This girl had already been a challenge. During her childhood years he'd saved her from falling out of trees, drowning in a pond, and various other near tragedies caused by her curious nature and wild imagination.

The dangers she encountered changed slightly when she entered her teen years. Adolescent girls were complicated. He longed for her to get over this boy-crazy stage. If she knew what these young guys were thinking, she'd run away. But telling her that wasn't part of Mike's job description.

She stirred again. He wanted to jump into her dreams to talk to her, but it wasn't time yet.

Olivia still had no idea how specifically God had answered her prayer to show her she had a guardian angel. Mike was always amazed at how humans asked for supernatural things yet were surprised when they happened. Most of the time when he appeared to humans, they passed out. He'd been given permission to be a little more subtle and creative this time.

Olivia was one of the best things that had ever happened to Mike. Oh, he'd guarded many souls over the ages, but this one was special. She reminded him of Queen Esther and Mary—women in history chosen to change their world.

Chapter 2

I LET MYSELF IN the side door of my sister's home, eager to get my mind off my weird experience with Mike by focusing on my niece. I hadn't seen him in the parking lot after school today. I wished I'd gotten his address before we parted. Then again, if I had, I'd become the stalker.

"Hey, Diane," I called out as the screen door slammed behind me.

Petey, the family beagle, bounded into the kitchen and greeted me with high-pitched barking and enthusiastic tail wagging. I reached down and petted his velvety soft ears. "Hello, boy."

My three-year-old niece came running into the kitchen, golden curls bouncing, and wrapped her arms around my legs. "I missed you, Livvy!" Tessa's smile showed the gap between her two front teeth. With a slight lisp, she whined, "I haven't seen you in forever!"

"It's only been a week." Every Thursday, while Diane and Brian went on a date night, I played with Tessa, then put her to bed and flopped on the couch to watch TV and eat junk food.

"Hey, Sis." Diane entered the kitchen, putting in her left earring. "We'll be home by ten, as usual. Tessa's already had dinner." She glanced in the mirror by the back door, smoothing her shoulder-length brown hair.

I always felt like a buffalo next to a gazelle in her presence. Diane had a petite frame and was poised and feminine, always knowing the right thing to say in any situation. I was five inches taller, twenty pounds heavier, and a borderline tomboy who felt awkward around strangers. Side by side you'd hardly know we were sisters, except we shared our father's sharp jawline and slightly slanted nose.

Brian walked in tying his tie, his tailored short-sleeved shirt straining against his large muscles.

"Fancy restaurant tonight?"

"I'm taking your sister to the country club." He put his arm around his wife. "You ready, sweetheart?"

I loved my romantic brother-in-law. He was the typical tall, dark, and handsome type. The two made a stunning couple.

Diane grabbed her jacket off the back of a kitchen chair. "I'm all yours."

"Have fun." I watched them leave, hoping I'd have a marriage like theirs someday.

After a fun evening of games and cartoons, then taking Petey for a short walk, it was time to tuck Tessa into bed.

"Will you pray with me this time, Livvy?"

The one thing I dreaded about Tessa's bedtime was being asked to join in prayers. I didn't like praying out loud. It wasn't something my family did much. "Why don't you start?"

Tessa closed her eyes tight. "God bless Mommy, Daddy, Gee Gee and Geepa, and Olivia. Oh, and help Petey to stop eating Mommy's slippers. Amen." She looked up at me with her big blue eyes. "Your turn."

I spotted a little winged statue on Tessa's dresser. "Do you ever think about angels?"

"Yep. There's one right over there." Tessa pointed to a corner of the room behind me.

Goose bumps returned to my arms, and I resisted the urge to turn around and look. "What do you see?"

"My guardian angel. I always see him after I pray. He smiles a lot. That makes me feel good and helps me fall asleep."

"Are you scared of him?"

"No. Why would I be?"

"Have you told your Mommy and Daddy about him?" I could only imagine what my parents would say if I told them I'd seen an angel.

"Yep. They say it's a nice thing for me to pretend."

"But you're not pretending, are you?"

"No." Tessa's eyes opened wide. "Do you believe me, Livvy?"

"I do. And I don't think angels are anything to be afraid of either." I said it more for myself than for Tessa.

I tucked the covers around her shoulders. "I'll see you next Thursday."

As I headed for the door, I glanced at the corner but saw nothing. I felt both relieved and disappointed. "Tell your angel I said hello." I flicked off the light switch. "Good night, sweetie."

"Night, Livvy. I love you." "Love you too."

Instead of turning on the TV I sat on the sofa in silent contemplation with Petey curled up beside my feet. Three-year-old Tessa knew more about angels than I did.

I bowed my head and closed my eyes. If I was going to figure out the mystery of Mike, I'd need God's help. I also had to figure out how to keep a calm head and not panic.

I walked into the school cafeteria, ignoring the line of students picking up the usual Friday special: greasy pizza. Grasping my sack lunch, I scanned the room to find my friend Christina. She was at a table with Tommy and one of his friends. Christina giggled over something Tommy had just whispered in her ear. Probably one of the crude jokes he was famous for.

I slipped into the seat beside her. "We have to talk."

"What's up?" Christina turned to me, flipping her curly red hair with her hand. "You look like you just saw a ghost."

"Actually, I think I might have. But it's too long a story to tell here."

"I can't wait to hear it." Christina's dark green eyes opened wide. "But I'm slammed with so many tests next week I have to study all day Saturday. Can you come to my house on Sunday after you get home from church?"

"Definitely." I felt better about going to Christina's house than Christina coming to mine. Her parents didn't hover like mine did, so we could talk more freely.

I opened my bag lunch and pulled out a peanut-butter-and-jelly sandwich and a bottle of water. Christina returned to chatting with the boys. She laughed again at something Tommy said, and the high-pitched sound grated on my nerves. But at least she wasn't laughing at me. Not yet, anyway.

Greg Monahan sat down beside me, tucking his jaw-length auburn hair behind his ears. Greg was close friends with Christina. Their relationship was totally platonic, but I wondered if he'd been feeling left out since she started dating Tommy two months ago. I hardly got a chance to talk to her much anymore either.

"Hey, Christina," Greg said. "I was wondering if you—"

"Just a second." After a quick glance at Greg, she turned back to Tommy.

Greg slouched, looking crushed.

Maybe I needed to talk to someone more empathetic. I noticed Eden sitting a few tables away, her nose in a book, as usual. Eden was more grounded and focused than Christina. Plus her father was the pastor of my church.

I tapped Christina on the shoulder. "I have to talk to Eden. Catch you later."

She didn't seem to notice that I'd said anything. She was too focused on giggling at whatever the boys were saying.

I squeezed Greg's arm as I got up to leave. Then I leaned in close and said, "Hopefully this Tommy craze will wear off soon and we can all hang out together like we used to."

He looked up at me. "That'd be nice." He rolled his eyes.

I grabbed my sandwich and my drink and headed toward Eden. The book in her hands was from one of the vampire trilogies. I'd long since tired of such books, but other girls couldn't get enough.

I didn't see any food in front of Eden. Come to think of it, I couldn't remember ever seeing Eden eat. Maybe she was a vampire and didn't need human food. I chuckled to myself.

"Eden?" I tapped my finger on the edge of her book.

She looked up. "Hey, Liv!" She inserted her bookmark and closed the cover.

I sat opposite her and set my sandwich and drink on the table. "Have you ever read anything about angels?"

Her face brightened. "Why do you ask?"

"I'm thinking of writing about them for our English composition paper." Not entirely untrue.

"Actually, I've read some really interesting things about angels." Eden leaned in and whispered, "I've also read about fallen angels and demons. It creeps me out." She ran her fingers through her spiky dark brown hair.

"Do you think all that stuff is real?"

"I don't know. But it's fun to think about. It sure would explain a lot of the strange happenings you always read about, like ghosts and"—she glanced at her novel—"all that paranormal stuff." Her fair complexion seemed to pale further.

I took a sip of my water. Talking to Eden had definitely been a good choice.

Eden took off her reading glasses and set them on the table. "My mom took a class in anthropology at college, and she says every culture in the world has stories about spirits. Some cultures interact with the spirit world as if it's as normal as you and me talking right now."

"I wish I knew more about them."

Eden looked around, then said, "My grandmother claims she saw my dad's guardian angel once."

"Really?"

"He had a fever that was causing seizures. While Granny was praying for him, a light appeared near the top of the bed, about two feet behind him. The glowing orb touched my dad while he was sleeping, and then it disappeared. His body temperature dropped almost immediately. Just that morning, Granny had asked God to show her His angel, and she believes He answered her prayer."

"Do you believe it?"

"My grandmother is pretty normal. I don't think she made that up."

I stared at my half-eaten sandwich. A glob of peanut butter stuck to the roof of my mouth. If Tessa and Eden's grandma had both seen angels, was it really possible that I'd seen one too?

"My dad took a course in seminary that had a section on angelology. I looked through his notebook one time. There's some pretty cool stuff in there."

"I'd love to see his notes. It'd make great research for my paper. Could I come over tomorrow?"

"Sure. We could do a sleepover and you can ride to church with us on Sunday."

"Sounds great."

Just then Ty Hudson passed close to where we sat. He was the star quarterback of the football team, gorgeous and very popular. Eden fell to pieces whenever he was near.

"There's Ty!" she squeaked, fanning her face with a small spiral notebook. She turned her body away from him but glanced sideways, watching his every move.

"Why don't you talk to him?"

"Are you kidding? Anything I said would end up sounding like some clumsy stutter. Oh—he's looking this way!" She quickly opened her novel and hid her face behind it.

"That was stupid. He looked right at you."

"Yeah, sure. He doesn't even know I exist. He was probably just looking at the clock behind me."

"I doubt that."

The bell rang. I had to get to math class. "Talk to you later."

I left the cafeteria, dropping my empty lunch bag in the trash can by the exit. Two doors down was my classroom. I took a seat next to the window, which was opened a crack, providing me a slight break from the stuffy air in the room. Nate Ryan slid into the seat beside me and let out a loud belch.

"Gross!"

"Better for it to come out the attic than the basement!"

I grimaced. "Keep both doors closed, would you?"

I shuffled my desk and chair a little closer to the window and stared at the oak tree in the lawn outside while Mrs. Gleason copied equations onto the blackboard.

Is Mike really an angel? When will I see him again?

"Miss Stanton?"

I jerked to attention when I realized Mrs. Gleason had called on me.

"Is there something interesting outside the window that you'd like to share with the class?"

I dropped my pencil, which I'd been frantically tapping on my desk while in my fog. "No, ma'am. I'm sorry."

Several students stifled giggles.

I retrieved my pencil, then sat up and looked at my teacher.

Oh gosh, I hope she isn't going to ask me a question I don't know the answer to.

"Welcome back." Mrs. Gleason gave me a mocking smile, then returned to her scribbling.

Whew. No one is looking anymore. How embarrassing to be caught dreaming. But I can't help it. Mike intrigues me. I have to know more.

While listening to the *tap, tap, tap* of the chalk, I gazed at my textbook, hoping it would look like I was studying the information on the page. The words and numbers blurred as I checked out again.

Would Mike be in the parking lot again today? I hoped he would be. If he were, I had to ask him how he pulled off that disappearing act and why he was standing around in the parking lot. Part of me hoped he was a guy who'd heard about me and went out of his way to meet me. But what if he really were an angel? How cool would it be to have a real live guardian angel taking care of me, even when I did something stupid?

At volleyball practice my distraction made me miss several easy passes. I fumbled almost every serve, sending the ball straight into the net.

"You OK, Liv?" Coach asked.

I faked a limp. "My ankle is feeling a little stiff today."

"Maybe you should rest a bit."

"No, no. I'm sure if I keep moving it'll loosen up." If I sat out, our backup setter, Vicki Beecham, would fill in, and she always gloated when Coach put her in to replace me. I decided to drop the bad-ankle act. If Coach told me to rest the next couple of days, I could lose my position at the next game.

Coach waved his arm in the air. "Carry on!"

I did my best to keep my mind focused on my performance. The rest of the drills went much better. I almost forgot about my good-looking stranger.

But as soon as Coach blew his whistle to end the practice, I dashed to the locker room, grabbed my things, and raced down the hall. I pressed the metal crossbar on the door so hard a tiny shock of pain shot up my arm.

When I got outside I scanned the parking lot for a red Camaro.

I froze when I spotted a red bumper just past where my car was parked. *It's him!* And he wasn't clear across the parking lot this time.

My breathing quickened as I walked toward my Honda. Was he sitting in his car this time instead of leaning against it? Would he get out when I reached my vehicle? I tried to remember the lines I'd come up with to say to him, but none of the words I recalled congealed into any kind of intelligent sentences.

As I drew closer I noticed a few small spots of rust on the front bumper. My heart sank. It couldn't be Mike's car. His had a new paint job.

Then again, if Mike were an angel, maybe the rusty car would suddenly turn glossy, the rust spots would vanish, and he would magically appear.

No such luck. As more of the rusty red car came into my view, I saw it was a '66 Mustang. Vicki Beecham's car. She and her dad had begun restoring it.

I shuffled to my Honda, turned the key in the lock, and opened the door, all the while staring at the dull red car beside mine, still half expecting it to transform into a shiny Camaro.

I slung my purse and backpack onto the floor on the passenger side and slumped into the driver's seat.

Why hadn't Mike shown up today? Apparently, whether he was an angel or a human, he enjoyed watching me from a distance for a few days, but after talking to me once, he stopped coming around. Was I that boring? If so, I'd probably never see him again.

Eden and I spent all Saturday night talking about boys and volleyball, then watched *The Princess Bride* like we'd done during every sleepover since grade school.

I kept waiting for Eden to mention her dad's notebook about angels, not wanting to push it. Besides, after thinking about the subject some more, I wasn't sure I really wanted to read about angels. I didn't want to be convinced this was all real.

But then I thought about Mike. The image of him, seared into my memory, was enough to make me want to know more.

When I woke up on Sunday morning, Eden stood over me, a thick spiral notebook in her hand. "This is it," she whispered. "You can take it home, but bring it back as soon as you're done. He's really picky about loaning things out."

I stuffed it in my overnight bag. At home, I'd hide it in my closet in the box on the top shelf behind a stack of books, where I kept all my secret things. I'd keep it a week, then give it back to Eden—whether I got up the courage to read it or not.

Soon after the organ began to play, the church choir came out of the doors on either side of the stage. But they weren't the same people I was used to seeing, and instead of the usual burgundy choir robes, theirs were a brilliant white. *It must be a guest group.*

They sat in the choir loft during the service and sang hymns along with the congregation, but they didn't sing a special number. I wondered why. They stayed on the platform the whole service, even during the sermon Eden's dad gave.

As my family was leaving the sanctuary, I said, "I really liked the choir's gowns. But how come they didn't sing anything by themselves?"

"What are you talking about?" Mom asked. "The choir had this week off."

I shivered. "Dad—?"

My dad wrinkled his forehead. "Olivia, there was no choir this morning."

They really hadn't seen the choir!

"I gotta go." I rushed to the restroom, my stomach churning.

"Olivia?" I heard my dad call out. I dashed across the foyer and burst into the bathroom, racing past the first person in line, and grabbed the first stall that came open. I closed the door and leaned against it, nearly hyperventilating.

What would I say to my parents on the way home? Should I tell them I had a guardian angel—and that he was good looking?

They'd never believe me. Dad was pretty open-minded, but Mom would think I was even crazier than usual.

God, help me!

After opening the stall door I smoothed my hair in the mirror, then fled the restroom, avoiding the curious glances of the women in line.

I managed to slip out the front of the church without Eden's dad noticing me. I didn't feel like entering into the usual Sunday morning pleasantries with the pastor.

As I crossed the parking lot, my Sunday school teacher, Miss Beverly, cornered me. "Olivia, honey, how are you doing?" I was relieved to see her. At seventy years old, she had spunk unlike any other elderly person I knew. She gave me her usual wink.

"I'm good. How are you?"

"Blessed, as always. How's school?"

"Fine."

"That's wonderful. You've been in my prayers, dear." She reached out and gave my hand a squeeze as she always did when she greeted me. I squeezed it back.

This woman knew the Bible really well. And she would give me an honest answer. "Could I ask you a question?"

"Of course."

"Do you believe in angels?"

Bev laughed.

Oh, no. She thinks I'm crazy.

Her countenance became serious. "I absolutely believe in angels. The Bible says angels attend worship services. In fact, they may have been here this morning during church to worship with us."

Had Beverly seen the angels in the choir loft too?

She elbowed me in the side, and her cheeks dimpled. "Why do you ask, dear?"

"I have a writing assignment for English class, and I thought angels might be a good topic."

Miss Beverly came closer and put her hand on my shoulder. "I wouldn't ask anyone around here." She chuckled. "It's not that they don't believe in angels, mind you. They just don't think they have any effect on our lives. But just because someone doesn't believe in something, that doesn't mean it's not true."

"I want to be really accurate in my research. Do you know how I can find out more about angels?"

"Oh, there's a lot of information about angels in the Bible. And I bet you can get on that computer of yours and find plenty of interesting things on the Internet."

"You're right. I didn't think of that."

Feeling I could trust Bev, and hoping she'd believe me, I asked, "What would you say if I told you I'd seen an angel?"

"I'd say you are a very special young lady. But I already know that." Her eyes twinkled. "Would you like to talk more about this?"

"Oh, yes, please."

"Why don't we have lunch next Saturday? Come over to my place. I'll make you my special French onion soup. And you can meet my new dog. She's a chocolate Lab named Caramel."

"I love dogs. I can't wait!"

Bev hugged me again, so tight that I had to stifle a squeak. "I'll see you Saturday, sweetie."

Since Bev was willing to talk with me, I decided to cancel my get-together with Christina. She'd just want to talk about Tommy anyway, and that would be annoying.

After texting Christina I crossed the parking lot toward my parents' car.

Out of the corner of my eye I spotted Mike leaning against his car across the church parking lot. His arms were folded, and he flashed me a grin. I sheepishly waved at him. He nodded back at me. Seeing him again gave me a feeling of reassurance. It had been at least four days since I'd seen him last.

Maybe he really was my guardian angel. I sure wouldn't mind having someone like him close by all the time. And he wasn't hard on the eyes.

Reaching my parents' car, I got in. Glancing back at Mike, I noticed he'd done his disappearing act again.

Dad drove out of the parking lot. After a few minutes of uncomfortable silence he asked, "What was all that about the choir this morning, Liv?"

"Nothing." I stared out the car window, pretending to look at something interesting.

Mom stopped fixing her lipstick in the mirror and turned to look at me. "Really, honey, you have to stop with this crazy imagination of yours."

"It's not my imagination, Mom. Bev said—"

"Don't believe everything that woman says." Mom put the lipstick tube back in her purse. "She's a religious zealot."

"Mom—"

"I hope you don't end up like your cousin Kathryn." My mother adjusted the lace collar of her dress. "Her condition makes her think she sees all kinds of things."

"I don't have a multiple-personality disorder." I hoped.

Dad stretched his hands as he held the steering wheel. "Now, honey, maybe we should give Olivia the benefit of the doubt."

Mom crossed her arms over her chest and kept her freshly painted lips shut.

I appreciated Dad coming to my defense, although I sometimes wondered if he did it just to take the opposite side of Mom.

He peeked at me in his rearview mirror. "I think you should talk to Bev. She's a good woman."

"She invited me to have lunch with her next Saturday. Can I go?"

"Sure. She's a much better person for you to hang around with than some of those boy-crazy friends of yours." Dad shot a smile over his shoulder.

Mom's posture stiffened. I knew she wouldn't go against whatever decision Dad voiced. They may argue about it later between the two of them. But my father won almost every time.

"Thanks, Dad."

As I glanced at my reflection in the car window beside me, I could see Mike's reflection behind my shoulder. I shot around to look. Nothing there.

First chance I got, I'd get out that angel notebook Eden had given me and read it. I needed answers. If nothing else, I had to convince myself I wasn't crazy.

Chapter 3

WHILE MY PARENTS took their usual Sunday evening walk, I finally had the opportunity to check out the notebook Eden had given me. I grabbed it from its secret hiding place in my closet and curled up on the bed with a bowl of popcorn.

As I scanned the pages, certain phrases jumped out at me.

"Angels are God's messengers."

"Angels have free will."

"Angels are neither male nor female, but seem to appear as men most times. They can take on other forms."

I had to squint to decipher my pastor's scribbled handwriting.

"There are three types of angels: cherubim, seraphim, and archangels."

"One-third of the angels rebelled against God and were kicked out of heaven with Lucifer."

"Angels and demons war amongst themselves. In the end, the fallen angels will be sent to hell, along with Lucifer."

"For we do not war against flesh and blood."

I stopped reading. That meant that there *were* other supernatural beings we wrestled with.

I turned on the computer and did a search for *angels*.

After wading through links to the California baseball team's web pages, I came to a site that confirmed the same things I'd just read in the notebook. I looked at the Scripture passages used to back up the claims.

Why hadn't I ever seen or heard anything like this in church? All I knew about angels was what Hollywood depicted on TV shows and movies. I could hardly believe people actually studied this stuff.

One topic on the website caught my eye: "Angels as guardians." Matthew 18:10 said that children had guardian angels. *Tessa certainly has one. I'm sure I do too.*

My eyes started burning from staring at the computer screen. When I closed them, I felt drowsy. I shut down the computer, put the notebook on my nightstand, and lay down on my bed. Somewhere between sleep and consciousness, I started dreaming.

I was floating over the baseball field at my school. Just outside my field of vision, I saw a shadow. It danced out of sight as soon as I looked toward it.

I'd had this dream before. But this time, I spoke aloud. "Who's there?"

I heard only wind.

In an instant, I was hovering over horse farms and stone houses that filled our little town of Rising Sun. I saw my home in a little neighborhood right in the middle of horse country. A stream ran behind the house.

I descended and sat beside the gurgling water. I felt the wet grass beneath me.

Then the dream changed. A yellow Labrador retriever galloped down the hill toward me. It reminded me of the many stray dogs I'd found while growing up. Since I was an only child, and we moved a lot, I didn't have many close friends. But whenever I felt lonely, a stray pup appeared. I'd hug it, play with it, and talk to it for a few days and not feel so alone. Then it would leave.

The Lab stopped and leaned against my leg.

"I'm the one you've always wondered about."

The male voice seemed to come from the dog, but its mouth wasn't moving.

"If I appear to you again, will you be afraid?"

"It depends on what you look like."

The dog ran behind a bush. A beam of light flashed behind the hedge.

"Are you ready?" the voice said.

"Yes," I replied with a calmness that surprised me after realizing the voice sounded just like Mike's.

Mike walked out from behind the bush, stood about a foot away from me, and smiled. He crouched down, his forearms resting on his knees. He looked exactly as he did that night when he filled my gas tank, only this time he wore a red cotton long-sleeved shirt, jeans, and white sneakers.

My pulse sped up a bit. I was excited to see him again.

"Hello, Olivia." He held out his hand, offering to help me to my feet. I grasped it and rose.

I wondered who decided what form an angel took on. Was it the angel or God?

"We do," he said, obviously reading my mind. "But God has to approve of it."

"Have you ever appeared to me as a stray dog?"

"Yes." His lips curled into that same grin Mike had given me on the roadside when I ran out of gas.

"Thank you. You have no idea what that meant to me. Sometimes you were the only one I had to talk to."

"That's one of my favorite forms. It never scares anyone. And I like wagging my tail."

I giggled.

"I really enjoyed the times you hugged me." Mike dipped his head.

"Why are you letting me see you again?"

"Because I want you to believe that we're real." He gazed directly into my eyes.

Without blinking I asked, "Do other people see angels?"

"Those who have the gift do. Like Tessa." A slight grin tugged at one corner of his lips.

I wonder why I was chosen to see angels.

"Do people ever see the other angels? The dark ones?"

His lips hardened into a straight line. "Sometimes."

"I don't want to see them."

"You're not ready for that yet. For now, I'm here to teach you, prepare you, and protect you." He stretched out his right hand toward me. "Come. I want to show you something." He dropped his hand to his side after gesturing for me to follow him.

In the blink of an eye we were at Eden's house, looking in her window.

Eden sat on the floor, leaning against her bed, crying. She held a butcher knife in her hand. She sliced her upper arm near her inner elbow. Blood dripped down her skin.

I tried to cry out, but my voice didn't make a sound.

Now I understood why Eden always wore long sleeves, even at the hottest times of the year.

I remembered finding out about cutting in a book we had to read in health class at school. Was Eden trying to relieve some inner pain by causing outer pain?

Mike laid his hand on my arm. "Eden needs you. God wants you to help her."

How in the world was I supposed to help Eden? I couldn't tell her that I'd seen her cutting herself from outside her window.

Instantly, I was sitting on the grass by the creek again. The ground felt cold. I wondered how much time had passed.

"Is Eden really cutting herself right now? Or was that just a dream?"

"God can reveal things to you in many ways. Including dreams."

I recalled a dream I'd had last year about my friend Katie. When I woke up, I knew something bad was going to happen to her, but I didn't do anything. After all, it was just a dream. And I couldn't remember any specific details. But later that day, when I learned that Katie had committed suicide, I wished I would have talked to her.

"That was the voice of God," Mike said, reading my thoughts again.

"How can I know for sure when He's speaking to me and when something is just my own thoughts?"

"It takes time to recognize His voice."

I tucked my hair behind my ears, a habit my mother was always correcting me about. "Does everyone have their own guardian angel?"

"Yes. The number of angels outnumbers the stars. There are enough of us for everyone. Some of us are fortunate enough to be able to protect, guide, and comfort our charges. Some individuals are so influenced by the dark angels that we never get through." Mike shoved his hands into his jeans pockets and gazed at the ground as if reflecting on a past charge who'd been difficult to assist.

"For some reason I always thought you only had a guardian angel if you believed in God."

His head snapped up. "Do you find anything in the Bible that says that?"

I paused. I couldn't think of any way to dispute his rhetorical question.

"I hope I've not been too much trouble for you." I smiled meekly.

"Let's just say you kept me very busy when you were a child. That tomboy streak of yours had you climbing every tree you could and jumping off of things all the time. Did you ever wonder why you never had a broken bone?" He crossed his arms over his chest, awaiting my reply.

"You?"

"You bet."

I shook my head. "I can't believe it. You were there all the time." I paused for emphasis before I said the next couple of words. "Thank you."

"My pleasure. And my purpose."

Anxious to know more, I asked, "Does the guardian angel stay with the person forever?"

"Until he or she dies. Then we're reassigned to a new person or task. I've had many charges since God created humans."

I picked at the blades of grass in front of me, sitting cross-legged. "Well, I assume some of them died before you could do anything to help them."

Mike halted, turned, and his brow wrinkled. "Unfortunately, yes. Not every charge has been as pleasant as you."

I felt bad for him when I saw him cast another faraway look, perhaps recalling an unpleasant memory of some distant tragedy he'd witnessed.

"I'm sorry." The way he looked into my eyes after I spoke those words told me I was right.

He straightened his shoulders and sighed as if he'd just erased the image in his mind.

My obsession with world history leapt into my consciousness. It was a preoccupation that kept my nose in historical novels since I was twelve. The realization of who I was talking to made me giddy. Before me stood a being who'd been a literal fly-on-the wall witness to perhaps millions of historical happenings. What if he'd been a guardian to some historical character such as Abraham Lincoln? Before I blurted out some ridiculous question like that, I stuffed my enthusiasm and decided get to know what kind of information Mike could appropriately offer.

"What sets you in action? Besides God, of course." I hoped my question didn't sound stupid. Although he appeared to be someone my age, I knew he had wisdom and experience beyond what I could comprehend. But he certainly hadn't made me feel as if my curiosity was out of line.

"Most of the time prayer beckons us to do our duties. That's where you come in. Eden needs you to pray for her so her guardian angel can act on her behalf."

"Then I'll pray for her right away."

My eyes snapped open, and I found myself in my own bed, staring at the ceiling.

What I'd just experienced was far too vivid to be just a dream. I climbed off my bed, dropped to my knees, and prayed for Eden like I'd never prayed in my life.

Chapter 4

MIKE HOVERED OUTSIDE Christina Corrigan's window, listening to her and Olivia chat about boys and school. In spite of the innocuous conversations, he felt spiritual tension in the cool night air.

He worried about his charge's close relationship with this girl. Christina wasn't a believer. Her fascination with the supernatural and her sexual activities with Tommy Larson could pose a peer-pressure threat to Olivia.

Christina leapt off her bed. "I'm bored. Let's go on an adventure." She grabbed Olivia's coat off the back of her desk chair and tossed it to her.

"Where are we going?"

"I read something on the Internet about people who record graves."

Before Olivia could respond, Christina ran to her parents' room and came out with a tape recorder. "I suppose a cell phone or camcorder might work just as well, but this is what the person I read about used."

Olivia lingered in Christina's doorway. "I don't know about this. It sounds...weird."

"Come on. It'll be fun. And my parents won't be back for at least an hour, so they won't even know we left."

To Mike's disappointment, the two girls walked out of the house and headed for the cemetery adjacent to Christina's home. He followed them.

"I've always been fascinated by this place," Christina said in a low voice as she crept up to the old iron gate at the back entrance. "I know almost every gravestone by heart." The gate gave an eerie squeak as she rolled it back. "Sometimes I imagine the lives that must have been lived by the people whose names are engraved in stone here. I wonder what they looked like. Where they lived. How they died."

Mike cringed. This place was a sacred location where people grieved for loved ones, not a place for teenagers who had no clue what they were getting into playing stupid, dangerous games.

"Let's go somewhere else," Olivia suggested.

Great idea.

But Christina marched through the gate, and Olivia followed. Fog swirled around the graves, and a light mist fell from the sky.

The girls walked down a narrow path and stopped at a grave under an oak tree. Mike perched on the limb of a hundred-year-old cedar.

Christina shone her flashlight on the gravestone. "Check out this one. 'Jonathan Pincher. Born 1880. Died 1886.'"

"I wonder what happened to him." Olivia pulled up her coat collar. Mike wondered if she was chilled by the cool night air or a sense of trepidation and foreboding.

"Probably some kind of sickness. Medicine and doctors were hard to come by then. A lot of people died young." Christina pointed the microphone of her tape recorder toward the gravestone and pushed a button.

"What's supposed to happen?" Olivia asked.

"When we play it back later, we'll hear voices."

"This is giving me the creeps. Let's go back and get some hot chocolate."

"Not yet. Now, be quiet." Christina knelt and placed the mic closer to the grave.

Olivia hugged her arms tight around her middle and looked around, as if she hoped someone would see them and shoo them away. Mike wished he could appear and talk her into leaving this place. But his instructions for tonight were to observe, not to interact.

Christina stopped the recorder. "That should do it."

"Can we leave now?"

She shrugged. "Sure. I want to listen to this anyway."

They headed back toward the iron gate.

Once they were back inside the house, Christina lit a small candle on her bedside table. She rewound the tape and pushed Play. A strong hissing escaped from the speaker.

"Sounds like static to me," Olivia said.

"Sh." After the recording of the girls' brief conversation in the graveyard, a moaning sound came out of the tiny speaker. Olivia shuddered. Then a child's scream ripped the air.

The girls' eyes widened.

"Turn it off," Olivia shrieked.

Christina pushed the Stop button with a shaky finger.

Olivia grabbed her book bag. "I'm going home. This is too creepy for me."

"Wait." Christina grabbed her friend's arm. "I know this seems crazy. But Olivia, the occult is real."

"Why? Because you heard a weird scream on a tape recorder?"

Christina pulled Olivia onto the bed beside her. "About a week ago, as I was getting into my car to go to a party, I heard a muffled voice coming from the backseat. It sounded like it said, 'I'm here.' I figured my little brother was playing a practical joke. But when I turned around, ready to smack Timmy on the head for scaring me, I saw the face of a young boy about six years old. He had long dark hair pulled back in a leather tie, and his clothes looked like those pictures in our history books from the nineteenth century."

"I suppose you think that was the kid in the grave you just recorded."

"I'm sure it was. I believe Jonathan's trying to communicate with me."

"That's crazy." Olivia's face looked as white as the painted headboard.

Mike tilted his head toward heaven and spoke to the Father in a heavenly language on behalf of his charge.

Christina crossed her legs under her on the bed. "Greg and I have been dabbling with this kind of stuff since eighth grade. One year we tried astral projection."

"What's that?"

"We jump into each other's dreams and travel together. We've been to Disneyland, Hawaii, all kinds of places. We compare notes each morning to make sure each of us saw the same details."

Mike's hands curled into fists. Demonic games. Deadly games.

"Greg and I have also tried chanting spells."

"You know magic spells?"

"There are several on the Internet."

Olivia was shaking so hard, Mike thought she might fall off the bed. "Christina, the occult isn't a game. It's scary."

Mike grimaced at the word *game*.

"No, it's not. It's fun." Her eyes clouded. "Most of the time."

"What do you mean?"

Christina stared at a corner of her room to the left of the window that Mike's eyes peered into. "The last time Greg and I chanted some spells, I saw a dark figure in a trench coat and top hat standing right there." She pointed to the corner. "I freaked out and sent Greg home, told him I didn't want to do this anymore."

"That's good."

"That...apparition has come back every night since, always standing in the same spot. He never speaks or touches me. He just stares at me with these piercing green eyes." She shuddered.

Mike had encountered this kind of dark spirit before. They loved to appear in black, stalking and tormenting individuals. He seethed at how they especially preyed on the young and innocent.

Is…is he there right now?" Olivia's voice trembled.

"No. But it's not midnight yet. I try to go to sleep before that, but I never seem to be able to."

Olivia checked her watch. It was eleven forty-five. "I don't want to see anything like that. I gotta go."

Christina clutched her friend's arm. "Please stay. Please?"

Olivia hesitated. Mike hoped she'd leave. But he couldn't intervene. Not yet.

"I'll only stay if…"

"If what?"

"If you'll pray with me."

Atta girl!

"OK."

Olivia took her friend's hands in hers, and they bowed their heads across the bed from each other.

Another presence entered the room. It was Mike's fellow guardian angel, Gideon.

"Knew you'd be here," Mike said, winking at his friend.

"Good to see you, Mike. Wish it was under more peaceful circumstances. This is the first time I've seen my Christina pray." Gideon shifted his gaze to the wall behind the girls. "Here they come," he murmured.

Two black forms came through the walls of Christina's bedroom and settled in the corner right behind where the two were praying, the same cloaked figures he'd encountered many times before. They hated showing their faces. The tattered hems of their cloaks fluttered as they hovered up and down beside the wall next to the two praying girls. Typical spirits of confusion and fear.

Cloaking himself to not be seen by the spirits, he called for backup. Dozens of glowing orbs descended around the house, morphing into forms that resembled ancient Vikings. Among them was Gideon, Christina's guardian angel, having left the room and joining the new arrivals. They all nodded at each other on the lawn outside the house.

The warring angels who appeared stood in the front of the house, heads facing the window of Christina's room. They had shields, helmets, and shin guards. They raised their glowing swords above their heads and waited in silence.

The two black forms that had been in the bedroom fluttered onto the lawn, facing their opponents, pressing toward the warriors, their figures swelling to ten times their original size, hissing. Mike knew the dark spirits were outnumbered, and they would back off quickly. But suddenly, ten other black cloaked figures appeared and descended on his comrades.

Behind him, the clang of swords being removed from their sheaths reassured him.

Mike sounded a war cry, being the lead guardian angel here, signaling the charge. "For the chosen of God and for Jesus the Lamb!"

"For the chosen of God and for Jesus the Lamb," the angels responded.

With wails and screams of rage, the demons scattered in all directions, bouncing off the sides of the house and the trees in the nearby graveyard, ricocheting like shrapnel, dispersing in all directions around the neighborhood.

The name—Jesus—was all it took to make them flee. Mike knew it. Not every battle was this easy, but the prayer of his charge had strengthened their side immensely.

The screeches of their foes rent the air, ringing over the town like a hundred fire truck sirens.

When Mike and Gideon's comrades had disappeared, the two angels returned to Christina's window.

Olivia opened her eyes and said, "Amen."

"Let's listen to some music." Christina turned on the radio. Blaring rhythms filled the room, the bass pounding the walls.

Olivia changed the station. Christian praise songs replaced the rock band.

Olivia had accessed one of the greatest weapons in spiritual warfare. Praise. Mike winked at Gideon. "She's learning."

Gideon nodded. "What a pleasant charge you have. I hope yours rubs off on mine a little."

Mike held his hand out toward Gideon, palm out. "All in good time."

Christina placed her hand on Olivia's shoulder and smiled. "Thanks, Liv. I feel...I don't know how to describe it. It's like I'm lighter. Inside. I've never felt so much..."

"Peace?" Olivia offered.

"Yeah." Christina inhaled deeply. "Peace."

"Prayer and praise have that effect on me too."

"I've been obsessed with the occult for years. But I want nothing to do with it anymore. I have to stop before one of these ghosts actually hurts me."

Olivia hugged her friend. "I'm glad I didn't leave after all."

"Me too."

"But I'm really tired. Let's get some sleep."

"OK. But…"

"What?"

"Can we leave the radio on?"

Olivia grinned. "Absolutely."

Mike glanced at Gideon and gave a "two thumbs up" sign, and Gideon returned the gesture.

The girls changed into their night clothes in the bathroom, Olivia settled down on the futon, and Christina crawled into her bed.

The backup warriors had made a great showing tonight. But the evil ones still had dominion there. Those tormentors would come again. And Mike's comrades would be powerless to step in unless someone invited them.

It was time to teach his charge about spiritual warfare. Olivia needed to learn how to use her position in Christ to command unclean spirits to flee.

If he could train her to effectively use the weapons she already had in her arsenal, there might be hope for her friend Christina as well.

Chapter 5

I SPRANG OUT OF bed, smiling at the sunlight shining through my window. I wondered if I'd see Mike after school again. Would he appear like a cute guy? Or a stray dog? If he did show up, would anyone else see him, or just me?

Hoping I'd see him as a guy, I added a few curls to my hair, a new gray-metallic eye shadow, and slightly more mascara than usual.

If Mike was always around, he'd seen me in every state possible. That was embarrassing. Where was he when I took a shower or used the bathroom?

I knew God was always with me, but this was different. Surely God wouldn't send a peeping Tom to watch me get dressed.

With a towel still draped around my body, I approached my closet and tried to decide what to wear. I squeezed into my favorite jeans, pulled on a comfy long-sleeved T-shirt, and slipped on a pair of leather thigh-high boots.

I hoped he'd show up that day. I couldn't wait to ask him more questions. Maybe I'd see him in the parking lot after volleyball practice again. *All this extra makeup and hair styling is gonna be wasted if I don't see him till after practice.* If he showed up earlier, I wouldn't have time to talk to him, because I had classes. *What if I'm the only person who can see him? I'll look stupid standing there in the parking lot or school talking to someone no one else can see.* Was his Camaro real? Could I get into it and go for a drive with him? If no one could see Mike, would they see a Camaro driving down the road with no one in the driver's seat?

I needed answers, and I didn't want to wait till I saw Mike next to ask. I'd gotten all I could out of Eden's dad's notes. So I decided to go straight to the source.

My parents kept lots of Bibles in their room. I never had one of my own. I'd never really read the Bible on a daily basis. I thought it was high time I got one I could keep in my room. Mom and Dad were downstairs having breakfast, so I snuck into their bedroom and scanned the bookshelf by Mom's dressing table, I found several Bibles. I grabbed the one that said *The Message* because the cover said it was a modern translation.

I sat on the bed and scanned a few pages to see if I liked this version. There were no long, old-fashioned words I couldn't understand.

Bev often encouraged me to read the Bible every day. I'd tried it and found it tedious. I'd only read a King James Version that my parents had given me when I was twelve or something, and I'd been bringing that to Sunday school with me every week, but I never looked at it except when Bev told the class to open their Bibles to a particular passage. Whenever I tried reading my Bible at home, I got frustrated at the strange words and gave up. Tonight, after school, I'd look up some of the Scriptures mentioned in Eden's father's angelology notes. I'd use this modern version. Hopefully I'd understand it better.

I carried the Bible downstairs so I could put it in my backpack and perhaps read some of it on the bus.

I checked my watch. Having taken more time than usual getting ready and then grabbing the Bible from my parents' room, I was running late. I grabbed my jacket and headed down the stairs, hoping I wouldn't miss the bus.

I ran into the kitchen and grabbed a Pop Tart. "Gotta go. I'm running late."

"Bye, sweetie," Dad said.

"Your lunch is on the shelf by the front door."

"Thanks, Mom." I grabbed the sack and my backpack and headed outside, still chewing my Pop Tart.

The bus rounded the corner of my street and stopped in front of the walkway to our house. Exhaust engulfed me. So much for that lavender body spray I put on.

As I boarded, I saw all the half-asleep kids in their usual seats. But this time they all had a green light floating above their heads or wrapped around their shoulders like a snake. I gasped. No one seemed to hear me.

I took my usual seat behind the driver, then dropped my backpack on the seat beside me. I peered over my shoulder, wondering if I'd see the same thing again. I did.

I heard a quiet voice say, "Look closer, and you'll see what's holding them." This voice wasn't Mike's. It had to be the Holy Spirit. Bev had talked about a "still, small voice" that was God speaking to us through the Holy Spirit.

As I gazed behind me, I sensed that each individual had something different encircling them. Brenda, who always sat right behind me reading trashy romance novels, had a feather boa and a Playboy bunny symbol on her back. The word *sensuality* dropped into my head.

I recoiled and faced forward again.

The bus stopped, the doors opened, and Greg walked in. Immediately the word *sorcery* dropped into my head. I recalled his escapades with Christina involving spells and dabbling in the occult. He slipped into the seat across the aisle from me and shot me a tired smile.

I felt pain in my left eye. I closed my eyes and grabbed the opportunity to pray.

There must a purpose to this, God. If I know what things are hindering my friends, I can pray more accurately for them, right? I have to admit, I'm not sure I want this gift.

I took a deep, jagged breath.

I'm not seeing the dark angels yet, but I must be getting close if I'm seeing visions of evil things on my friends.

In Sunday school once, Bev taught that all children of God had spiritual gifts. One of those gifts was discernment of spirits. Was I discerning spirits?

I wondered what kind of spirit I'd see on Christina when I saw her in school today.

I reached into my backpack and pulled out the Bible I'd tossed in before rushing out of the house. I turned to the index in the back and found a heading for spiritual forces. One of the verses listed was in Ephesians, so I turned to chapter six and read, "This is not a wrestling match against a human opponent. We are wrestling with rulers, authorities, the powers who govern this world of darkness, and spiritual forces that control evil in the heavenly world." It was the same verse I'd read in the notebook, only worded a little differently in this version of the Bible.

When the bus arrived at school, I put my Bible away to face the day before me.

After getting my books out of my locker and hanging up my hooded jacket, I maneuvered down the crowded hallway, looking for Christina.

God, I need a break from seeing these "things" on people.

When I didn't see any spirits lingering on people I passed, I was relieved. I could turn it off!

I caught Christina as she closed her locker. She looked like she hadn't slept for days. But I didn't see any spirit engulfing her.

I took her arm and whispered, "Are you OK?"

"Some weird stuff has been going on. Can we talk at lunch?"

"Absolutely." I threw my arms around her and gave her a squeeze.

As Christina headed into the hallway, something fell out of her backpack. I picked it up. It was a medicine bottle. The label said it was Xanax.

My mom took that for anxiety. What was Christina doing with it? She was already lost in the sea of rushing students, so I slipped the bottle into my backpack so I could give it to her at lunch.

I had a test or quiz in nearly every class. I was relieved I had a study hall first period so I could review all my notes.

When the bell rang for lunch, I hurried to the cafeteria. Christina waved at the guys she usually ate with, signaling that she and I needed to talk. Then she pulled her chair close to mine. I sat down, opened my brown lunch bag, and pulled out an apple and a sandwich made from mom's leftover meatloaf.

Christina's eyes darted around to make sure no one could hear her. Then she whispered, "Last night, after I listened to the recording I made of the grave again, I saw the spirit of that little boy. He talked to me. He told me his name. It was the same one we saw on the gravestone." She covered her face with her hands. "He's been following me ever since last night. He sits in the corner of my room and stares at me. And he sat in the backseat of my car while I was driving to school today."

God, what do I say to her?

I opened my lips and hoped God would give me the right words to say. "You're on dangerous ground, Christina. You have to stop playing games with this stuff."

"I know. You're right."

"I want you to meet a lady I know from church. Her name is Bev. She'll know what to do. And she'll pray for you."

She drew her hands away from her face and looked up at me. "Where does she live?"

"Right down the street from me. Let's stop at her place after school tomorrow. I have too much homework to do it tonight."

"I'll do anything to get away from that spirit."

I pulled the bottle of Xanax out of my backpack and handed it to her. "You dropped these after we talked this morning." Christina took the bottle and tucked it into her purse. "I've been having trouble sleeping for about a month. My mom took me to the doctor, and he prescribed these pills."

"Have you been seeing other spirits?"

Christina rubbed her forehead and grimaced. "The last time Greg and I tried to dream jump, I saw that spirit in a trench coat and hat standing near my bedroom window. His face was a blur. All I could see were his green eyes."

Oh no.

"I tried sleeping on the couch one night, but he followed me there. So I asked my mom to take me to the doctor. He said I wasn't getting enough sleep. The medication worked. But it made me feel sick, so I stopped taking it about a week ago. Even when I was sleeping soundly, I still saw that spirit."

Well, I guess the proverbial boogey man wasn't such a pretend thing after all.

The bell rang, and the cafeteria began to clear out. We picked up our backpacks.

I placed my hand on Christina's elbow so she'd pause a moment before rushing to her next class. "Do you have a Bible?"

"There's one on the coffee table in our living room. No one ever opens it."

"You need to get it and read the book of Psalms." Bev told me once that the Psalms could comfort people. Christina really needed to be comforted.

"I'll read it tonight. Thanks, Liv."

What if she forgot? Would she be kept awake another night with eerie apparitions lurking in her room again? Fear seized me as I wondered when I'd see an evil spirit. Mike had said I would in time. I didn't want to.

While Olivia stopped during her route to pray in her car outside of Christina's house, Mike flew to the window outside the girl's bedroom, where he could observe her without losing sight of his charge.

A large hardcover Bible lay open on the bed. Christina lay on her stomach beside it, poring over her literature textbook.

Gideon sat on the floor in the corner of her room, bobbing his head to the rock music blaring from Christina's headphones. He smiled at Mike in greeting.

"She's going to blow out her eardrums," Mike exclaimed, his hands covering his ears.

"I know!" Gideon shrugged. "We can only do so much."

Mike understood. He danced to the beat thumping from the radio beside Christina's bed, and Gideon joined in. A light mist filled the room. Mike and Gideon stopped dancing. Two dark-cloaked, faceless figures appeared again near Christina's other bedroom window.

"Spirits of confusion," Mike said with clenched teeth.

The two angels reached behind their backs and drew out swords.

Mike's sword blazed with fire. A metallic bronze triangle materialized in his other hand. Gideon's two swords glowed blue. A metal helmet clanged as it covered his face. Breastplates and shin guards clanked into position. Lightning shot from their armor.

Christina's cell phone rang. She looked up from her books and spotted the boy in the corner. Mike had not seen him there until this moment, having been focused on the faceless cloaked ones.

She put her hand on the Bible.

Gideon pointed his sword at the tiny figure.

"She invited me here," sneered the boy. "You can't do a thing." Of course, Mike knew that was a lie.

"Watch me!" Gideon dragged the boy by the scruff of his neck and hurled the boy through the wall. He dragged him into the field behind the house, then chopped at the demon with his blade.

Mike turned his attention to the other presences in the room. Suddenly a shriveled face appeared from under one of the cloaks and leered at Christina. The demon licked his lips with a snake-like tongue, the rest of his facial features still.

Mike moved toward his enemy with confidence, knowing Olivia was still in the car praying, and Christina had her head bowed also.

"Look at me, you filth!" Mike demanded.

"You have no power over me." The demon's eyes glinted as they turned in Mike's direction. His dark companion hovered behind him.

"Wrong answer!" Mike swung his saber, knocking the legs out from under the demon, landing it flat on its back. He traced a pattern over the demon with his finger. A golden rope followed the trail and bound the evil spirit, who writhed and screeched. Mike wrapped the golden cord around the demon's mouth, silencing him. The second cloaked demon had already disappeared.

Hoisting the bound spirit over his shoulder, Mike joined Gideon in the field behind the house. He dumped his prey next to the other hellhound.

"Go back to where you came from," Gideon yelled. The two angels plunged their swords into the demons' bellies. They turned into a green dust cloud that quickly dispersed.

Mike and Gideon returned to the bedroom.

Christina got in bed and snuggled under the covers, leaving the lights on. She gazed at the bottle of pills on her desk.

Mike wished he could tell her she may not need them anymore.

"God," she prayed, "if You're real, show me."

She sat up, picked up the Bible that lay open at the foot of her bed, and opened to the index. She found the page number for the psalms and turned to it. Mike peered over her shoulder as her finger pointed to a verse that said something about being in the shadow of God's wing.

Mike felt a heavy hand on his left shoulder. He turned and embraced Gideon, whose expression had lightened, as there appeared to be hope for his charge.

She kept reading until Mike could see that her eyelids were beginning to flutter. Just before dropping off to sleep she peered at the window. No demons stood there.

"Thank You, God."

She turned on the radio to the Christian station Olivia had played the night she slept over. Then she closed her eyes and fell asleep.

Olivia started her car and headed home. After driving about a mile down the road, she jumped at the sound of Mike's voice as he said, "Hello."

"If you hadn't been present I would not have been able to assist Christina's angel, Gideon, tonight because, of course, I can't leave you."

"I guess that's why God had me stop in front of her house to pray instead of just praying for her at home."

"There is a fight ensuing concerning your friend, you know." Mike let the words hang in the air for a moment.

"Do you think Christina will make the right choice, and all these demonic attacks will stop?"

"I'm only an angel, not God. I don't know the future. But you can pray, Olivia. Don't stop."

"I won't."

Mike and Gideon had emerged from this skirmish unscathed. But he had a feeling this battle was going to intensify. Soon. Was he ready for the war to come?

I climbed into bed and stared at the night-light in the corner of my room. It was a punched-tin angel that my mother gave me on my third birthday. The glow that peeked through the tiny holes in the tin always gave me a sense of peace and security.

I hoped Mike would visit me and we could talk more about Christina.

I closed my eyes and prayed again. "God, help me make sense of all the things I'm going through. Be with Christina. And Greg too."

I felt a gentle hand rest on top of my head.

"Do you know you are a chosen one?" The voice came from behind me as I lay back on my bed.

I dared not turn around. Something I recalled from a church sermon told me it was impossible to look at God and live.

"Don't be afraid."

I guess God would say the same thing angels say when they talk to people. I wasn't afraid.

"I'm doing something special in you. You will help many people. You will be a warrior."

I can't imagine that. I'm not much of a fighter.

"The gift I'm giving you is not for you alone. It is for My other children. Can I trust you with it?"

"Yes," I said aloud.

"I will always be with you. And I will send My angels to watch over you and protect you."

A vision came over me, and I fell slowly through clouds into a sky that glowed like the blue-and-pink dawn of a fall morning. I drifted to the ground, landing on the patch of grass where I'd talked to Mike the last time I'd talked to him in a dream state. My heart raced with anticipation.

I saw him on the horizon just above the hill. He wore a red cotton T-shirt, jeans, and bright white sneakers. He swung his arms as he walked toward me.

When he came close I smelled the earthy, masculine smell of patchouli, one of my favorite colognes.

"It's good to see you again." He squatted down with his hands leisurely folded on his knees.

I resisted the urge to hug him since I wasn't sure about our physical boundaries.

The corners of his eyes crinkled when he smiled. "We've had some exciting things happening lately. I bet you have a lot of questions."

"I'm not sure I'd call all of this exciting. But I do have a lot of questions." I stood and instinctively brushed off my pants, which was stupid since there was no dirt to brush off.

"Let's take a walk." He leaped over a small creek and waited on the other side. "Come on over."

I thought about how I'd get to Mike and in an instant found myself on the other side. Dreams were so cool like that. I wished I could float like that in real life.

"What's your first question?" he asked.

"Am I crazy?"

He looked at me intently. "No. God has given you a gift. Most people ignore God's gifts. Many don't even realize they've been blessed with one. Or they're too selfish to use it the way it was intended. Some try to use their gifts for their own means or to manipulate people."

"I guess my knowledge of private things about others could be used to manipulate them. But I wouldn't do that."

"I know. You remind me of Mary, Jesus' mother."

"I do?" I sure didn't feel I deserved to be compared to her.

"She was just a young woman when God chose to use her. Joseph was a typical young man, but he had a heart that was surrendered to God, tender and sensitive. Like yours. God trusted him. He trusts you too."

If God trusted me, He needed to know that my feelings for Mike were totally pure. "I think I've been looking forward to our meetings in the wrong way." I wrung my hands, searching for the right words. "You seem like the perfect guy—the kind of guy any girl would love to have as a boyfriend." I felt myself blush. "So if you're reading my mind, please forgive me."

Mike held up his hands. "Don't worry. Intimate interactions with humans are off limits to angels. In the ancient days, some of the fallen ones crossed that line. They had improper relationships with women, and a race of super-humans resulted. They were called the nephilim. They were half-angel, half-man."

These beings sounded like the characters having romantic relationships with human girls in the novels my girlfriends read. I'd seen these books on desks at school and had read the back covers to see what they were about.

"During the flood of Noah those creatures were destroyed. They were sent to a dark abyss. But the book of Jude says they'll be released in the end times." Mike ran his hands through his wavy, flaxen hair.

"My friends would fall for that deception. Falling in love with fallen angels. They read it in novels all the time and think it's romantic. Girls all over school would brag about a half-angel boyfriend if they ever had the opportunity to have one. I'm sure all the stories about fallen angels and vampires—nephilim is what they sound like—has desensitized us girls. I think it's a bit creepy myself. But this is serious stuff and not something to be romanticized." I shook my head as the realization of this demonic deception overwhelmed me.

"That's why God needs warriors who have discernment. Like you."

"Me?" I felt like such a novice. I had so much to learn.

"You've always had a sensitive heart. God sees that. I see it. And now you are delving into the deep understanding of what a true walk with God is all about."

"I had no idea how intense it would be—yet exciting."

"Your spiritual gift discerns, identifies spirits."

"I'm scared. I'm not sure I want this gift. I saw some 'stuff' on people one day on the bus. It really freaked me out."

"That's because you don't understand it. The church hasn't done a very good job of mentoring people with your gift. That's where I come in."

All I could think to say was, "Thank you."

"When you've learned to use your gift, you'll be able to pray for people like few others can. And some of your friends really need some powerful prayer. They're participating in activities that open themselves up to the schemes of the fallen ones. As a result they're experiencing depression, oppression, and suicidal thoughts."

"I do want to help them."

"That's what I love about you."

Although flattered, I realized this was a pure, brotherly love.

"That's what God loves about you too."

That was exactly what I expected him to say.

"The last days on Earth are coming. As the time gets closer Lucifer and his fallen ones will become more determined. The battle is going to intensify. Eternal lives are at stake. God is equipping people like you to assist Him in the war to come."

"I've heard about the final battle in the book of Revelation in church sermons, but I never really understood it."

"God will allow humans to see the extreme evil that He has kept at bay for generations. The church needs to be vigilant and grow stronger. They need to know the crafty ways in which the evil ones work."

I'd already had a taste of their work, knowing what Christina and Eden were going through. Anger rose up inside me. Suddenly I felt like fighting.

"For every gift of God, the fallen ones have a counterfeit. Remember when Moses tossed his staff on the floor in front of Egypt's king, and the supernatural power of God turned it into a serpent?"

"Yeah, I remember that Sunday school lesson."

"Under a different power, the court magicians did the same."

"Yeah. Didn't Moses' snake eat theirs?" I smiled at the mental image.

Mike laughed. "God has a good sense of humor."

I agreed. I couldn't wait to get to know God better. I'd missed out on so much all these years. All I did was sit in church. I never desired or understood how personal a relationship with God could be. Now I craved it.

As we walked along the creek I admired the flowers blooming beside it.

"In the last days there will be more false prophets. Some will actually worship us angels. But we don't deserve any worship. We only want to see God worshiped."

I reached for a flower and plucked it from a bush. Silver sparks flew from the stem where it broke. I giggled with delight. "Am I dreaming? Or is this real?"

"Yes to both. This place is real. But I find it helps to appear to people in a dream state sometimes. It's a little less frightening at first, and it helps people warm up to me. It's really annoying when we appear to humans and they faint."

I chuckled. "I liked it when you helped me with my gas. I wasn't afraid of you...much."

I faced Mike. He stopped to wait for my next words. I'm sure he was already reading my mind anyway.

"So this gift I have—do I have to use it?"

"You can choose to accept the gift God has given to you, or you can reject it. Just like I accepted to be a holy angel, not one of the fallen who chose to rebel against God in the beginning of time and were kicked out of heaven."

"You mean you can choose to disobey God?"

Mike's expression became serious. "I have a free will, just like you do. But if I turned away, I would not have redemption, as you do. There are no second chances for us."

"Why did God give humans a second chance but not His angels?"

Mike shrugged. "There are many things that are still a mystery to us."

Mike quickened his stride as he changed the subject. "We love to join in worship with you humans in church."

"Oh, like the time I saw the angel choir?" I beamed, trotting to keep up his pace.

"Yes. But we can't imagine your joy as you worship as those who have been given the second chance. Jesus died on the cross for the human race, not for us. So your worship is different from ours. Those of us who are holy angels love to worship our Creator because we know His nature and His heart. We need no other reason."

"So these fallen angels—am I going to see them soon?"

Mike came to a halt, put his hands on his hips, and turned to me. "Don't worry. When the time comes, you'll be ready."

I skidded to a stop beside him. I couldn't imagine not fainting at the sight of one.

He then regained a leisurely stride. I was relieved. I had to take two steps for every one of his. We crossed the field of grass and entered a garden where red roses covered a white trellis that extended as far as my eyes could see. I breathed in the scent of the roses. The bushes were trimmed into all sorts of animal shapes. Butterflies flew in the air. Heavenly music seemed to come from all the living things.

Mike reached up to pluck a flower from one of the taller trees. As he did so, his shirt rose slightly. I noticed a flat, chiseled stomach.

Hey, he doesn't have a belly button! I smiled to myself. *Why would he?*

As we walked, our feet touched the ground, but my soles felt no pressure. We'd walked quite a way, yet I did not feel like I needed to sit and rest. I imagined I could walk like this for a hundred miles and never get tired.

"You've been wondering when you'll meet the life partner God has chosen for you, haven't you?"

"How did you know?" I was embarrassed that he knew this. "I've never really had a true boyfriend. It seems like so many other people in school have had serious relationships. Sometimes I wonder if I'll ever find 'the one.'"

Mike's lips curled into an amused grin. "Oh, you don't have to worry. God has the right one in mind for you. When the timing is right he'll appear."

"I can't wait," I exclaimed but then sobered. "But how will I know he's the one?"

Mike threw me a crooked smile. "Trust me, you'll know it when you see him."

I obviously wasn't going to get any help from Mike on this topic. So I decided to ask some of the other questions that had been plaguing me.

"When will I see you again?" I reached out, but he disappeared. I was back in my bedroom, lying on my back on the floor.

"Soon."

I couldn't help but worry if I would be entering into spiritual battle alongside Mike soon. Would I measure up? Would I run away at the first demon that challenged me face-to-face? I didn't want to disappoint God.

Chapter 6

CHRISTINA AND I sat in Bev's kitchen eating just-frosted sugar cookies, drinking herbal tea, and occasionally petting Bev's chocolate Lab.

After a few minutes of small talk, Bev looked intently at Christina. "Sweetie, would it be OK if I prayed for you?"

She nodded.

"Is there anything in particular I can pray about?"

Christina shuffled in her seat. "I've been seeing some scary things, and I want them to stop."

Bev leaned back in her chair. "What sorts of things?"

"Dark figures. Spirits."

Bev walked around the table and laid her hands on Christina's shoulders. After they closed their eyes, I did too.

"Lord," Bev prayed, "we know fear is not of You. Please deliver this young lady from the torment she has endured. We thank You for Your love and Your goodness. We love You."

I laid my hand on Christina's arm. "Amen." We opened our eyes.

Bev squeezed Christina's shoulders. "Sweetheart, you can invite God into your life right now. These tormenting spirits will stop playing with you. You'll have the power of God living inside you."

"I can? How?"

"Just thank Him for Jesus, who died to defeat death, hell, and the grave. Thank Him that Jesus overcame the enemy and all of his evil cohorts. Denounce the wrong things you've done. And ask God to begin to change you."

"I don't know if I can remember all that."

Bev smiled. "Just tell your heavenly Father what you're feeling."

"OK." Christina bowed her head. "God, please forgive me for the bad things I've done. Take my fear away. Relieve me from my anxiety attacks. I want to be a Christian like Olivia and Bev."

Her prayer was simple and halted but obviously sincere. When she opened her eyes she took a deep breath, as if she were breathing for the first time. The tension in her shoulders relaxed.

Bev kissed Christina's forehead. "You belong to Jesus now."

Christina's face lit up. She smiled at me.

I smiled back, relieved that I had another Christian friend. I also realized she had a lot to learn. Teaching her was going to be my job.

I noticed the time on Bev's wall clock. "I really hate to cut this short, but we still have homework to do." I also knew that Bev went to bed early, and we'd already kept her up pretty late.

Bev handed each of us a napkin with two sugar cookies to take with us. "Christina, when you get home I want you to pray over your house, especially your room."

"How do I do that?"

"Honey, you just pray out loud in your room. Declare that you belong to God now and that Jesus' work on the cross has covered all your sins. Evil spirits hate the name of Jesus, first of all. Second of all, it may sound gross, dear, but they also hate when you say you are covered in the blood given in the accomplishment of Jesus' sacrifice on the cross. Keep reading your Bible every day. Listen to Christian music. Create an atmosphere that demons hate to dwell in."

"I think I get it."

"Start reading the gospel of John. It chronicles the life and ministry of Jesus."

"I'd like to know more about Him. And Olivia found a Christian radio station for me."

"Read the book of James too. It's a good book for a new Christian to read. It is like a 'starter's guide' to the Christian walk."

Bev leaned down to stroke the head of her dog, then stood up abruptly and slapped her thigh. "Oh dear, I almost forgot—you must also understand the need to be around other Christians. Would you consider going to church with Olivia?"

"Liv, can you take me on Sunday?"

"You got it. I'll pick you up at ten o'clock on Sunday."

"I'll be praying for you." Bev hugged Christina with one of her vise-grip embraces. I hoped she hadn't knocked the air out of her.

"Call me anytime," Bev said.

Christina let out a huge sigh. "I feel like a heavy load has been lifted off my back."

Caramel then wedged herself between Bev and me and wagged her tail and barked at the cookies we held in our hands.

"Can I give her a piece?" I asked.

"Oh, go ahead. George sneaks her goodies all the time."

I broke off a piece of my sugar cookie and held it out for Caramel. She gently grabbed it from my hand and swallowed it without even chewing, then intently stared at me, waiting for another piece.

"Another time, girl." I leaned down and kissed the top of her nose just below her eyes and patted her softly on the head.

Bev then gave me a hard squeeze and walked us to the front door. "Sleep well tonight."

Christina replied, "I think I will."

What kind of battle was facing my friend back at her home? Would she follow Bev's instructions?

Then I wondered about what Greg might think of Christina's change of heart. Would it rip their friendship apart?

"Olivia?" A hand gently shook my shoulder. My skin tingled beneath it.

My eyes popped open, and I found Mike perched on the windowsill, his elbow on his knee. His golden hair sparkled. I looked at my clock. It was two o'clock. I'd normally be annoyed if someone woke me up at this time of the night, but I was happy to see Mike, so I propped myself on one elbow and rubbed my sleepy eyes with my other hand.

"You sure are stirring things up in this town. We all had a party last night when Christina became a child of God."

My insides did a dance. "I know. How cool is that?"

My mind raced to remember all the questions I'd thought of to ask Mike over the past two days.

"Questions again?" Mike gave me his crooked smile and his eyes sparkled.

"Yeah. I've been dying to ask you this one. Are vampires real?"

Mike snorted. "I'm surprised you didn't ask that earlier. The fallen ones take many forms. They came up with the vampire disguise decades ago. Lately, novelists and movie-makers have made these creatures seem harmless, even beautiful—"

"Olivia!" my mother screamed. My blood turned cold. I'd never heard her scream like that in my whole life.

I bolted from my bed and ran down the hall to my parents' room, which was the direction I'd heard her scream come from. The light was on inside. It was freezing cold when I entered the room. I thought that strange since my mom loved her bedroom warm and cozy at night. A

strong, sulfurous smell hit my nostrils. I looked around to see if there
was a candle causing the odor but saw nothing.

Mom sat on the side of the bed, shaking my dad. I'd never seen such
terror on her face.

A lizard-like figure crouched over my father, its long, thin, bony hands
encircling Dad's neck.

Mom looked at me. "He's not breathing. Call 911!"

The creature's leathery head turned, and green eyes challenged me as
it spread its knife-shaped wings.

As I turned toward the door I heard a *swoosh* behind me. When I
whirled around again, I saw Mike's form, sporting large white wings,
smash into the dark form. They both disappeared through the wall.

Dad gasped for air, his eyes wild.

"Olivia, call 911," Mom repeated.

"No, Elise, I'm OK." Dad sat up, breathing normally.

"Are you sure?" Mom asked.

He smiled. "I promise I'll go to the doctor first thing in the morning
to get it checked out."

Relieved to see my dad's breathing return to normal, I felt certain it
would be OK if I ran to the second-story window and looked outside.
Mike and his rival flew through the air, hurling each other down the
street.

Praying harder than ever before, I asked God to help Mike win this
battle.

The dark green monster fled. Mike fizzled into thin air. Only a few
sparkling feathers lingered.

"Lord God, thank You for Your holy angels of protection. In Jesus'
name, I ask that You protect my guardian friend, Mike. Amen."

When I turned around Mom and Dad gazed at me with slackened jaws.
"You haven't prayed out loud since you were six years old," Mom said.

I yearned to tell my folks what was going on with me. I hoped they'd
understand. "Mom. Dad. We have to talk. Dad, are you sure you're OK?"

"I'm fine, honey."

I led them to my bedroom and sat on the bed. I rocked back and forth,
trying to calm my nerves.

"Sit down, Dad. Rest." He sat beside me. My mom remained standing
in the doorway.

"You know the stuff we hear in church about spiritual battle?" My
voice trembled.

"Yes," my parents said at the same time.

"I've been seeing it lately. God's been showing me things."

"What kind of things?" Dad asked.

"In your bedroom, I saw a demon attack you. He had his hands around your neck, and he was choking you."

"Oh, dear God," Mom said.

"Let her finish."

"Bev says I have a spiritual gift that discerns spirits. It's in the Bible. I see good spirits too."

"So you see demons as well as—"

"Enough!" My mother's eyes widened. Her face was red. "She's becoming just like her cousin Kathryn."

"I'm not schizophrenic. Besides, Kathryn hears voices but she doesn't see things."

Mom spun on her heel and left the room.

My father gently pushed my shoulder so I would lie down, then pulled my blanket up around my face. "Olivia, you know I want what's best for you."

I nodded.

"I'm just not sure gifts like discernment of spirits apply today—at least not to the point of actually seeing angels and demons."

His doubt unnerved me. If Dad didn't believe me, I was in trouble, because he was usually my ally. And if both Mom and Dad thought I was crazy—what then?

"I don't see how seeing spirits serves any godly purpose. Until I do, I can't help but be skeptical. And concerned."

I hated the look of pity in his eyes.

"Get some sleep, Goldilocks. We'll talk about this more later. I love you." Dad kissed me on the forehead.

"Love you, too, Dad."

He rose from the bed, turned out the light, and headed down the hall. I heard the floorboards squeak as he entered his room.

I longed to follow him into his bedroom and curl up beside him in bed like I did when I was five.

After my parents' door closed, I sat up and whispered, "Mike?"

"I'm here." In the glow of a streetlight outside my window, I saw Mike leaning against the wall beside my bed. He wore a red shirt, jeans, and white sneakers. No wings. He didn't look injured in any way, but I still asked, "Are you OK?"

"Yes. That filthy thing was really strong. But I've wrestled with ones like him before."

"I told my parents I saw it strangling my dad."

"How did they react?"

"Mom thinks I'm crazy. Dad wants to believe me, but he's having a hard time."

"Did you tell them about me?"

"No. I don't feel comfortable sharing that. Not yet anyway."

Mike touched my hand. It calmed me. "Everything's going to be OK. Be patient."

"I've never had much luck with patience." I shifted my weight to my right side, facing Mike, and voiced the next question that came to mind. "You've obviously fought other battles like the one tonight. Can you tell me about some other battles you've fought?"

"How about I tell you about times of rest instead? Maybe that will calm you down and help you sleep."

It sounded like a good idea.

Mike lay down on the floor beside my bed, his legs crossed, arms folded behind his head, and stared at the ceiling. "After the flood in Noah's day, with only four families left on Earth, we angels had a lot of free time. We hung around the throne of God together, worshiping and enjoying Him. That was like a vacation for us."

I yawned. His voice calmed me immediately.

"What was your hardest fight you ever faced?"

"You are obstinate, aren't you? OK, we don't have to talk about my boring times; they aren't that exciting." He paused as if thinking about the story before voicing it. "We fought long and hard during Jesus' time on Earth. But the ultimate clash came during the crucifixion. The Dark Prince sent his entire fleet of fallen ones to wage war against the Chosen One of the ages. We fought until we felt we could fight no more. But we didn't give up. We knew Jesus would rise from the dead, but the demons would not let us alone, so we fought until the tomb finally opened. I loved seeing the demonic realm seethe during that moment."

I wanted to hear more, but his smooth voice relaxed my tension, and I fell asleep.

I awoke around four o'clock and headed to the bathroom to get a drink of water. I gazed out the window at the houses across the street. Beside one house stood an angel about twenty feet tall, gazing in my direction. He held a golden sword at his side and wore a plain white gown.

Maybe someone had been praying for my protection, like Bev. I wondered why there were more angels appearing, as if waiting for something awful that Mike may need backup help from. I pondered what kind of challenge lay ahead.

God, I'm scared. But I'll do whatever you need me to.

"That's why I chose you," a deep voice answered from behind me. I turned around. Nothing. But I knew it was my heavenly Father's voice. How grateful I felt to have the most powerful force in the universe looking out for me. I figured I was going to need it.

Chapter 7

RESTING MY CHEEK on the palm of my hand, I tried to pay attention to Mr. Jackson's monotone voice in English class. But it was no use. After counting tiles in the ceiling I doodled on my math notebook. When I glanced at the clock I saw I still had a half hour before the bell rang.

Mr. Jackson wrote something on the blackboard. The chalk particles collected into an image of Mike's face. The dust kept moving across the board until I could make out the outline of his upper body. He smiled and winked at me.

Nice trick! I knew he could hear my thoughts.

"Thanks." Mike mimicked Mr. Jackson as he waved his textbook, dramatically explaining the meaning of a poem we were studying. A giggle slipped out. Mr. Jackson shot me a disapproving look.

John Matthews, a guy I went out with once last semester, winked at me, obviously just as bored with this class as I was.

On my first date with him, he asked if he could kiss me, and I said no. He had salami breath. *Disgusting!* Our second date got canceled on account of a flat tire. He never rescheduled.

I looked up at Mike's face on the blackboard. *Did you deflate John's tire to keep me from going on that date?*

"Guilty!" Mike wagged his finger at me. *"That guy has slept around. I didn't want you with him. If it helps you feel any better, he picks his nose when he does his homework."*

No way. Another giggle came bubbling up, so I put my head down on my desk to help contain it. When I had gained my composure, I looked up again.

Mike's eyes darted in the direction of Bill Chathem's desk. I blushed at the memory of that date. It was one of those awkward kissing experiences I'd rather forget.

That date ended quickly when the car sputtered to a halt on the way home. He had to call his dad to pick us up. He never asked me out again either.

"I unplugged his spark plug. I didn't want him touching you."

Darn it, he did it again!

"You pick some real winners, Olivia. Oops, sorry. In John's case, no pun intended!" Mike tossed his head back, laughing. As he did, the particles of chalk dust scattered like someone had blown on them.

Although disappointed at his departure, I sailed through the rest of the day, feeling good that Mike cared about me. He made me feel special. I didn't feel alone anymore.

When you're a child of God, you're never alone. This wasn't Mike's voice. It was my holy Father speaking directly to me, just as I had heard those other nights. *You are very special to Me.*

I'd always thought of prayer as a one-sided conversation that sounded like a long grocery list of things people wanted. I now realized the communication was supposed to be two sided. And I was beginning to listen to the other side.

So this was what people meant when they talked about a personal relationship with God.

Arriving home from school and volleyball practice on Tuesday night, I found my parents sitting at the kitchen table. Usually after they both got out of work at the elementary school where they taught, they ate dinner and then spent the night in the living room either watching TV or reading. The fact that they were waiting for me when I walked in the door clued me in that something wasn't right.

"What's up?" I yawned, hoping I could make this brief by acting tired.

"Your father and I think you need to see a psychologist."

I felt like I'd been punched in the gut. "Dad?" I pleaded.

"Your mom and I talked about this last night. I'm sorry, but I agree with her. Since you've been seeing things no one else does, we think it would be a good idea for you to talk to someone about it."

"I'm not crazy."

Mom folded her hands across her chest. "Sane people don't have hallucinations."

I slammed my backpack onto the floor. "I won't go. You can't make me."

"Honey," my dad said in a timid voice, "a psychologist can help you know what's real and what isn't."

"Can I go to my room now?"

"Yes," Dad said.

I picked up my backpack and ran upstairs to my room. I flung my pack onto the floor and jumped on my bed, landing face down.

After crying for a minute or two, I felt a hand rest on my shoulder. But I didn't want to talk to Mike right now. If it weren't for him, my parents wouldn't think I was crazy.

God, why did You allow me to get into this mess? I need some help here.

God had sent a guardian angel to help me. But I doubted he could help me with this.

Chapter 8

I N A FOG because of the fight with my parents the night before, I walked down the hallway at school with my eyes toward the floor, not wanting to talk to anyone. Suddenly someone smashed into me, causing me to drop my book bag and stumble a few feet. I heard a high-pitched laugh and looked up to find Vicki Beecham staring at me, hands on her hips.

"Watch where you're going, twit. Oh, and watch out at practice today. A stray ball might just hit you right in the face."

Really? Today of all days? Vicki had been bullying me since seventh grade. I had no idea what I ever did to cause it.

As I steadied myself and readjusted my backpack on my shoulder, my cell phone rang, and I pulled it out of my jacket pocket to see who was calling. Andy Fergusen. We sat together in Spanish class, and we'd been having a lot of fun joking around lately. He was a soccer player, funny, gorgeous—and Vicki's boyfriend for the past two years. Rumor was that they'd just broken up this past week.

I tossed a smug look at Vicki and raced down the hall so I could answer the phone.

"Andy, you there?"

"¡Hola, mi amiga bonita!"

I blushed at him calling me beautiful. "Your girlfriend just bumped into me and almost sent me skidding ten feet down the hallway. That was *not* an accident."

"You mean my *ex*-girlfriend?"

I laughed. I needed that.

"Hey, you wanna hang out Saturday night?"

I swallowed hard, surprised at his question. My eyes caught sight of Vicki walking my way, flipping her long blonde hair, strutting as she always did.

"Yes." It flew out of my mouth before I could stop myself.

Oh, such sweet revenge.

"G-great...uh...I'll pick you up at seven o'clock at your place. Movie?"

"Sounds great. Gotta go." I hung up and thrust my phone into my jacket pocket.

My boy-crazy streak was emerging again. I hadn't dated anyone in a while, and I had a chance to make Vicki insanely jealous.

I tried on three separate outfits, wondering which one Andy would like best for our date to the movie theater. I finally settled on jeans, flats, and my favorite band T-shirt.

I half expected Mike to show up and try to talk me out of this date, considering all the other dates he'd ruined for me. But I hadn't seen him for a couple of days. I hoped Mike wouldn't botch this date up like the others. I really liked Andy. I never thought I'd go out with a jock, but I was warming up to the idea. After all, he was one of the best-looking guys at school.

And to be honest, I wanted to get back at Vicki for being so mean to me. *Let's hope she never finds out, or the bullying may get worse.*

As I brushed my hair I noticed my Bible sitting on my nightstand. I hadn't opened it for several days. But I didn't have time for that right now. I had to get down to the business of finding Mr. Right. After all, Mike had told me he'd be coming. Maybe Andy was the one.

I rarely wore makeup, but for tonight I used a little bit of blush and mascara. Vicki wore a lot of makeup, so I hoped Andy would like this touch of color better.

I grabbed my red sweater off a hanger in my closet, then stepped into my bathroom looking for some perfume. I hardly ever used the stuff, but Christina said it had quite an effect on guys. As I picked up the bottle I noticed the name on the label.

Innocence Lost.

Ignoring the twinge of guilt, I sprayed some on my neck and wrists, then set the bottle down on the bathroom sink and grabbed my sweater.

I heard a knock on the front door. After one last glance in the full-length mirror on the back of my bedroom door, I hurried down the stairs.

Mom opened the door, and Andy walked in. His muscular thighs stretched at the fabric of his jeans.

Down, girl.

"Come in, dear," my mom cooed. My mom and Andy's mom had been friends since high school, and they went to the same church as us. I knew Mom would let me go out with him.

"Thank you, Mrs. Stanton." His deep blue eyes seemed to burn right through me as I came to the bottom stair. "You look amazing."

My face felt hot. "Thanks."

I fumbled to put on my sweater. When Andy noticed, he held a sleeve for me.

My revenge date was becoming so much more. I really liked this guy.

Dad entered the foyer and shook hands with Andy.

"So nice to see you, sir."

Dad winked at me, just like he did before every date. It was his reminder that I could call him if I ever felt uncomfortable and he'd come pick me up. That was the whole reason he bought a cell phone for me.

"We'll be back by ten," Andy said. He opened the door for me. I waved good-bye to my parents.

Andy smiled at me as we walked down the sidewalk. The front door closed behind us with a *thunk*. "Thanks for going out with me tonight."

"No problem." I spotted his shiny blue classic Corvette parked in our driveway. "Nice car!" I'd always been a fan of vintage sports cars.

"I restored it myself. It's a '77."

I already knew that.

We both reached for the handle on the passenger side at the same time, and his hand caught mine for a moment.

"Watch your head. Getting into this car is like stuffing yourself into a sardine can."

I laughed and slipped into the seat. Andy shut my door. The smell of his musky cologne filled the car.

When he got in, we were so close our elbows touched. He turned the key, put the car in reverse, and backed out of the driveway.

"Vicki's not going to be happy about this."

Andy sniffed. "Let's forget about her tonight. I'm here to spend time with *you*."

I was excited to get to know him better and have some good laughs. I stared at his full lips, wondering what it'd be like to kiss him.

Andy pulled into the parking lot at the movie theater and looked at the sign. "Wait a minute. I don't see *Revenger* listed. Is there another movie you'd like to see?"

I scanned the list. "Not particularly." Even if there had been, I wouldn't have said so. I wanted to spend time talking with Andy instead of staring at a screen for two hours.

"Maybe we could go to Hopkins Park and watch the sun set. Feed the geese on the pond. Then get a bite to eat at the Charcoal Pit."

Going in a car with a guy for two hours was not a good idea. A small voice inside my head said no. I ignored it.

"Sure, let's go."

"There's an unopened bag of potato chips in the backseat if you're hungry."

I reached around, grabbed it, and tore it open. While munching on our snack, Andy and I shared amusing soccer-team stories on the way to the park. By the time we got there we were both breathless from laughing so hard. While he parked I grabbed the review mirror, turned it in my direction to make sure my mascara wasn't running down my face, then moved the mirror back into its original position as best I could.

I looked at Andy's hands on the steering wheel. I wondered what they'd feel like cradling my chin.

Maybe I should splash some of that pond water on my face to cool off.

Just before we got out, rain started coming down, so we stayed in the car. We talked about Spanish class, sports, and what colleges we were thinking of going to next year.

"Who are you going to the school dance with?"

Was he going to ask me to the dance? "I'm not going, since no one asked me."

"I was planning to ask Vicki, but now I'm not so sure."

I waited for him to ask me, but he didn't. "I hope this doesn't offend you, but you seem like a nice guy. How could you date her? Do you know what a jerk she is to me?"

"Yeah." He paused and slipped another potato chip in his mouth. While still crunching on it he added, "I'm really sorry she's like that with you. I guess I only dated her because she's a nice accessory to have on my arm. She must be jealous of you."

Jealous of me? She's so beauty-queen beautiful, and I'm so . . . average pretty.

Andy interrupted my thoughts as he pointed at me and giggled. "You have a piece of potato chip on your lip."

"I do?" I stuck out my tongue to try to get it.

"Here. Let me just . . ." He reached out to brush it off. When his hand neared my mouth, I grabbed it and stared into his eyes.

He kissed me. I kissed him back. He pressed me against the passenger door. I ran my fingers through his hair, satisfying the urge I'd had all night to do that.

I'd kissed three boys before, all of which had been quite awkward. I could never quite get the head tilt right or how big to open my mouth or whether to let a tongue in. Of course, the salami-breath guy was a major turn-off. I hadn't really looked forward to the opportunity again—until now.

After a couple of minutes, the windows fogged up. The two of us were getting cramped in the small space, and my foot got stuck in the steering wheel. Andy grabbed me around my torso and pulled me over the center console. When my head hit the roof, we laughed. I quickly pulled him close again.

I could get used to this. I wished time could stop for a while—at least until I became dehydrated and had to have nourishment.

I buried my nose into his neck and breathed in his musky scent.

Andy drew back, and his eyes wandered to the opening of my blouse.

I knew I should suggest we go for a juicy cheeseburger before this went further than I wanted. So I pushed away from him, but he gripped my waist and his lips pressed harder on mine.

OK—just a minute longer.

His hands moved from my waist and started tugging at my blouse.

"Andy, don't." I tried to wiggle away, but his strong grasp overpowered me. His body weight crushed me into the vinyl seat.

I felt his hand slip inside my blouse. I pushed it away.

He tried unbuttoning it. I pushed his hand away again.

As he stretched the material, I heard my blouse rip. The lust in his eye landed on my exposed bra.

God, help!

I heard a noise like claws scratching at the car door. Andy snapped up to a sitting position. A low growl rumbled. Yellow eyes appeared through the window, and globs of drool ran in rivulets across its fogged surface. My mind exploded in fear.

Andy let go of me and scrambled into the driver's seat, letting out a string of curse words. I clutched my ripped bloused together. He turned the key, rammed the car into reverse, and stomped on the gas pedal.

I peered out the back window, searching for the creature that attacked the car. It looked like a wild dog—maybe a Siberian husky. Its breath sent billows of steam into the cool evening air. Its fierce topaz eyes glowed.

As I watched, the creature thinned into a vertical line of light. Then I spotted a red shirt, jeans, and white sneakers.

Mike! He'd ruined another date. I was relieved this time.

Andy drove to my house in silence, dropped me off without saying good-bye, then sped off. I was pretty certain that was our first and last date.

Fortunately, my parents were already in bed when I got inside, so I didn't have to explain the ripped blouse.

When I opened my bedroom door, I found Mike leaning against the bookshelf with his arms crossed, glaring at me. I'd never seen him angry. My angel notebook did say that angels had emotions, so why was I surprised?

"What were you thinking? Oh yeah, you *weren't* thinking."

"You didn't have to be so dramatic. I mean, come on, a wild dog?"

"I think your dad would have thought the rabid dog thing was a nice touch." Mike continued glaring.

"Stop looking at me like that." I turned my back to him.

"That boy was attacking you, Liv."

Then it hit me. What might have happened if Mike hadn't shown up? Maybe Andy wouldn't have stopped.

I turned to face Mike. "Are you saying I could've been raped?"

"Yes. But you weren't."

"Because you intervened?"

"Because you prayed."

"I did?"

"Yes, you did. I always show up when you invite me."

I tried to remember when I'd prayed. Then I recalled crying out to God for help in the car when I heard my blouse rip.

I flopped hard onto my bed and put my head in my hands. "I shouldn't have gone out with Andy in the first place. But I've been feeling lonely lately. And when I saw the chance to get back at Vicki, I started on a big ego trip."

"How did you feel when you accepted the date?"

I thought back. "My stomach felt tied up in knots."

I'd had several other red flags that I ignored, like knowing I was going out with a guy that I knew slept around a lot and who dated a girl that was a jerk.

How could I be so naïve and reckless?

Mike sprawled out on my floor, his head resting on the backs of his hands. He looked up at me. "You're human. Don't be too hard on yourself. You're still learning. And the Enemy tends to attack people in the areas where they're the weakest."

"In my case, boys." I rolled my eyes.

"But now that you recognize your area of weakness, you can conquer it."

"How?"

"By listening to the voice of God. He can give you power over temptation."

"Yeah, that twinge of guilt I felt in my bathroom right before I left on the date was God telling me I was making a bad choice. But I ignored it."

"Listen to that still, small voice—the one that tried to warn you when Andy invited you to go out with him. Whenever you feel uneasiness in the pit of your stomach, pray. And don't put yourself in situations that will cause you to fall."

"Like in a parked car with a hot guy?"

"Exactly." Mike chuckled, then looked serious again. "When you feel the Enemy pressing in, remind him of your position in Christ. Say it out loud so he can hear it. Memorize Scripture so you can quote it when you need to use it during spiritual battle."

I giggled at the thought of quoting Scripture at Andy in the car and reminding demons out loud that I was a child of God. He'd have driven home even more shaken than when he thought he'd seen a crazed dog.

"If you command evil spirits to flee, they have to leave. And if you ask God to give us angels charge over you, we'll come to your aid right away."

"So you're saying I have power to resist the devil. I just need to use it?"

Mike grinned. "I knew you'd get it." He stood, then vanished, but a glow lingered, assuring me that he was still here.

"Can you stay here while I sleep?"

"I always do."

I dove under the covers and slammed my head into the pillow.

God, I almost got raped tonight because I ignored Your voice. Please forgive me. Make me wiser. Help me to listen to You and resist temptation.

As I drifted off to sleep, I wondered if Bev had prayed for angels to watch over me tonight.

"Your mom prays for you, too, you know."

She does?

"She's put me on assignment many times."

This surprised me. Mom didn't always act like my ally. But if she prayed for me, I was thankful.

Noxious fumes blew into my face. Green eyes glared at me from above my bed. An invisible force held me down.

"God, help me—"

"Quiet," a spirit shouted.

I felt an invisible hand cover my mouth. I tried to move my arms and legs, but the force would not let me go.

"You think your big friend and his angel gang are so strong, but we demons are stronger."

"*He is called the Deceiver for a reason. He is a liar.*" It was the still, small voice again.

Four more pairs of green eyes floated around my room. The demons then took on various forms. One had the body of a dog and the legs of a spider. The other had a man's body, but the face was a twisted, rotting piece of skin.

The faces pressed in closer. I shut my eyes.

God, do you hear me?

"We can help you as much as He can." The high-pitched voice hurt my ears.

The creatures holding me down shook me so violently I feared I might fall off the bed.

The dog with the spider legs shouted, "God doesn't care about you. You're one of millions of pathetic humans who are going to fail over and over and then die."

"But I'm going to heaven," I mumbled.

"Silly girl." The voice was deeper, so I assumed the man with the twisted face was talking now. "There's no heaven. No glory. We're going to win in the end. We almost won two thousand years ago. Now we're smarter and stronger."

The spider monster spoke again. "Our lord has plans for this town. There are hordes of us in every corner of the city. We'll take down every person who lives here, one by one."

I remembered Mike telling me to call out to God at times like this. I mustered up the strength to yell out, "Jesus!" Since my mouth was covered, it came out muffled. So I screamed the name again inside my head.

I knew I was in trouble when I saw the menacing shadow lurking in a corner of my dark bedroom. An invisible fist twisted my heart until it felt like it would explode. Unseen hands gripped my mind, paralyzing me with fear.

The shadow emerged, and I saw a grotesque face with hollowed-out eyes and skeletal features framed by a black cloak. I sensed a fire of hate in its crimson eyes as they flashed at me. I knew it intended to kill me. But I couldn't move. I was pinned to my bed.

Its rage enveloped me as it choked me with its bony fingers. My head swam as I gasped for oxygen. Was this the end?

My eyes rolled back in my head. As I attempted to draw one final breath, I saw a flash of light. I was sure my spirit had departed from my body.

But as I gave in to inevitable death, the brilliant light lingered. When I focused on it, I recognized Him. The one who was sent to fight for me. The one who had promised to battle beside me.

That's when I realized that I was not in this alone. And that the struggle was far from over.

God, where are You?

"Watch this," Mike bellowed.

I opened my eyes and saw a window of light open amid the blackness.

Mike appeared in an enormous form of his human self I'd never seen before, filling the room. He grabbed the smaller demon by the neck and hurled it out of my room. He disappeared right through the wall.

When the demon on top of me released me in order to fight Mike, I flew to my bedroom door and leaned against it, recoiling as the demon hissed and slammed into Mike, encircling him with his willowy, bony arms.

I prayed as hard as I could. Mike's wings filled the room the way they had the night my father was assaulted. He wielded a flaming sword in his right hand. A trail of fire followed its every swing.

The remaining demonic creature raged in response, spewing black smoke from its mouth. Mike melted through the wall, taking the tussle outside.

I dropped to my knees beside my bed and decided to quote Psalm 23, the only Scripture I knew by heart since I'd heard it read so many times at church and funerals. "Yea, though I walk through the valley of the shadow of death, I will fear no evil."

Before I could quote the rest, I began to sing the only worship song that came to mind. "Peace, peace, wonderful peace, coming down from the Father above."

God, send backup help if Mike needs it. And please—

I heard a knock on my window. The glass shuddered but didn't break. I looked outside. Mike hovered about six feet outside my window. Red and green blood ran down the blade of his flaming sword, dripping off the end as it hung toward the ground. Mike's chest rose and fell rapidly. The demon was nowhere in sight.

I turned the latch and threw open the window. "Are you OK?" My chest was heaving so hard I could hardly get out another word.

"I am." He gasped for another breath. "Thanks for sending backups."

"Yeah, I had prayed for that." I held my hand to my head. "I need to

read my Bible more often. And memorize more verses. I want to be prepared next time."

Mike gave me a thumbs-up. "Great idea."

My phone rang, and Mike disappeared. I grabbed my cell from the
bedside table.

"Liv," Christina yelled. "Get to Greg's house, fast! I'll meet you there."
She hung up.

What now?

I grabbed my purse and keys and flew out of the house.

Chapter 9

IKE RODE IN the passenger seat beside Olivia through a section of town filled with bars, adult bookstores, and strip clubs. She parked in front of a red brick house. A glow of light came from the basement window. Olivia sat in the car with the engine turned off and began to pray, waiting for Christina to arrive. Mike dove inside the building, still able to watch out the basement window to be sure his charge was safe. A teenage boy was crouched against the far wall, staring up at an older man. Mike recognized the boy as Olivia's friend Greg. He assumed the man was Greg's father.

Mike knew Greg's father had always scared Olivia. She'd seen him at she and Greg's middle school graduation ceremony. He was a large man with a shaved head and tattoos all over his massive biceps, which were about as large as Olivia's head. Everyone knew that he had an anger problem, and Greg had come to school with a shiner on more than one occasion. He always made some excuse about how he'd run into something, but Olivia had her suspicions. Her heart hurt for Greg. He was the sweetest guy in spite of his circumstances.

"You little punk!" The older man rubbed his whiskered face, then raised his fist and brought it down on top of the boy's head. "Don't you smart mouth me like that."

"Dad, please stop."

Greg took another blow to his face. More blood spewed from his already fractured nose. He held up his arms to try to block the next blow, but he couldn't fend it off. His dad's fist hit him on his left jaw.

The father threw a lamp, shattering it into pieces, then stormed up the basement stairs.

Greg slumped over in a sitting position on the floor. His sobs sprayed blood all over his torn T-shirt and jeans.

Tears pooled in Mike's eyes. His heart ached for the boy. *No wonder he sought the escape of paranormal games and supernatural escapades.*

An old-style telephone with a long tangled cord sat on a table in the middle of the room, the receiver dangling over the edge. Greg crawled to it and placed the earpiece to his ear. "Christina? Are you still there?" His legs wobbled as he forced himself to stand and hang up the phone.

Mike noticed a glow on the other side of Greg. Facial and body features came into focus until he could see Churiel was facing him. He'd seen this angel around Olivia's group of friends before.

"Your blondie is out there praying." He bowed in greeting to Mike.

"Yes, I've taught her well." Mike thrust his chest out with pride.

"Well done, comrade. As you can guess, my effectiveness in this household has not been put into motion until Olivia's prayer outside."

With tears in his translucent eyes, Churiel knelt beside his charge. He wore no armor, only a long white robe gathered at the waist with a golden rope. His long, flaxen hair cascaded over his shoulders.

Greg bellowed and swung his fist into the dark paneling, creating a hole in the wall. When he'd gathered his emotions, he moved with long steps to the broom closet, where he grabbed a short stool and a length of clothesline rope.

"This will be the last time you punch me, Dad," he mumbled. "You won't ever have to worry about me again."

Mike stared at Churiel, awaiting some action. Surely his friend would intervene.

Greg shuffled into the furnace room and shut the door. A pull on the string dangling from the single light bulb in the center of the room illuminated the dark chamber. With shaky hands he placed the stool beneath the rafter, stood on it, and looped the rope over the beam.

Mike waited in silence for a signal from Churiel...or a miracle.

Greg tried to tie a noose in the rope. While fiddling with it, he lost his balance. Churiel shoved his foot into the stool and tipped it, toppling Greg to the floor.

Churiel ginned with satisfaction as he withdrew his foot.

"Good move," Mike said.

The phone rang. The loud jangling sound brought a string of curses from Greg as he walked into the other room to pick it up.

"Greg?" Mike's sharp hearing picked up the concerned female voice coming through the receiver.

"Christina!"

"I'm on my way. Don't move. I'm one minute from your house."

Greg dropped the phone onto its cradle, wiped tears from his eyes, and returned to the furnace room, where he sat on the tiny stool, staring at the wall in front of him.

Headlights streamed through the basement window as a car screeched to a halt outside.

Christina's face appeared on the other side of the window. Her eyes were red from crying and wide with fear. She tapped on the window. "Greg, I'm here! Come to the front door."

Mike caught a glimpse of Gideon just behind Christina.

Greg shook his head and yelled, "My father's up there. I'm not going anywhere near him."

Her face disappeared. A minute later, soft footsteps could be heard coming down the basement stairs.

Christina peered around the corner into the room. She gasped in shock when she saw Greg sitting on the tiny stool with the noose dangling above his head. She rushed to him.

"I left as soon as I heard you and your father arguing over the phone. Your back door was unlocked, so I let myself in without knocking. Hope your dad doesn't get angry."

She kneeled on the floor and took his hands away from his face so he would look her in the eye. "How long has this been going on?"

He shrugged.

"We've been friends since grade school, and you never told me about this?"

Christina brushed a wisp of hair away from his sweating forehead, revealing a fist-sized area of skin where a chunk of hair had been ripped out. His face was swollen from where he'd been punched.

She wept. "I'm so sorry. If I'd only known..." She embraced him, and after a few seconds, his arms wrapped around her neck and he sobbed into her hair.

She rubbed his back. "It's OK. We'll work this out. You can come to my house. My parents will let you stay as long as you want. I know they will."

"Really?"

"Really. You're my best friend. I'm here for you."

His sobs subsided, but he continued to embrace her. He twirled his fingers through her red curls. He drew back and searched her eyes for a moment. She kissed his cheek, then the corner of his mouth. Greg kissed her lips. Then he buried his face in her neck. He let out a muffled groan.

Christina placed her lips near his ear. "I prayed for you on the way over here. It's the first time I've ever prayed that hard. I'm not sure, but I think it worked."

"I'm glad you did. You're my angel."

"Well, I'm no angel." She laughed. "But maybe someone is."

Mike smiled. He was proud of the example Olivia was displaying for her friends. He gave Churiel a high five.

Christina cradled Greg's face in her hands. "Let's not focus our friendship on the scary stuff we've been doing anymore."

Greg nodded, then dried his tears with the sleeve of his shirt.

She grabbed his arm and helped him stand. "Come on. Let's get out of here."

They rose, holding each other's hands. After ascending the stairs, they quietly let themselves out the back door and walked to Christina's car.

Olivia leapt out of her car and wrapped her arms around her friends. "Are you guys OK? I've been out here praying. Christina told me to stay in the car when she got here. She wanted to go into the house by herself and have me stay out here just in case she needed my help calling 911 or whatever."

Greg's chin was quivering. "Thanks." Then his red eyes looked back at the ground.

Christina grabbed his hand, "Let's get you out of here."

As they drove away, Mike realized his job here was over. The boy was safe. His charge was safe, and she'd prayed like he had taught her. Churiel hadn't done too badly either, even though all he had to do was kick over a stool.

Two dark ghouls swirled out the basement window, the same kind Mike had seen at Christina's house. "We aren't leaving," they taunted. "We don't have to." Mike knew from experience that demons didn't have to leave a territory if they had been invited there.

He slipped away into the night with his charge.

As I sat in the library at home watching *The Notebook*, notions of romance clouded my mind. I drifted off to sleep on the couch, fantasizing about "the one" that Mike had told me about.

"Olivia?"

The soft whisper sounded like Mike's voice. I opened my eyes. Blue eyes met mine. They looked like Mike's, but a dark tempest brewed there.

I felt his hand caress my arm, then brush against my chin, then move slowly up to my lips. Muscular arms encircled me. This touch was more intimate than I was used to with Mike. Was I dreaming?

I gazed into his exquisitely beautiful face, framed by short-cropped curls. I felt myself softening under his sensual grip. I felt guilty at how much I was enjoying this. But if it was just a dream, I could let this scene play itself out, right?

I closed my eyes and gave in to his advances, allowing his mouth to explore mine. His hands stroked my back from shoulder to lower hip. His breath on my neck sent my senses reeling. I ached for more.

Sudden pain shot through my body as his fingers became spikes, digging into the flesh on my arms. The embrace crushed the breath out of me. I opened my eyes, and instead of Mike I saw a creature with dark green veins under his light green skin. Jagged teeth protruded from his mouth.

I tried to scream but could make no noise. My mouth went dry. My muscles ached as I tried to fight this demon off of me.

Hot blood trickled from the wounds on my arms. The more I tried to scream, the angrier the monster became, and he dug his claws deeper into my back.

The creature let out a low growl, and I felt a force moving my legs apart. "Come with me," its seductive voice hissed. "I'll make you my queen for eternity."

"No!"

I received another dose of pain. My rib cage felt like it was being crushed. My breath was forced out of my lungs. My eyes rolled back in my head.

"God!"

A bright light flashed into the room.

"*Faleilmae el Laidu*," Mike's voice boomed.

Mike ripped the demon off of me. The ceiling opened and swallowed the demon, then closed.

I had no idea what he'd said, but at least I could breathe again.

I jolted upright on the sofa, gasping for air. "What just happened?"

"You opened yourself up to a spirit of sensuality pretending to be me."

"I didn't mean to," I said, trying to sound innocent.

"What were you doing before you fell asleep?" Mike raised one eyebrow at me.

"Watching a movie that had—well—let's just say, some racy sexual scenes."

"Remember what I told you about the women in Noah's day opening themselves up to romance with angels?"

"Yes." I looked away in embarrassment. From the start Mike had laid down the boundaries in our relationship and given the Old Testament example of the nephilim.

"That's what just happened to you. You fantasized about the two of us. You can't do that. Those filthy beings would like to see us both fall And since they know they can't take me down, they're messing with your mind. If they can separate us, then God's purpose in sending me to you will be over."

"I had no idea that an evil angel could pretend to be you and tempt me that way." I shivered as I recalled the horrific scene that had just transpired.

"You need to guard your heart, even in your sleep. Pray before you lie down, and ask God to take over your dreaming. I love protecting you, but don't make my job harder. I had to fight off five other demons before I got to you just now. Try disciplining your mind and your thoughts."

I sat up, elbows resting on my knees, my hands over my eyes. I felt ashamed of myself for letting my mind wander in a direction that was off limits in my friendship with Mike—and for opening myself up to be attacked by a dark angel.

Mike and I had a relationship like no other. Why would I want to ruin it? Mike wasn't made for romantic relationships. He didn't even think he was missing out on anything. He never seemed lonely. And why would he be?

Mike sat beside me on the couch. He pulled my hands away from my face, tilted my chin so I would look him in the eye, and kissed my forehead. His face softened, assuring me that I was forgiven for my moment of weakness.

Chapter 10

I ENTERED THE SCHOOL cafeteria at midday and scanned the room for my friends. Greg, Christina, and Eden were sitting together. They all motioned for me to join them. I headed in their direction.

Christina and Greg sat closer together than in the past. Christina hadn't been hanging with Tommy since we had been to Bev's house. It was fun being just the four of us.

"What's with the makeup, Liv?" Eden asked after I sat beside her.

After my date with Andy, I'd decided to try wearing a touch of makeup just for something different.

"I think she looks spectacular." Greg's eyes had their sparkle back.

"I agree," Christina said.

Christina looked happier than I'd seen her in a long time. There were no dark circles under her eyes.

Eden frowned and stuck out her lower lip. "The makeup hides her freckles. I loved them!"

Greg playfully reached over Christina's head and ruffled my hair. "I think your freckles are adorable. I miss them too!"

I had no idea that my freckles were something people could possibly admire. I'd always regarded them as a curse.

Eden's compliment meant a great deal to me. She was a natural beauty.

As I pulled an apple out of my lunch bag, I saw Andy walking across the lunchroom. I glanced away but kept an eye on him in my peripheral vision. *Creep.*

Vicki bounced over to where he sat. She flashed him a flirty little smile. Andy concentrated on his teammates seated at his table.

Vicki can have him. They deserve each other.

I turned to my three friends. "My cousin Samantha called me last night. She said her church is sponsoring a concert this Friday night at that refurbished theater on Water Street. You guys want to go? It's free."

"How good can it be if it's free?" Greg grimaced.

I named the bands that were headlining. Greg's face lit up with enthusiasm.

Greg and Christina locked eyes, then looked back at me with eagerness. Christina chirped, "I'm in."

"Me too," said Greg.

"Sounds cool to me," said Eden.

Samantha had told me the concert would be followed by an invitation for kids to give their lives to God. Sometimes the band members gave testimonies. I hoped Greg would be receptive to the message.

As Christina rose to leave at the end of lunch, I noticed her face pinch in pain. After the others dispersed, I asked, "Are you OK?"

"I'm having stomach cramps from my period. That's all," she whispered to me, clenching her teeth and bending over.

Christina had never acted this way during her monthly cycle.

"Do you have any Tylenol?"

"Yeah." I reached into my backpack and got the bottle. I shook out two pills and handed them to her. "So, is Greg still staying at your house?"

"Yeah. His parents came over Monday night to speak with my parents. They all went into Dad's office. They were in there quite a while. I suppose my dad convinced them to let Greg stay a while longer. Especially when he smelled whisky on Mr. Monahan's breath. He mentioned that Greg's dad agreed it would be good for them to spend some time apart."

"You guys seem to be getting along really well." I winked at her.

"He kissed me that night I was at his house."

I gasped. "I'm so happy for you." I squeezed her arm.

Christina grabbed her abdomen, stretching at the fabric of her short, black skirt.

"Maybe you should go see the nurse."

She straightened her skirt. "I have to run to the bathroom first. Then I'll go."

"OK. Let me know what she says."

She limped down the hallway. As I went to class, I prayed that God would relieve my friend's cramps.

During math class, I heard sirens. I ignored them and tried to concentrate on my test.

A couple of minutes later I saw flashing lights. I looked out the window beside my desk and saw an ambulance parked in front of the school. Someone was being put into the vehicle on a stretcher.

The other students gathered at the window, chattering. Mrs. Collins tapped her pen loudly on her desk. "Get back to your seats and complete your tests."

I caught a flash of the shirt hanging over the edge of the gurney. It was the same one Christina had been wearing at lunch.

I could hardly concentrate all day, worrying about Christina. As soon as I got out of school I dialed Christina's cell phone before heading to volleyball practice.

"What happened?"

She broke into sobs. "I...I had...a miscarriage."

My head began to spin and a wave of nausea hit me. "You mean you're..."

"I was."

"Why didn't you tell me?"

"I didn't even know till now."

"Have you told Tommy?"

"Not yet."

"Are you going to?"

"I'm not sure."

I breathed a prayer for Christina and her parents, for Greg and his parents, and even Tommy.

Jerk.

I sat in the waiting room of the psychologist's office, staring at the dark wood panel on the walls. Old, cracked chairs faced a TV that was playing the news. I wanted to run out. It took every ounce of control for me to stay seated.

Mom sat next to me, paging through a magazine. Other adults did the same, ignoring the children with them. One looked to be a teenager my age. The other two appeared to be of grade-school age.

"Olivia Stanton?" A nurse in a white shirt and blue polka-dotted scrubs appeared at an open door to my left, holding a folder in her hands.

Mom and I stood.

As we approached the nurse put up her hand, palm out. "I'm sorry, Mrs. Stanton. We'll need to see Olivia alone first."

"But..."

"I'm sorry. It's our policy."

I walked through the door, hearing it shut behind me. I felt relieved Mom wasn't with me. I'd get to tell my side of the story first about seeing angels and demons. I hoped to sound perfectly sane so the doctor wouldn't classify me as crazy.

The nurse led me to a private office at the end of a hallway with white painted walls and dark wood paneling halfway up the wall. A large mahogany desk sat in the middle of the office, with a brown leather chair behind it. Bookcases lined almost every ounce of space except for right behind the two seats opposite the desk. She motioned for me to sit in one of the two chairs. I sank into the deep leather cushion.

"Dr. Stein will be in momentarily." She smiled. "Relax." She put the folder on the desk and walked out.

I looked at all the framed certificates that covered one entire wall. He certainly looked qualified. I hoped he would also be sympathetic.

I heard a knock on the door. "Olivia?"

"Yes?"

A man in a brown sweater, pleated blue pants, and shiny leather shoes walked in, holding a pad of paper in one hand. He looked to be in his mid-forties. He shook my hand. "I'm Dr. Stein." He took the chair behind the desk, set down the pad of paper, and folded his hands. "So, Olivia, why are you here?"

"I see spirits." I figured I'd just blurt it out and get it over with.

His eyebrows lifted. "OK." He scribbled on his notepad.

"Does that mean I'm crazy?"

"Not necessarily. But it is unusual." He pushed his round-rimmed glasses up his nose. "People in the Bible saw angels. Are you a Christian?"

"Yes."

"I'm Jewish."

I wondered if that would work for me or against me.

"So, tell me about these spirits you see."

I told him about the angelic choir I saw at church. He scribbled on his pad as I talked. Then I described Mike.

Dr. Stein put down his pen, took off his glasses, and gave me a slight smile. "Are you taking any drugs, prescription or otherwise?"

"No. Never." He probably wondered if I was hallucinating. Smart of him to rule that out.

"Do you have a boyfriend?"

"Not right now."

He flipped back to a previous page in my file. "Your schoolwork doesn't seem to be affected."

I wondered what else Mom had told these people when she made the appointment.

"Perhaps these visions of yours are the result of your longing for a boy-friend—someone to be close to."

"But Mike is real."

"Has this spirit of yours asked you to do anything harmful, like jump off a cliff with him?"

"Of course not. He's my *guardian* angel."

"What else do you see?"

I jammed my hands into my jacket pockets and looked at the floor. "I see demons. I've watched my guardian angel fight them."

I was probably entering into the "severely wacked" category, but I might as well get it all out now.

Dr. Stein put his glasses back on and wrote furiously. After a couple of moments, he looked at me. "Tell me about the demons."

"I saw one attack my father. It was choking him, and my dad was coughing and gripping his chest. The demon was green—sort of lizard-like."

"Hmmm." He raised his eyebrows, then scribbled on his pad of paper again. "What did you do when you saw this *demon* attacking your father?"

"I prayed. Mike came to my dad's defense and defeated the demon. I didn't see the actual fight, since Mike took the demon through the wall with him into our front yard. But later Mike came and told me he'd won the fight." It all sounded crazy coming from my mouth. "Am I nuts?"

"Olivia, the only nuts in this room are the peanuts on my desk." He offered a brief smile, holding out the bowl of peanuts, offering me to sample one.

"No, thank you."

He set the bowl down in its previous spot. "I'd like to learn more about this spirit world you see. That may take some time."

"How long?"

"Oh, perhaps a year or so, depending on how many times a week I see you."

"What?" I didn't want this to take over my life for the next year. "Look, I'm sure you're good at what you do, but to be honest, all I want is for you to tell my parents I'm normal."

"I can't make that assessment based on just what you've told me today."

"Well, what's your best guess based on what you've heard so far?"

He leaned back in his chair. "As I said, it's too early for me to give a diagnosis."

I felt light-headed. Then I felt a touch on my shoulder. *Thanks, Mike. I needed that.*

"What if I don't come back to see you?" I asked calmly.

"If you're not properly treated, your life could be in danger. These visions could torment you to the point where you're no longer able to cope. In my experience, individuals who see things like you do have a tendency to become suicidal or bipolar, or have panic attacks."

I could understand why someone would become that way if they didn't know what they were seeing—or why.

"They aren't visions. They're real." I crossed my arms in defiance. Realizing how much I looked like my mom doing that, I uncrossed them.

Dr. Stein rubbed his chin. "Your response to your belief that a demon was attacking your father tells me you do have some coping skills. You prayed instead of jumping in. Some of my patients who have hallucinations throw things or yell at the voices they hear. Sometimes they even harm themselves."

Mom and Dad had caught me praying out loud the night the demon attacked my father. Fortunately, no one had heard me talking to Mike. I needed to be careful that no one did.

Dr. Stein looked me in the eye. "Why don't we bring your mom in now?"

Great. I could already hear my mom telling him, *"She's crazy, just like her cousin."*

After he walked out of the room, Mike whispered, "Your mom is in for a big surprise."

I smiled. Mike could be very creative.

"But you'll need to be patient. Give me a day or two and I'll come up with a solution."

I couldn't wait to see what Mike had up his sleeve.

Chapter 11

IKE STOOD IN the field next to Olivia's house, waiting for Saphar to arrive. Saphar was an old friend Mike had worked with on many missions before he became a guardian, so he made sure to request him specifically. Saphar knew Mike well enough to know how to help without being asked what to do, and he also had a great sense of humor. Mike knew he needed help with protecting Olivia, and Saphar was the best reinforcement angel for the job.

Humidity hung in the night air like a damp washrag, and the only sound was the frogs peeping in the pond nearby. Mike could see for miles from rolling hill to rolling hill. Within moments it was dark enough for Mike to gaze at the stars appearing as the sky faded from a light yellow to a deep blue.

Mike closed his eyes and took in a deep breath of the sweet air. When he opened them he saw Saphar standing in front of him with a wide grin. Saphar was a lot like Mike as far as height and build, only he had dark red hair with soft curls that sometimes fell in his face. Mike returned his smile and gave him a strong hug of greeting.

Before they could exchange pleasantries, Mike's sensitive hearing caused him to perk up his head, jerking it in the direction of the town. He focused in on two demons sitting on a bluff that looked down on Rising Sun a few miles away. He used all of his energy to hear what the demons were saying. Saphar picked up quickly on what Mike was doing and did the same. At first the demons' voices were muffled as Mike weeded out all of the sounds, and it took a while before they became crystal clear. His supernatural sight zeroed in on their forms within moments. These were demons he'd never seen before. They were crouched down and looked very haggard, as minion demons often did, and were about the size of small dogs. One was larger than the other, and their saggy brown skin clung to their bones, protruding out of their frail extremities. Bony spikes shot out of their backs. Their large yellow eyes hungrily scanned the town below. Minions always had a leader, and Mike knew that there had to be a more powerful demon close by.

"We're aiming for his heart on this one, Bazil," one minion wheezed to the other. "If we can take out the girl, Lagarre will be very pleased."

Mike froze. Lagarre was in Rising Sun. He grasped Saphar's bicep as his knees buckled. His companion clasped his hand over Mike's.

Mike tucked his hair behind his right ear as he concentrated on the conversation that ensued.

"You mean he won't beat us anymore?" The other minion hissed and then let out a hideous, phlegm-filled cough.

"Maybe he will promote us like he is always promising." The smaller, dog-like demon crouched lower to survey the town. "He will have to if we kill the charge of his rival. She is becoming trouble for all of us anyway."

"Olivia," Mike whispered. It was the joy of his heart they were speaking of. Of course Lagarre would find the most brutal way to wound him.

"Yeah, that high school girl and her friends are getting strong, even engaging the enemy to fight against us," the large, dog-demon growled with disdain.

A swift, invisible force from behind the minions caught them off guard. A demon that must have been Lagarre sent them hurtling down the hill end over end.

"Shut up, you idiots! You never know who is listening!" Lagarre had changed in appearance. He was taller and thinner. He looked weak. Mike studied Lagarre's face. It was more gaunt and skeletal. But there was no mistake that it was him. Mike tried to look closer, but just as he focused in, Lagarre looked directly in Mike's direction. Even though Mike was watching from miles away, Lagarre could sense him. Mike immediately took his focus off of the bluff. He didn't want Lagarre knowing what he had heard or where he was. If Lagarre could pinpoint Mike's location, he could find Olivia, and that was the last thing Mike wanted.

In ancient times before the flood, when the ungodly offspring of fallen angels were destroying the Earth, Mike was assigned to hunt and destroy Lagarre and anything that Lagarre spawned. Lagarre was the son of one of the two hundred fallen angels who became infatuated with the daughters of man before the flood. They mated with these females, hoping to corrupt human DNA and thus prevent the prophesied Savior from coming to Earth. He fell for a beautiful brunette, the daughter of a powerful landowner in the Fertile Crescent. Their son, a powerful giant, ravaged the land, killing off all plants and animals within a hundred-mile radius.

The prayers of a Jewish priest engaged Mike to destroy this killer. He'd led a battalion of three hundred warrior angels who destroyed Lagarre's son, sending his disembodied spirit to roam the Earth. When Lagarre found out, he vowed to destroy Mike, but he hadn't had a real chance until now. Lagarre must have been hunting Mike for centuries, and now that he'd found him, he had the best weapon against him: his charge. By killing Olivia, Lagarre would be making good on his promise to see the demise of his archrival.

As Mike stood next to Saphar, a voice floating on the evening wind hissed, "Your precious little princess is dead!"

"He saw us!" Saphar breathed helplessly.

Mike turned around to find Lagarre standing in front of him.

Lagarre held out both of his bony hands and with one motion sent Mike and Saphar sailing end over end through the air, landing in a pond at Hopkins Park over five miles away.

A roar rose up from deep inside of Mike as he burst out of the water, thrusting his wings out to full length. He looked frantically around for Lagarre but didn't see him. Lagarre didn't want to fight. He wanted Olivia unprotected.

When Greg pulled up to the curb outside my house, I shouted good-bye to my parents and hurried out to the rusty blue Jeep. Eden and Christina sat in the back, so I climbed into the front passenger seat.

I was excited about going to the concert at my cousin's church, but I felt a little apprehensive about Greg's driving. He had a reputation for going really fast. "Christina says you have a lead foot."

Greg laughed. When he turned the key in the ignition, loud music thumped from the stereo. I had to restrain myself from covering my ears.

We rode in silence since there was no way we could have any conversation over that noise.

Greg took one corner so fast the rear of the car fishtailed.

I clutched the door handle. *Oh, God, don't let us die. God, I assume You are going to protect us all so my friends can get to the church and hear the gospel?*

"Yes."

I relaxed my fierce grip on the door handle after I heard God's response.

When we arrived at the theater we found a bar across the parking lot entrance, indicating it was full. Greg parked in the grassy field behind the building, along with several other cars.

When Greg cut the engine, the music died, and I breathed a sigh of relief. We all poured out of his Jeep. Christina took Greg's arm, and we all proceeded to the open front door of the old town theater.

Even from outside we could hear throbbing music. This was going to make the noise from Greg's car stereo seem tame.

We paid the ten-dollar entry fee, got our hands stamped, and entered the building. By the time we'd gone through the lobby and walked toward the stage, the volume of the music was blistering. We blended into the crowd of teenagers gathered around the stage but steered clear of the mosh pit, where ten guys flipped, spun, and ran around the edges of the circle.

In the midst of thumping bass, banging drums, and flashing lights, I felt myself moving to the beat. My ears would probably ring for days, but I didn't care. I started to enjoy the full-throttle sound pulsating from the speakers.

Eden leaned in and screamed something in my ear. I had no idea what she said, but I shot her a smile and nodded. She smiled back. Then she pointed. Ty was standing about seven feet from us. Eden's high school crush. I winked at her.

Greg stood in front of us, his arms encircling Christina. They moved together to the beat. Apparently they'd officially moved past "friend" status.

The song ended with guitars wailing and the vocalist screaming out his last note. The crowd roared.

A guy in tight jeans, a striped black T-shirt, and black hair approached Greg. I'd noticed him at school hanging out with Greg. His name was Toby. His black leather jacket and blue jeans blended in with the majority of the crowd.

Greg left Christina and moved toward Toby and slapped him on the back in greeting.

I felt a tap on my shoulder and turned to see my cousin Samantha wearing a black T-shirt that said Staff, jeans, and a pair of neon-green Chuck Taylors. She was three years older than me, but we had the same blonde hair, green eyes, fair complexion, and petite body frame. She threw her arms around me and shouted in my ear, "I'm so glad you came!"

I leaned in, my lips almost touching her ear. "I brought some friends with me." I gestured toward Eden. "This is Eden. Her father is my pastor."

Samantha waved at Eden. Eden waved back and smiled.

Greg had returned to stand behind Christina, so I touched him on the shoulder. "This is my cousin Samantha." Christina and Greg nodded at her, then turned back toward the stage. Toby now stood next to Greg and Christina.

A young man who looked to be in his mid-twenties took the stage and introduced himself as Scott Anderson. "I'm the youth pastor here at Christian Life Church. Now, we want you all to have fun tonight. We also want you to know that you're loved. If you don't have someone in your life who loves you, or you just need to talk to someone, come see me or any of the people wearing staff shirts. We love you. God loves you. And God is *awesome!*"

A shout rose from the crowd. I hollered, too, clapping my hands, enjoying the excitement in the air.

God, You are awesome.

While Scott laid some ground rules for the evening, the next band came to the stage, unplugging chords and setting up guitars. Every one of the musicians had multiple tattoos and piercings—just like most of the people in the audience.

My church would stick up their noses at these kids. Why did Samantha's church embrace them, even bring in bands they wanted to hear? Samantha had told me the theater was packed every month. The bands invited weren't necessarily religious, but all sang songs with a positive message.

God, I see Your hand in this. I'd love to be a part of this ministry somehow.

Samantha tapped me on the shoulder. "I'm working lights for this gig. Wanna come up to the sound booth with me? You'll have a great view from up there."

I looked at Eden, who'd obviously heard the invitation.

She grinned. "Go for it!"

"Tell them." I nodded at Christina and Greg, who were listening to the youth pastor introduce the next band.

Eden gave me the OK sign with her fingers.

I grabbed Samantha's sleeve, and we wormed our way through the shoulder-to-shoulder crowd.

We climbed the stairs into the sound booth, which had a bird's-eye perspective of the stage and the crowd. The fifteen-foot-square area was packed with strange-looking equipment. One guy moved knobs up and down on the larger sound board. Another one sat in front of the smaller board. A piece of masking tape on his gear had the word *lights* scrawled on it.

"Come over here." Sam gestured for me to stand next to her by the lights board. The two guys who had been in front of it turned, smiled, and moved aside.

When the band hit their first note, Samantha started flashing the multicolored light cans mounted above the stage area, using the buttons and sliders on the control board. As the music played, she synchronized the lights with the beat of the song.

Cool!

The guy who had previously been running lights had moved behind the spotlight on a platform near the back corner of the room.

When the song ended, Sam looked at me. "Do you want to try it?"

"You bet!"

Sam stood behind me and guided my hands on the board to give me a feel for the buttons and how to push them. The music was so loud, there was no way she could audibly instruct me.

As the song ended I punched a few of the lights, my fingers dancing across the buttons like it was a computer keyboard. I followed the drummer's arms, watching for the beats coming up, and perfectly finished on the last crash of the drums.

"I think you've got it!" Samantha had a big smile on her face.

"That was fun." I was hooked.

"I'm glad you liked it. Because Josh just called and asked if I could give him a break and run the camera for a few minutes. Think you can handle this on your own?"

"Do you think I can?"

Samantha winked at me. "You're a natural." She left to take her place behind the camera.

I focused my attention on the lights board, listening to the bass and drum for my beat, my eyes never leaving the drummer.

At the end of the song, the guy running the sound board smiled at me. "I'm Aaron."

"Olivia."

He glanced at the lights board. "You picked that up pretty fast."

"Did I do OK?"

"You did great."

"Thanks. I'm really enjoying this."

"You know, I'm looking for people to work on technical crew for the music festival this spring. Interested?"

"I'd love it."

"Samantha can give you the details later."

The next song started, so I focused on my new job. Playing with my "instrumental lights" made me feel like part of the band.

I'd always loved music, but I never thought I'd get into the technical aspect of it. But if I could do this, maybe I could get free tickets to lots of concerts. And I'd be able to watch them from this great vantage point, maybe even get to meet some of the band members.

I decided to learn this lighting stuff the best I could. Maybe get into sound and camera work too.

At the end of the concert the youth pastor got back on stage and started talking about God.

Lord, please let Greg hear the message. I really wanted him to become a Christian since Christina was now. I figured Eden and Christina were praying for him too. I knew he'd need God to deal with the abuse he'd endured at his father's hands for years.

While the youth pastor spoke I watched Greg's body language. He seemed to be listening intently to every word.

"I know some of you are dealing with all kinds of stuff. You may have an addiction. Maybe you have relationship problems at home or at school. You might think no one cares. But God does. He can change your life. All you have to do is invite Him in. He loves you so much, He sent His Son, Jesus, to die for you, taking all your sins upon Himself. He died for each and every one of you. You matter to God."

I squeezed my eyes shut and prayed for God to help Scott say the right words and that those listening would respond positively to them.

"You can ask God to be a part of your life right now. You can pray and ask God silently. Or if you'd like to have someone pray with you, find the ones with staff T-shirts. What matters is that you make a choice tonight. The right choice."

I liked the way this youth pastor spoke. He was direct but not preachy.

"Thanks for coming out tonight. The band is going to play one last song. I hope you'll come back next month. And please attend our festival we're having this April. Flyers will be at the doors as you leave."

I'll take a couple extra and hang them up around school.

The crowd cheered as the drummer clicked off the beginning of the song. I hated that it was the last song, since I enjoyed "playing the lights" so much.

When the band ended I said good-bye to Aaron.

"I hope to see you at the music festival."

"I hope to be there!"

I caught Samantha's eye where she stood by the camera and waved at her, then made a phone sign with my hand and mouthed, "Call me." She nodded. I wanted to let her know I could not wait to volunteer at the music festival.

I found my friends waiting by the door we had come in. They were all smiling. "Did you like the concert?"

They all said, "Yes."

Then Greg added, "I really want to come next month. And also to the music festival."

Yes!

Eden and I looked at each other and smiled.

"Wanna hang out at my house?" Greg suggested. "Dad's pulling another graveyard shift, so we'll have the house to ourselves."

We all replied, "Yes."

I was relieved Greg's dad was gone for the night.

Toby followed us back to the car. "Hey, Toby, you coming?" Greg asked.

"Wh-—Sure." He zipped up his black leather jacket and jammed into the backseat with Eden and me. He and I sat side by side, and I could see him trying to lean toward the car door to give me room. When our arms touched he spurted, "So sorry, excuse me."

He seemed polite. And he didn't give me the creeps.

I'm sure he's fine if he's friends with Greg.

It was only a five-minute ride to Greg's. Thank God he didn't have the radio roaring the whole way. My ears were still numb from the concert.

I closed my eyes and leaned my head back as we drove, resting my eyes, hoping I'd be able to stay up at least another hour so I wouldn't disappoint my friends. When the car jerked to a halt I snapped my head up. We'd pulled up in front of the red brick home. Eden and I exchanged concerned glances as we scanned around the neighborhood. Trash cans were strewn everywhere, lawns were overgrown, and shutters dangled from a few of the windows of Greg's house. Several dogs barked as we approached the front door. Their echo came from every direction.

As Greg fumbled with the keys in the blackness, a cat hissed. I jumped. Eden gasped. I grabbed her jacket sleeve. "It's just Cujo, the junkyard cat. Ha! Just kidding. That's Cuddles. She doesn't like strangers."

Greg cackled, hovered over the doorknob, his shoulders bobbing up and down as he reveled in freaking us out.

"Here, kitty," Greg mewed at his cat, who raced ahead of us through the door as soon as it was open.

I inhaled stale cigarette smoke before even entering. Once inside it was overwhelming. My parents would certainly smell it on me when I got home. I wondered what they'd say.

I quickly texted my Dad:

> At Greg's. Will be home in an hour. Eden and Christina are with me. I'm fine.

I left out Toby's name, not wanting Dad to get worried or suspicious. Within seconds I received his response:

> See you soon, Goldilocks.

We all shed our jackets and threw them on the living room couch. Greg switched on an overhead light that illuminated the area by the front door and the stairway right in front of it. We bounded up the stairway, giggling as Christina imitated the way Greg talked to his cat like it was a little baby.

As we followed Christina down the hallway toward Greg's room, he came rushing past us to cut us all off. He almost shoved me aside as he fled into his room, shutting the door behind him. I pounded my fists on the door, and we all pretended to be upset. All we heard was shuffling. There was no answer to our sarcastic whining.

"OK! You can come in!"

Christina turned the knob, and the door squeaked on its hinges. Greg was sitting on his bed as if nothing had happened, his arms folded across his chest. I raised my eyebrow at him while everyone else filed in the room. He just shook his head as if I had no reason to be suspicious. I gave up trying to figure out what Greg was hiding until Christina reached under Greg's pillow and pulled out a beat-up stuffed dog. Greg reached for it in vain. Christina was too fast.

"Put Boo down!" Greg yelled before he could stop himself.

The room went silent, then erupted in laughter. Greg turned beet red. Toby reached over and snatched the dog from Christina and cradled it in his arms and rocked it like a baby.

Greg joined in with the laughter. He was a good sport, even though he was obviously embarrassed.

"You have no reason to be ashamed of Boo," Christina said, grabbing the stuffed dog from Toby. "He's adorable, even with a missing eye."

Greg grabbed Boo from her and stuffed him back under his pillow with a sheepish grin.

"How about a movie?" Greg said, desperately trying to change the subject.

"Sounds good to me!" Eden said out of compassion for him.

We situated ourselves on Greg's floor with lots of blankets and pillows. Once the popcorn and candy was distributed, we started the movie. It was one of Greg's mindless yet entertaining action comedies. I fell asleep almost immediately. I woke up to everyone laughing because I had let out a loud snort and woke myself up with a violent jerk. I hated when I did that. Now it was my turn to be embarrassed. Toby seemed to be sound asleep as well, so deeply that he'd missed my horrible moment.

I looked over at Greg and Christina and saw that Boo was nestled in between them. I couldn't help but smile. Greg just shrugged his shoulders as if admitting his love for his stuffed dog, Boo. I couldn't have loved my friends more at that moment.

Chapter 12

A STADIUM FULL OF fans stood in the outdoor bleachers, cheering as the high school band entered the football field. From my perch halfway up the stands, I watched cheerleaders do cartwheels, jumps, and splits in anticipation of our team's entrance. Tonight was an important game against our rivals, the Golden Elks.

My parents hated football, so I always got rides to games with Eden and her parents, who were avid fans. Eden's father was the team chaplain, so he attended every game.

The noise of the crowd escalated when the first player burst through the large white banner painted with our school's colors of red and white. Once the team had gathered around Coach Aaron, the opposing team entered from the other side of the field.

Eden elbowed me and pointed at Ty taking his spot on the field as quarterback. "Doesn't he look amazing in his uniform?" She said it quietly enough that her mother, sitting next to her, wouldn't hear.

"Yeah, he does." The tight white pants the guys wore made their Herculean thighs obvious to any female who had an ounce of estrogen in her body.

I wished Eden wasn't so shy. She was afraid to even talk to Ty, the guy she'd had a crush on for as long as I could remember.

I noticed Greg and his parents sitting ten seats down to my left. Christina sat beside Greg. I caught their eye and waved. They waved back.

A ref's whistle signaled time for the kickoff. The ball flew through the air and was caught by a receiver. Seconds later, the clash of helmets and shoulder pads made me wince. I loved the game of football, but I hated the thought of what these guys were doing to their bodies.

Early in the second half, our Rising Sun Tigers took possession of the ball and found themselves in a fourth-down-and-one-yard position. When the team came out of the huddle Eden's dad leaned over. "Watch for a quarterback sneak."

Ty took the snap and attempted to leap over the line of defense. The middle linebacker launched himself into the air, smacking our quarterback's helmet with his own.

Ty twisted and flew through the air, collapsing in an unnatural heap. A loud gasp went up from the crowd. Most of the spectators stood.

Eden clasped her hand over her mouth. I put my arm around her shoulders. A hush fell over the stadium as coaches and managers gathered around Ty. He didn't move.

A few rows to my right, a woman wearing a red-and-white team jacket thudded down the bleachers and ran onto the field.

"That's his mom," Eden murmured.

Eden's father touched her shoulder. "I'm going down there."

Eden followed him, and I followed her. I assumed they'd let us on the field since Eden's dad was team chaplain.

Our feet pounding down the bleachers thundered in the death-like stillness. The eerie silence made me shiver.

Once we hit the turf we sprinted toward Ty, pushing through a crowd of people surrounding him. His lips were blue, his eyes closed, and his neck was twisted in an odd angle. The team physician was performing mouth-to-mouth resuscitation and CPR on him.

"Let's give him some space," Coach said, and we all moved back.

Ty's mom spotted Eden's father. "Pastor!"

Eden's dad hugged her, and she sobbed into his shoulder.

I felt out of place, but no one shooed me away, so I stayed to support Eden.

The team physician laid a finger against Ty's neck. "There's no pulse."

A wail rose from Ty's mom.

Men with stretchers ran toward us. One of them shouted, "Ambulance is on its way." Guys from both teams wiped at their eyes.

Ty's mother grabbed the coach's arm. "This is my pastor. I'd like him to pray over Ty while we're waiting for the ambulance."

"Sure, ma'am."

Eden's dad removed his baseball hat and knelt beside Ty's motionless body. Eden grasped my hand. I squeezed it tightly.

As the physician continued his resuscitation efforts, the four of us huddled together on Ty's other side. Players from both teams removed their helmets and bowed their heads.

"Holy Father," Eden's dad said, "we come to You on behalf of this young man. Oh, God." He paused, as if grasping for the right words to say. "Have mercy on this boy's life."

Ty's mom whimpered.

Eden dropped to her knees and touched Ty's left hand. Her lips moved but no sound came out. Tears dripped onto the ground.

Ty's chest heaved. Coughing wrenched his body. Everyone standing around Ty gasped. His mother sank to the ground and grasped his shoulders.

Eden covered her mouth with both hands and stood. She leaned against me as if she were about to faint. I caught her and steadied her.

All around me jaws dropped in amazement. Both teammates and opponents cheered and jumped around. The stadium exploded in applause.

Ty sat up. "Who touched me?" His voice was scratchy.

Eden darted a look at me.

"I felt a rush of energy pulse through my left hand."

Eden knelt beside him. "I did that," she whispered.

"Thanks."

The coach rubbed Ty's back. "Easy, buddy. You'd better lie back down."

The paramedics came, put Ty on the stretcher, and carried him off the field. Ty's mom threw her arms around him and kissed him before they carried him toward the locker room. She ran behind them.

Coach pointed at a young man seated on the bench. "QB 2, warm up. You're on the field!"

As if nothing Earth-shattering had happened, the game resumed. The yard had been gained, Rising Sun had first down, and a fifteen-yard penalty was assessed for a personal foul.

"Pastor," Ty's mom yelled over her shoulder, "follow us!"

Eden and her dad sprinted for the locker room. I followed close behind. Inside was chaos, with paramedics and team doctors surrounding Ty.

"I feel fine," Ty protested. "I don't want to go to the hospital."

"It's just routine, son," said one of the paramedics. "We have to check for concussion and make sure you're OK." They began to strap him to the stretcher.

Ty looked around. "Where's that girl who touched me?"

Eden took a few steps toward him. "I'm the one."

"You're Eden, right?"

She blinked. "I didn't realize you knew my name."

"Will you visit me at the hospital?"

"Yeah, sure."

Before the paramedics took off, I heard Ty's mom talking on her cell phone, telling her husband to meet her at the hospital. Then she climbed into the ambulance and sat alongside her son. The rest of us returned to the stands.

Through the remainder of the game Eden and I sat speechless, even when the fans around us cheered.

Over and over I replayed in my mind what had happened on that field. My friend had touched Ty, and immediately after he was healed.

I'd read several Bible verses about spiritual gifts lately. One was the ability for someone to lay hands on the sick and pray for them to be healed. Did Eden have that gift?

I wanted to stand up and dance. Instead, I stared straight ahead, smiling from ear to ear.

Chapter 13

O N FRIDAY NIGHT, Eden invited me to hang out at her place while her parents went to a meeting at church. I enjoyed a great meal of spaghetti and meatballs with Pastor Bob and his wife, Kathy. Since they had to leave right after dinner, Eden and I offered to clean up. Kathy went upstairs for some final touch-ups while her husband disappeared into his study. I started rinsing the dishes, then Eden put them in the dishwasher.

A greasy pot slipped out of Eden's hands, skidded across the linoleum floor, and thudded against one of the kitchen chairs. "Slimy little bugger," she said. She bent over and picked it up.

We broke out laughing.

She came back to the sink with the slippery pan.

"Klutz," I teased, then jabbed my forefinger at Eden's side. She jerked back as if she was afraid of being touched.

Kathy walked back into the kitchen and grabbed her Bible off the table. The scent of her floral perfume filled the room. "You know the rules, right?"

"Yes, Mom. Clean up our messes. No boys in the house. In bed by nine thirty."

I could tell she'd heard the speech a hundred times. Sounded like the same speech my mom always gave me.

"Uncle Jeff said he'd come over to check on you sometime tonight, just to make sure you're safe and sound."

That seemed strange. We were teenagers, not eight-year-olds. Why did we need to be checked up on?

A shadow crossed Eden's face. She turned on the hot water and squirted liquid soap into the sink.

"The meeting is scheduled to end at eight thirty, but you know how your father likes to talk to everybody afterward, so we probably won't be home until at least nine." Kathy retrieved a white sweater from the coat closet by their back kitchen door and pulled it across her shoulders.

"OK." Eden shoved her hands into the steaming dishwater and rubbed them vigorously. "Come home as soon as you can."

What teenager would want her parents to come home soon? I loved the freedom of not having adult supervision.

Kathy walked up to Eden. "Are you OK, honey? Would you rather I didn't go? Or do you want to go with us?"

Why was Eden's mom treating her like a little girl?

Pastor Bob poked his head into the kitchen. "Come on, Kathy. The girls will be fine." He looked at his watch. "We're already late."

"I'll be fine, Mom. Olivia's here. I'm not alone."

Kathy grabbed her purse and Bible, then headed toward the front door with her husband.

"Free at last," I sang out as I snapped at Eden's leg with the rolled-up dish towel.

Her eyes stayed focused on the sink, and her hands rubbed beneath the water in a frantic motion. I looked closer and saw that she was scraping the back of her hand with a steel-wool pad. Red blotches rose on her skin.

I grasped the scouring pad. "What are you doing?"

Her hands flew out of the water, sending a spray of suds and water across the room. The round, gray pad landed on the counter beside the sink.

"I'm fine."

She started washing the dishes that wouldn't fit in the dishwasher. I grabbed a towel and rinsed and dried them, then placed them on the kitchen table so Eden could put them away where they belonged.

I felt an urge to reach out to Eden, but I waited, hoping she'd say something to open up the conversation.

When she stayed silent I finally opened my mouth to speak, but stopped when I heard a loud pounding on the glass of the back door.

Eden jerked her head toward the sound. A shadow swept across her face again. As she headed toward the door, a whispered word slipped from her mouth that sounded like a curse.

After Eden turned the deadbolt and opened the door, a balding, overweight man walked into the kitchen wearing a shirt that was too small for his hairy belly. "Hey there, beautiful. How's my favorite niece?" His voice was too loud for the quiet room.

He reached out to touch Eden's arm, but when he saw me standing at the sink, he shrank back. "I didn't know you had company."

Eden twisted her dishtowel in her hand and stared at the floor. "This is my friend Olivia. She's from my school. And church."

His eyes moved up and down my frame. A cold chill swept over me. I felt like I was being looked over like a horse being sold at auction. "Olivia's a pretty name. Just like Eden is. Two pretty names for two pretty girls."

This guy was definitely a creep. I suddenly realized why Eden had stiffened in his presence. I'm sure she had the same feeling I did. Or worse.

Eden wrapped her arms tightly across her shirt and held her legs close together. I'd never seen her so tense.

He broke the silence with a small laugh. "Well, if Eden isn't going to introduce us properly, I'll have to do it myself. I'm Uncle Jeff. Pastor Bob's older brother. He probably doesn't talk about me much. Can't say I blame him. After all, I ain't the whitest sheep in the fold, am I?" Coarse laughter echoed through the room.

My creep siren went off again.

"OK, you don't have to hit old Jeff with a baseball bat for him to get the message. I can see I interrupted some serious girl talk here. Y'all were probably talking about your boyfriends, right?"

"N-not really." Eden's voice was hesitant and guarded.

"Well, I told your daddy I'd check on ya, and I did. So now I'll just head back across to my lonely house." He turned away, and I let out a breath. I hoped I'd never see that man's face again.

He grabbed the door handle, then turned around and looked me over once more. "It was a real pleasure meeting you, Miss Olivia." His eyes reminded me of a wolf stalking its prey.

The second he walked out the door, Eden pushed it tight against the frame and turned the deadbolt with a fierce twist.

I draped my dish towel over a kitchen chair. "Eden, I know something's bothering you. You don't have to tell me what it is right now. But if you feel like talking sometime, I want you to know that I really, truly care about you."

Her fingers clenched the fabric of her pale gray shirt. Her eyes looked as timid as a kitten's. "Liv, I..."

She smiled a fake smile, like older people do when they think you're not mature enough to handle the adult topics of life. "Oh, never mind this serious stuff. Let's talk about something fun—like our science project." She grabbed her books out of a backpack sitting on a small stool in the kitchen.

Only Eden would think a science project was fun.

"Shall we go to my secret la-bor-a-tory?" she asked with a fake German accent.

Though I was still worried about Eden, I welcomed the change of mood. "Why, of course, *Herr Frankenstein!*"

We giggled and headed upstairs.

Eden's room looked like a Disney store. Cartoon princesses graced her walls, and she had a whole shelf of fairy-tale storybooks above the headboard on her bed.

I'd always felt her taste in room decoration was odd, but I never teased her about it. I wondered if her parents wouldn't let her put up band posters and other typical teenager stuff.

We threw our schoolbooks onto the Hello Kitty bedspread and flopped down on our bellies beside each other. I opened my science book but couldn't concentrate on the words. God's voice prompted me to speak to my friend about more serious stuff—something more specific than from a high school science book. "Eden…"

"Let's not talk. I'd rather just do our homework, OK?" She reached up to put her hair into a short ponytail with a hair tie she'd had around her wrist, and I saw a flash of skin when her sleeve slid down. I grabbed her hand and pulled the sleeve farther down.

"Hey!" She pulled her hand away. "What are you doing?"

"You can stop hiding it now. I saw the scars."

She slid the sleeve back in place and picked at a piece of frayed fabric on the bedspread.

"You're a cutter, aren't you?"

She looked up at me. Tears pooled at the corners of her eyes. "I…I can't stop it, Liv. I've tried. I don't want to do it. I…I just can't help myself." She dropped her face into her hands, and a flood of sobs shook her shoulders.

I touched her back. At first she recoiled as if my hands were made of ice. But then she relaxed beneath my fingers. "Why did you start?"

After a long silence, she said, "Him."

I knew exactly who she meant. "You mean Jeff?"

She nodded. "He…touches me. And he makes me touch him. He forces me to do things. I hate my body!"

Vomit burned its way up my throat, and I swallowed to hold it down. The acidic taste made my eyes burn. I took a deep breath and tried to calm my voice. "When did you start?"

"When I was eight. Jeff said everybody does this with their favorite niece. He said I'll like it better when I grow up. Olivia, I don't want to grow up!"

Suddenly Eden's choice of room décor made sense. It reflected her desire to not grow up.

I listened without interruption as she told me about the times she fought against him. I felt like beating the living daylights out of Mr. Perv!

"I hated the way he talked about me growing prettier every day. So I stopped eating. When starvation didn't destroy my body I started cutting it. I wanted to look ugly enough that he'd stop wanting to touch me. But it didn't work."

"Do your parents know?"

"No. My mom saw scratches on my arm once. She thought my neighbor's puppy did it."

"Why didn't you tell her the truth?"

"Jeff said Daddy would lose the church if I said anything."

I wondered if I should tell Eden's parents about this dirty old man. Would that help or cause more problems?

"I've prayed for him to die."

"I don't blame you."

"But I feel guilty for praying that way."

I had no idea what to say. She needed someone a lot more qualified than me to deal with her psychological issues. But I sure didn't want her to end up with the shrink my mom sent me to.

"Oh, Olivia, you don't know how long I've wanted to tell someone."

"I'm glad you trusted me enough to share this."

"I feel so much better just talking about it."

Sensing the Holy Spirit urging me, I asked, "Eden, can I pray with you?"

"I'd like that."

I covered her hand that was lying on top of her textbook, then closed my eyes. "Father God, reach down into Eden's heart. Take away her pain the way only You can. Take Jeff out of her life, God. Raise up a wall of protection around her. Lord, You know Eden. You knit her together in her mother's womb, and You know everything about her, inside and out. You know her pain. You know her desires and her longings. You can deliver her from this torment and the evil Satan has planned for her. You are greater than he is. Father, I ask You to show Your power in Eden's life, even tonight. I pray in Jesus' name, amen."

When I opened my eyes, I saw a smile spread across her tear-dampened face. I hugged her close.

Standing behind her, beside the bed, an angel stood about eight feet tall, smiling at me. He had a black beard and curly hair. His breastplate was dented as if it had been used in heavy battle. On it was a frieze of a bear's head, its mouth open in a roar. Draped around his shoulders was a bear pelt, fastened around his neck with a gold clasp in the shape of a bear claw. Under his arm he grasped an iron helmet in the shape of a bear's head. The opening looked like a bear's mouth, with sharp metal teeth.

His golden eyes held me in a trance. Then his gaze turned to Eden, and his face softened with affection. His large, scarred, hairy hand completely covered the top of Eden's head.

As I released my friend, the angel transformed into a grizzly bear standing on its hind legs, poised for battle. Then he disappeared.

A wave of relief came over me. Eden was certainly well protected. Her angel looked battle-worn. No doubt he'd had a hard job. I hoped the worst was over.

"Thanks for praying for me, Liv."

"My pleasure."

Eden disappeared into the bathroom. I heard the water running. I waited until she entered the bedroom again. I hoped the angel in the room read my thoughts. *You watch over her. Like never before.*

As I washed my face, brushed my teeth, and put on my pajamas, the shocking image I'd just seen kept playing in my mind.

When I returned to the bedroom Eden was studying her textbook. She looked peaceful. I sat down on the bed beside her and opened my own textbook, trying to concentrate on our assignment. I stared at her arms. No blood there. She had not cut herself.

After we finished our science assignment, separately, Eden shut her book and laid it on the floor beside the bed. I did the same shortly after.

"Want to watch a movie?" she asked.

"Sure. Which one?"

"How about *Cinderella*?"

Typical of Eden. I'd watched the animated version with her numerous times. But after the dark subject matter we'd discussed tonight, I didn't mind entering into fairy-tale land at all. Besides, Disney movies never get old, no matter what age you are.

Eden hopped off the bed, grabbed the DVD off the bookshelf, and slid the video into the player.

I fell asleep with pleasant images in my mind of Prince Charming riding to Eden's rescue on a white horse. Just before I drifted off I heard Mike whisper in my ear, "Eden will be safe now."

I reached out, wanting to touch him in some way in thankfulness. Instead, I felt him squeeze my forearm.

I awoke to the sound of doors slamming, footsteps running up the stairs, and Eden's parents calling out her name. I opened my eyes and saw Bob and Kathy in the doorway. They looked disheveled, and their eyes were red.

When her dad turned on the light, Eden sat up in bed. "Dad. Mom. You look horrible."

"Eden, honey." Her father wrapped his arm around her. "There's been an...incident." His voice shook.

Eden blinked. "What?"

"The police just called," her mother said, stroking Eden's hair. "Uncle Jeff's been arrested and is being held without bail. The authorities found some questionable material on his computer."

"Like what?" Eden asked.

Neither of her parents responded.

The color drained from Eden's face.

I could certainly guess what they had found. I guessed that Eden had a clue too.

Pastor Bob kissed Eden on the forehead. "I need to go to the police station. Your mother's going to Grandma's house to stay with her until I can get there to comfort her once she tells her the news."

"Will you girls be all right here alone for a while?" Kathy asked.

Eden clasped her arms around her knees. "We'll be fine."

Her mom looked my way. "I called your mother and asked if you could stay here with Eden until we get back. I hope you don't mind."

"Not at all." Truth to tell, I couldn't wait to hear what happened to stupid Jeff.

Her parents left the room. Her mother closed the door behind her, leaving the light on.

I thought about the prayer I'd prayed just a few hours ago. What had I said to God? If I recalled correctly, I'd asked Him to take Jeff out of Eden's life. Had God done what I asked Him to? Had my prayer caused somebody to go to jail?

At least he couldn't hurt Eden from jail. I hoped he stayed there for a long time.

I couldn't help but wonder how many other times God had answered my prayers in ways I didn't know.

Eden and I lay awake talking till morning. By dawn we were so tired we decided to stay home from school.

As we sat in her kitchen eating bowls of cereal, Eden squirmed in her chair. "Is it bad that I'm happy Uncle Jeff's in the slammer?"

"Personally, I think God answered my prayer for your protection. It just happened faster than I thought it would."

"You think God put Jeff in jail to keep me safe?"

"I know He did."

"How can you be so sure?"

"My guardian angel told me." There. I'd said it out loud to someone.

Eden dropped her spoon, and it clanged against her cereal bowl. "You mean you heard a voice in your head?"

"No. I've actually seen him."

Eden's mouth dropped open. "For real?" Then her expression turned to a look of curiosity. "What does he look like?"

I put down my spoon and pushed my cereal bowl away. "Most of the time, he looks like a normal teenage guy. At least that's how he appears to me. He's got blond hair, tanned skin, and he wears jeans and sneakers."

"Is he hot?" Eden giggled.

"No!" I threw my napkin at her. "Well, actually, he's not bad. But he's my guardian angel. He's not really a guy."

Eden sighed. "If vampires are hot I can just imagine what angels must look like." We both laughed. I loved seeing her relaxed expression. "I guess you liked my dad's angel notes."

Of course, they had helped tremendously in starting this new journey of seeing angels. "Yeah. Thanks for lending them to me."

"So, what's his name?"

"Mike."

"Like Michael the archangel?"

"No. Just Mike. He's not an archangel."

"And he...talks to you?"

"Yeah. And he's really funny too."

"Like how?"

"He jokes around with me. And he has creative ways of getting me out of precarious situations."

"Do tell."

"Remember my date with Andy that I told you about?"

"Of course. Who could forget a groping guy being interrupted by a snarling wolf?"

"Well, that wolf was Mike. He protects me in other ways too."

"So he protects you from danger? Like stopping cars from running over you?"

"Well, no, but he could."

"Do you think I have a guardian angel too?"

"I know you do."

"How do you know?"

"I saw him last night."

Eden leaned in, her eyes wide. "You did?"

"After I prayed for you, he showed himself to me. He's a big, burly guy. Very intimidating. But he has gentle eyes and a kind smile."

"He must have hated seeing me hurt myself all those times. I guess if he's been my guardian angel, he's seen everything that has happened to me."

"Your angel wants you to be delivered from all the things you've suffered."

"Really?"

"Really."

"Wow. My dad's been a pastor for as long as I can remember, but this is the first time I've really felt God's love for me. I mean, if He assigned a big, burly angel to guard me He must really care about me."

"He does. A lot."

Eden patted my hand across the table. "Thanks, Liv."

"Don't thank me. Thank God."

Eden looked heavenward and said, "Thank You, Lord."

We grabbed our cereal bowls and placed them in the dishwasher.

After taking showers and getting dressed, I called my mom and asked her to come pick me up.

"I heard you skipped school today," she said.

"Yeah, I thought it best to stay with Eden."

There was a long pause on the other end of the phone. "Well, I can understand."

I was relieved my mom wasn't angry at me.

"See you when you get here."

I hung up the phone.

Eden and I sat at her kitchen table, waiting for my mom to arrive.

"I don't know how to thank you, Liv."

I gave her another hug, then walked to Mom's car, which was waiting in the driveway.

When I got home I went straight to my room so I could work on the assignments I knew were due the next day after checking my teacher's website to find out what I'd missed and what the homework assignments were for the day. As I was finishing a math assignment my cell phone rang. It was Eden.

"Liv?" Eden's voice sounded more euphoric than ever.

"Yeah?"

"I just saw him."

"Who?"

"My guardian angel."

"Really?"

"He was really tall, like you said. And hairy, like a bear. But he looked like the nicest guy in the world. His eyes were so gentle in contrast to his intimidating appearance. And trust me, our angels care for us, more than I ever imagined."

I let out a sigh. Eden had confirmed exactly what I saw. I wasn't crazy after all! "Where did you see him?"

"I was outside, taking out the trash. When I saw him standing by the bushes beside the garage, I screamed. He smiled at me through his thick black beard. I gave him an awkward wave, then ran back inside."

"Next time you see him, talk to him."

"Do you think I'll see him again?"

"I'm sure of it."

"What should I say?"

"Whatever you want. You could start by asking what his name is."

"I can do that!"

"And Eden?"

"Yeah?"

"Before you go to sleep tonight, be sure to thank God for letting you see your angel."

"I will definitely do that."

"I have to go. Math homework."

"Say no more. I hear you." We both laughed as we hung up.

Boy, it was nice not being the only one who saw angels.

Thank You, God, for letting Eden see her angel. She needs to know she is protected. And thank You for the relief I heard in Eden's voice. Now I have a friend who can learn to do spiritual battle as I am learning. I just may need her—and that burly angel of hers—to assist Mike and me sometime.

"You will."

I shuddered at those words from God.

Chapter 14

I FORGOT TO TURN off my cell phone at volleyball practice. Coach shot me a dirty look as I jogged over to my backpack to turn it off.

Caller ID showed it was Eden. I panicked for a second. She knew better than to call me in the middle of practice. Then I remembered God was in control.

Let her be OK, God.

I missed two perfect passes and failed to set the ball for the hitters. My fingers felt like Jell-O.

Of course, Vicki pounced on me. "Get your stuff together, Liv."

"Vicki, step in for Olivia," Coach shouted.

She smirked as she walked to my position.

I seethed as I took my place on the bench. I took the opportunity to grab my phone and run to the bathroom. Once out of sight I read a text from Eden.

> Call me ASAP! Greg and Toby have been in a car accident. Meet me at Lord's Memorial hospital as soon as you can.

I stared at the lockers, wondering if the guys were dead or alive.

I dialed my mom's cell phone immediately. "Mom, come get me. I have to get to the hospital. Greg Monahan has been in a car accident."

"I'll be right there."

Mom and I rode in silence on the way home after practice. As soon as I was home I burst into the kitchen to find my dad.

"I need to borrow the car, Dad. Do you mind? I want to go right away."

"Sure." Dad walked over and gave me a bear hug.

"Thanks, Dad."

I grabbed the keys from the peg by the back door.

Mom merely stood beside him and watched me leave, yet said, "Call us as soon as you know anything."

Mom wasn't always quite as nurturing as Dad. But I knew she cared. I knew she prayed for me. Mike told me so. For that I was thankful.

Since she did not make the effort, I decided I would. I gave her a hug before I stormed to the garage and jumped in the car, jamming the keys into the ignition. I could still see the shocked look on her face in my mind's eye as I drove to the hospital.

I tried not to drive too far over the speed limit, even though my hands were trembling and I was feeling lightheaded. I wondered what I'd find when I got to the hospital. Would Greg even be alive?

I'd only met his friend Toby once at school, then saw him the night of the concert. He didn't hang out with us much. But I'd heard from Christina that he was as bad as Greg when it came to driving really fast. Whenever they hung out together, they were even worse.

Arriving at the hospital, I grabbed a pack of tissues from the glove compartment and ran across the parking lot.

I waited impatiently for the doors of the ER to open automatically. People in green scrubs rushed up and down the hallway. I went to the check-in counter. The nurse behind the window handed a file on a clipboard to a doctor, who grabbed it and then disappeared out a small door.

I braced my hands on the edge of the counter. "I'm a friend of Greg Monahan. Is he OK?"

The nurse turned to me. "I'm sorry. You'll have to wait until the family arrives."

The last thing I wanted to do was wait. But seeing no choice, I said, "Thanks," then headed into the large, empty waiting room. Where was Eden?

I sat in one of the blue upholstered chairs, put my elbows on my knees, and covered my face with my hands.

God, help Greg and Toby to be OK. I'm not sure if they're Christians or not. Lord, give them the chance to decide. I bet You can work through near-death experiences, comas, visions. Could You do that now?

A flurry of voices shouted out medical orders. I looked up and saw the automatic door open. Eden walked in, her eyes red and swollen. "I'm sorry I'm late. I had to wait till Dad got home so I could use the car."

I stood and embraced her.

"How are they?" she asked.

"I don't know. The nurse won't release any information until the family gets here."

"Oh gosh. I can't stand not knowing."

I wiped tears from my face. "Do you know if Greg's a Christian?"

"No. At the concert he looked pretty intent when the youth pastor was inviting people to ask God into their hearts. But he never talked about it after. Not to me, anyway."

Then the thought hit us both at the same time, and we both said, "Christina."

"Oh, no." I dialed her number. No answer.

More commotion at the ER entrance caught our attention. Greg's parents sped past the waiting room toward check-in. I heard his mother wail, "Where's my son?"

I peeked around the corner and saw a man in a white coat motioning for Greg's parents to be seated on chairs in the hallway. As he spoke with the Monahans, Greg's mom cried and blew her nose over and over. Greg's dad looked emotionless.

I turned back to where Eden sat in the waiting room. Her lips were moving. I couldn't hear any words, but I knew the Holy Spirit was giving her words to pray, like He had that night on the football field.

The doctor placed a hand on Mrs. Monahan's shoulder. Then he disappeared into a room down the hall. I wished I could hear what he said to them.

I felt Eden come up behind me.

Mrs. Monahan spotted us. "Girls!" She elbowed Greg's dad, motioning in our direction. "Honey, its Greg's friends from school."

We rushed to her side. I couldn't think of a single word to say. Pat answers would sound empty. All I had to offer were my presence and my prayers.

Comfort them, Lord. No matter what the outcome is with Greg.

Mrs. Monahan rocked back and forth, blowing her nose on a well-used tissue. I reached into my purse, pulled out the mini pack of tissues I'd grabbed from the car, and handed it to Mrs. Monahan.

"Thank you, dear."

A nurse approached us. "You can go in and see your son now."

The Monahans shot to their feet.

"How is he?" Greg's dad asked.

"Unresponsive but stable."

The Monahans followed the nurse, and Eden and I followed them.

We entered a small room with stark white curtains and walls. Greg lay motionless on the bed, his eyes shut. His left cheek was bruised, and a three-inch swab of hair had been ripped from his head on the same side. His lips were swollen and purple. A nurse stood beside the bed, adjusting his IV drip. Bruises covered his hands and arms. Blood seeped through the bandage on his head, where I assumed was a deep gash.

His mother hurried to his bedside, letting out a whimper. His dad removed his baseball cap and stood next to the bed, his hand on his wife's shoulder. Eden and I lingered in the doorway.

A doctor brushed past us and approached the Monahans. "I'm Dr. Howard. I'm so sorry you have to see your son this way. He will be admitted. There's swelling on his brain. If it doesn't go down within the next seventy-two hours, there won't be much hope that he'll recover. If he does, there could be serious long-term damage—we won't know until he wakes up."

Mr. Monahan's shoulders shook, and he hugged his wife.

Dr. Howard gave Greg's mother a squeeze on her forearm. "Again—I'm so sorry. We'll do everything we can to keep him comfortable. In the meantime we must monitor him and wait. Come next door with me, and I'll show you his X-rays."

When they turned, I asked, "Is it OK if we stay for a minute?"

"Of course," the doctor responded.

As everyone else exited the room, one of the nurses gave us a warning look. "Keep it short. His family may need some privacy with him when they get back."

"Yes, ma'am," I said. "Thank you."

The clamor that had filled the past hour stilled.

I felt like I was in a TV soap opera. All of this seemed surreal.

Eden went to the foot of the bed. I walked up to Greg's side and touched his hand. "Greg," I whispered, "If you can hear me, I want to encourage you to choose God. It's never too late." I started to cry. But I'd given all my tissues away, so I wiped my nose with the back of my other hand. "Jesus died to forgive you for everything you've done wrong. It all died with Him on the cross. Accept His sacrifice. Have faith. Ask Jesus to be Lord of your life." Eden handed me a tissue she'd found from the box at his bedside.

The words sounded cheesy to me. Greg wasn't used to hearing all this churchy language. But it was the only way I knew to express it. I prayed Greg would be able to comprehend it—if he could hear me. And I hoped he would make the right choice.

Suddenly a vision flashed into my mind. I saw Greg standing in the corner of the room, watching me talk to him in the bed. As fast as it came, the image faded. Was this a sign from God that Greg was listening?

"He's still here," Eden said in a shaky voice.

"You feel it too?"

"Yes."

I heard wailing outside the room. I peeked out the doorway and saw a nurse escorting a crying couple down the hallway. Another nurse came into the room.

"How is Toby?" I asked her.

"Toby was pronounced dead on arrival. I'm sure his parents are getting the news right now." She then walked over to Greg to check his IV and pulse.

I could not imagine being his parents and getting that kind of news.

Eden and I went into the hall. I heard the doctor and the Monahans in the next room discussing X-rays. I poked my head in the door. "We're going to leave now so you can spend some time alone with Greg. Could you please call me whenever you get a moment and let me know if he improves?"

"Of course," said Greg's mom. "They gave me Greg's cell, so I'm sure I can find your number."

Eden gave them both a hug. I did too. When I did I thought I smelled alcohol on Mr. Monahan's breath. I wasn't surprised. Perhaps that is what caused him to go into rages and hit Greg.

At two o'clock in the morning my cell phone rang. I grabbed it from my bedside table, where I'd left it before going to sleep.

"Greg passed away a half hour ago." Mr. Monahan sounded drunk. He slurred his words.

"I'm so sorry," I offered.

He sniffled.

"OK. Thanks. Bye." He hung up.

I dropped the phone on the bed.

Greg is dead. My mind swirled that phrase 'round and 'round, trying to grasp the truth of it.

I couldn't imagine how it felt for a parent to lose their child. How would my parents feel if I died? It made all the problems in my life pale in comparison.

I dialed Christina's cell phone number again. No answer. I called her home number. Busy.

I couldn't fall asleep for an hour. I tossed and turned. Then a hand touched my head.

Mike. I drifted off into a sound sleep.

When the alarm went off I dragged myself out of bed and got ready for the day, even though it was the last thing in the world I wanted to do.

I wondered how I had been able to sleep—although fitfully—for the past few hours. Then I remembered Mike. He'd put his hand on my head as he'd done many times before. I must have gone to sleep right after that.

When I walked into school the first person I saw was Christina, standing by her locker. I could tell from her slumped shoulders and red-rimmed eyes that she'd heard the news. I wrapped my arms around her. "I'm so sorry."

"It's OK. I know he's in heaven."

I drew back, my hands still on her arms. "How do you know?"

"I was lying in bed last night after Greg's dad called me in the middle of the night. After that I shut my eyes to pray. I suddenly pictured Greg floating above his bed. You know, like you hear about when people tell about their near-death experiences."

"I saw that too!"

"You did? When?"

"I went to the hospital and saw him before he died. I talked to him, hoping he could hear me even though he was sedated or just unconscious. I told him how to be a Christian and encouraged him to make the right choice. I have peace that he did."

We smiled as tears flowed down our cheeks.

Christina dabbed at her eyes with a tissue she had in her hand. "The Monahans asked Eden's dad to do the funeral. They told me last night when they called. In a way I'm glad I wasn't there last night to see how Greg looked. I saw several missed calls on my cell after I checked it this morning. My phone had lost its charge, and I never got them. Good thing my mom picked up the house phone in the middle of the night and was able to let me talk to Mr. Monahan."

"Well, it's good to hear about Eden's dad doing the funeral." I knew he'd preach the gospel. That's what people needed to hear when they stared death in the face.

We parted to head to our classes. I clutched my books to my chest, trying to get rid of the weight in the pit of my stomach. Even though I knew Greg was in heaven I still missed him. And I felt bad for the people who loved him who were hurting even more than I was.

I felt Mike's presence, but I didn't look for him or speak to him. My mind was too focused on the loss of my friend. But when I sat down in homeroom I felt Mike's hand on my hair and I felt comforted.

I remembered reading in the Bible that the Holy Spirit was called a Comforter. So I asked Him to help me get through this. I needed all the comfort I could get.

Chapter 15

GREG'S FUNERAL WAS scheduled two days later.
As I approached the breakfast table that morning, Mom and Dad looked up from their coffee cups.

Dad slid his legs around in his chair to face me. "Honey, I'm so sorry we can't go with you today. We have to watch Tessa because Brian and Diane are leaving to go to celebrate their anniversary."

I'd totally forgotten. "Tell them I said happy anniversary, would you?" I slid out a chair and sat down opposite my mom.

Mom pushed a plate toward me. It was piled with three chocolate chip pancakes. She knew they were my favorite.

"Aw...thanks, Mom."

"I wanted to do something special for you today."

I remembered reaching out to hug her before leaving for the hospital. In Mom's way, she was reaching back.

"Go ahead and take one of the cars. We'll be staying home all day," Dad said as he wiped his mouth with his napkin.

"Thanks, Dad." The words were muffled by my mouthful of pancakes.

When the funeral home came into view my heart started pounding. I hated funerals. I especially dreaded looking into the caskets and seeing people looking like painted dolls. At least this funeral may have closed caskets due to the severe injuries of the boys. Both families decided to hold the funerals the same day at the same funeral home. Perhaps they knew their boys—great friends—would have liked it that way. I hoped so.

After finding a parking spot I sat in the car for a few minutes, staring at the steering wheel. Finally I gathered the strength to unlock my seatbelt.

A soft knock on my window made me jump. I looked up and saw Eden, her eyes bloodshot and her cheeks stained with tear streaks. I got out of my car and hugged her. She let out a muffled whimper into my shoulder.

I'm going to lose it. I may as well start now.

I turned back to the car and reached to grab my packet of tissues as the tears began to flow.

We held hands and headed toward the funeral home. I felt like we were moving in slow motion, but that was OK with me. We approached the white building with white pillars surrounding the front porch.

We entered a crowded parlor full of Greg's and Toby's personal things. Their letterman jackets lay across the backs of two wooden chairs. I grabbed Greg's and held it close. It still smelled like him. I was careful to put it back exactly as it was.

I saw Greg's stuffed dog sitting on the floor next to his letterman jacket.

Eden and I smiled as we paged through an album of baby pictures. I'd never seen any pictures of Greg as a baby or small child before we met in kindergarten. He was so cute. Christina came up to us in the short black dress she'd worn to the school's fall dance. She hugged me and Eden like she was comforting us. Shouldn't she be the one falling apart? They were best friends—and more as of late.

She whispered, "I saw his angel."

My mouth dropped open. God was redeeming her prior experiences and transferring them into a biblical spiritual gift.

"That's great!"

"The angel was smiling. I think he was trying to assure me that Greg is in heaven," she said with confidence.

Eden and I exchanged glances. "I think you are absolutely right," I said.

"Before Bev prayed for me, I used to see all kinds of evil spirits. Now that I'm a Christian, God is letting me see the good spirits as well as the bad ones. And the bad ones don't scare me anymore."

I nailed it!

It seemed strange to be at a funeral yet feel happy. Organ music began to play over some speakers in the ceiling.

I glanced at the crowd. Most were young people. The girls gathered together in clumps. The boys sat somberly, most wearing their school jackets.

At the head of the room sat two closed caskets. I was relieved.

I never knew what to say at funerals. I dreaded the receiving line.

Eden gripped my arm and led me toward that exact place. Christina grasped my other hand. Perhaps she was feeling the same as me and needed my strength, through that touch, to help get her through the next hour.

I felt a third hand on my shoulder. I glanced up. Mike. I looked over my shoulder to see him motioning with his head, prodding me to move forward. The person in front of me in line was standing in front of the caskets. My turn was next. I never knew how long to stand there. Some people stood a long time and cried in front of caskets. I preferred to speed by them and get that part over with as soon as possible. Thank goodness these caskets weren't open. The family had opted to place a framed photo of both boys on each.

When I neared Greg's coffin I saw an angel standing behind it, his hand resting on the spot where I assumed Greg's head would be inside. He was seven feet tall and had long, flaxen hair. I could not see his eyes; they were cast down at the coffin. He wore a plain white robe with a golden rope tied at the waist.

"That's my fellow guardian, Churiel," Mike said.

Greg's angel looked up at me. His eyes were a burgundy color that matched streaks of the same color that framed his face. Churiel's smile left no doubt in my mind that Greg was in heaven, ready to party with his angel and his Savior forever.

I hesitated to move on to Toby's casket because I knew his angel would not be at peace. As I moved closer, I saw Toby's angel. His wings were limp, and his head was bowed. He looked down at the casket, his face contorted in grief, and large tears that looked like liquid crystal ran down his face. I felt the angel's anguish as he lamented his lost charge.

"That's Phillip," Mike whispered. "He's been a faithful guardian to Toby." Then I heard a soft intake of air. Was that Mike stifling a sob? Was he grieving the fact that Toby died without being a Christian?

The angel traced a finger across the cover of Toby's casket with the tenderness of a father putting his young son to bed at night. I could only imagine the depth of his despair, losing a boy he had spent every moment with for the past seventeen years. And now his job assignment would change.

Mike's hand tightened on my shoulder, coaxing me to move forward in the line.

When I approached the families in the receiving line, Eden moved past me and took the lead. As a pastor's daughter she had attended many funerals and knew exactly what to say. Christina and I huddled around her and let her take the lead.

Eden directed her words to both sets of parents. "I'm sorry for your loss. We loved Greg so much. We'll continue to pray for you. God will comfort you. We love you." She hugged each of the parents. All of them hugged her back. Greg's mom held on to Eden longer than the other parents, and her shoulders began to shake as she wept. The other parents watched and cast their eyes downward, no doubt feeling fresh tears well up.

I hugged each of them, and so did Christina.

I couldn't wait to sit down. I felt faint and uncomfortable. I felt Mike's hand on my shoulder again as if guiding me to the three empty chairs near the back of the room. We all sat down, joining the others who had already been through the receiving line. I now felt both of Mike's hands on my shoulders. I knew he was behind me without even looking.

As Eden's father began the service, demons in tattered black cloaks swept in. They twisted and twirled among the individuals seated and standing in the room. The hair on my arms prickled as goose bumps formed on them.

"Get out!" Mike commanded. His hands left my shoulders, but his voice was still behind me.

They responded with what sounded like many voices in unison. They wheezed, "We are here to distract and confuse."

Since there were more than a hundred people in the room I estimated there were that many angels too. Mike whispered in my ear, "Look around you." My spiritual eyes opened and scores of angelic figures were crammed into the room. Twice as many demons weaved among the crowd.

I heard Mike draw his sword from its sheath. "Olivia," he whispered, "help us! Pray!"

Without taking my eyes off Eden's dad, I prayed. *God, we need backup angels, lots of them, if You can spare them.* I didn't know why I prayed that, but I figured the idea of asking God to summon more angels couldn't hurt. And only moments after that thought floated through my head, to my astonishment dozens of glowing orbs floated into the room. They appeared out of nowhere and fluttered like snowflakes as they fell to the ground. Each morphed into a tall, muscular figure wearing armor different than I'd ever seen before. They seemed to be covered in gray wet suits like I'd seen surfers wear. But my guess was that they were impenetrable.

Mike let out a loud war cry that ripped through the room. A blue light beamed through the ceiling. It dissipated as it split into bits of tiny lightning strips, each one wrapping itself around every dark figure in the room. The power of it hurled them through the air, making them disappear instantly.

I wondered if this was the sheer power of God coming to zap them to death.

Eden bumped my arm. "What are you looking at?" I realized my mouth was hanging wide open.

"A battle," I muttered.

Her eyes closed. My sister warrior began moving her lips silently in prayer.

Phillip, Toby's angel, raised a glowing sword in the air and sliced at a small, toad-like demon to his right, then at a spider-looking one to his left. Green blood spewed from the demons, and they screeched as they evaporated and vanished.

A large demon in a black cloak and with the face of a skeleton approached Churiel. "Well, well, look what we have here." He pointed a bony finger at the angel. "Clearly you aren't needed anymore." Green smoke wafted from his hollowed-out mouth.

"Ignore him, Churiel," said Mike.

"No way." Churiel balled his fingers into a fist.

"Poor Toby," the demon whined. "Damned forever."

"Shut up, you filth!" Churiel struck the demon in the jaw with such force that the demon fell through the wall on the far side of the room and landed on the rough gravel outside.

The guardian angels all wrapped their wings around their wards to protect them from the onslaught of any more demonic attacks. The backup angels stood side by side, lining the whole length of the four walls around us, holding tall spears, their gazes directed heavenward, forming a spiritual fortress.

Eden's eyes remained closed, her mouth still moving in silent prayer. I was glad she hadn't stopped. Perhaps there would be another wave of devils. I kept repeating the word *Jesus* over and over in my mind. Glancing at my lap, I noticed my knuckles turned white from grasping my hands together so tightly in prayer.

With the battle now at bay, I could hear the pastor's words again. "Is there anyone here who would like to accept Christ and walk with Him for eternity?"

Toby's parents and his two brothers raised their hands. Countless more hands went up. My nerves subsided.

Thank You, God. Thank You that my friend's death has turned other people to eternal life.

I turned to Eden, and she smiled at me. No doubt she was having similar thoughts.

Mike kissed the top of my head the way my dad used to do when he tucked me into bed as a child. I placed my hand on my shoulder over where I felt his hand resting. I couldn't feel him, but I knew he was there. The tension in my shoulders eased.

God, thanks for my protective big brother. What a gift You've given me.

"Those of you who raised your hands, please turn to the prayer on the back of the bulletin you received when you entered. You can read that prayer now or after you leave. Or come see me after the service. Whatever you do, make the right choice today. Don't wait. Any of us could end up in a car accident tomorrow, just like these two boys."

Yes. God, let each one in this room consider the reality of death and think about choosing to live for God. Help them to stop any destructive behavior they have in their lives. May they walk out of here changed forever.

"Let's all bow our heads and close our eyes."

I closed my eyes and prayed Pastor's prayer, standing in agreement with him.

"Our Father, we ask Your comfort for those here who are grieving. We pray for their close family and friends. Send Your Comforter, the Holy Spirit, to ease their pain. Don't allow one person to leave this building today without knowing for sure where they'd spend eternity if they were to die tomorrow. In Jesus' name we pray, amen."

The organ music played again, and people stood and filed out of the room. I couldn't wait to get a breath of the fresh air outdoors. It was so stifling in the room from being packed with so many bodies.

As I walked outside I sensed Mike and Churiel following close behind as I heard swords being slipped back in their sheaths.

A sinister phantom draped in black rose from the gravel sidewalk six feet in front of me.

I gasped. Just when I'd hoped the battle was over.

His face resembled a wolf. He drew back his lips, exposing yellow teeth. Drool ran from the corner of his mouth. "So, you can see both angels and demons?" he growled. "My, what a unique gift you have." The way he said the word *gift* made it clear it was not a compliment.

I seethed. His taunting made me furious that he'd make fun of a gift given to me by the God of the universe to fight this exact type of evil.

The demon moved so close to my face his dog-shaped snout touched my nose. I drew back and wiped the moisture from my nose. Disgusting.

Where's Mike? Can't he see this dog-faced monster is about to bite my head off?

When I turned around to look for Mike, he morphed into his twelve-foot version of himself and flashed by me, pointing his sword at the hell-hound. He pinned the devil to the ground, the tip of his blade touching the center of his chest, where I supposed the creature's heart would be, if it had such a thing.

I glared at the beast. *In the name of Jesus Christ, be gone!*

The demon let out a puff of putrid air and glared at me with yellow eyes. "Before your mighty friend kills me, I want you to know something." He let out a sinister laugh. "I was the one who escorted that boy Toby to hell!"

With Mike beside me I wasn't intimidated at all. I leaned over his gruesome face, dying to spit in it. "Yeah, well, you're on your way there yourself, buddy."

"Do you know what hell is like?" he choked out because of the pressure Mike was applying to his chest area.

Mike pressed the sword farther into the demon's scaly skin, causing a low moan to escape his lips. But he didn't finish him off yet. I knew he could, so why didn't he? Was there something he wanted me to hear first?

"Hell is a place where the loving influence of God is never felt," was all I could manage to say.

I felt a wing envelop my body. Mike's touch gave me the courage to hear what I knew I would not like.

Most of the funeral crowd was heading to their cars. Eden and Christina were far ahead of me. I'd been detained by this creature and couldn't wait to get away from him.

"Hell is not about physical pain, because there is no body to harm. Torment of the spirit and the soul are significantly worse. There's no light to indicate the passage of time."

This was a new concept to me. Or was it a lie?

I could think of many sleepless nights when God's presence with me was my only hope.

As if reading my mind, he snapped, "Yes, when you've had nights like that, you were comforted. There is no comfort in hell!"

I glanced up at Mike. He gave me a reassuring nod.

"Right now, Toby can't feel anything but darkness. His mind and soul are slowly unraveling under the full weight of *nothing*. There's no one to comfort him. In fact, to him, it feels like he's the only one in hell."

I'd never thought of hell as anything more than the fire and brimstone I'd heard about so many times. I knew about being separated from God, but had never thought about the darkness. The absence of everything good.

The demon let out a wicked laugh. "Oh, sometimes there's a flash of light…a ray of hope, a speck of feeling. Then the lights go out again. Pretty soon you begin to hate the light."

I turned away, closing my eyes. I couldn't imagine the torture that would be.

"You could have prevented his fate, you know."

Accusation. That was what this spirit was all about.

But was it all my fault?

He'd gotten to me.

"Go to hell, spirit of accusation!" Mike plunged his sword so deeply into the demon that he split in half. The force shoved his body into the gravel below him.

The words of the monstrous figure echoed in my ears and covered me with chills. They held some truth, and I knew it.

The weight of this responsibility for those who die without Jesus made the whole world seem to darken. My hands shook, and I was covered in sweat. Everything went black. My knees crumbled, and I fell to the gravel.

When I awoke Christina and Eden were leaning over me, concerned looks on their faces.

"You saw something happening in the spiritual realm, didn't you?" asked Eden.

I nodded, lifting myself up on my right elbow. "How did you know?"

"I saw your eyes darting about inside during the funeral."

"I noticed that too," added Christina.

They assisted me to my car, then waited until I assured them I was OK to drive home.

Mike slipped into the passenger-side seat. He was human-sized now but still had his armor on.

He covered my right hand, which was on the steering wheel. I stopped shaking. "Do you realize you stared evil in the face and stood your ground?"

"Pfft—yeah, and then fainted. I'm pathetic."

"Each time you'll become braver. Trust me."

The words *each time* made me tremble again. "You mean I'll always have to fight like this?" My voice quivered.

"If you live in this world you will always be fighting the evil one." Mike took my one hand from the steering wheel and clasped it in both of his hands as he turned to me. "I know that you must not think this is a gift right now. But it is the gift God has chosen to give you. And you must use it. For yourself and for others. You're going to need it."

I swallowed hard, wondering when the next battle would come. Mike said I'd need it. *Oh, no...*

When I opened my eyes, I saw nothing but blackness all around me. I stood and waited for my eyes to adjust to the darkness. I heard water dripping. I knew my bathroom didn't have a leaky faucet, so I must be somewhere else—but where? I stretched out my arm and my hand touched a cold, slippery surface. It felt like a cave I'd once been in when I was twelve.

When I could finally see in front of me I realized the water was coming from the ceiling and into a pool of water somewhere not far from me. I recalled this sound from the cave we'd visited that vacation long ago: each drip of water echoing as it splashed into the water below it.

I took shuffling steps, wary of slipping on the damp floor. The cold water splashed onto my bare feet, making me shiver. I breathed in a musty, earthy smell, much like the caverns I had been in.

A red glow came into view. Its source seemed to be around a bend just ahead. A child's laugh echoed deep inside the cave. I hurried toward the voice and the red glow.

A scream exploded in my eardrums. Icy fear shot through my bones. It sounded as if someone was being killed. I had to do something. But what would I find? Would I be harmed too? My curiosity helped me gather the courage to yell, "I'm coming to help!"

I picked up my pace as best I could without risking a slip. If I fell and broke a bone I'd be useless to assist anyone. And then I wouldn't be able to run away if some guy with a knife or something came after me next.

I rounded the next corner and saw Toby standing in front of the red glow.

I'm dreaming. Oh, thank God.

His hair was matted with blood, his clothing tattered and torn. "You can't help me." His voice shook.

I took a step closer. Toby's eyes seemed to gaze right through me.

Torn flesh hung from Toby's forearm. Bruises, gashes, and open wounds covered his body. His teeth poked through a mangled mass of flesh on his face. I grimaced with revulsion and stepped back, clutching my arms around my body. I began to hold one hand out. "Toby—"

"No!" His body convulsed.

I backed up and shrank against the wall of the cave. Could I blink my eyes enough times to wake myself up? I tried, but nothing changed.

His eyes widened in fear as he turned and looked at the opening of the cave behind him. When he turned back to face me, he whimpered, "They're here!" He repeated those words over and over, his voice becoming fainter each time he said that phrase.

A cloaked figure floated in, its long black cloak about five inches off the ground. It held a sickle in one hand. I hoped it didn't notice me. He turned to face Toby, backing him against the cave wall. Toby screamed.

A stream of green light shot out of the demon's finger. Lashes of rope instantly appeared, forming restraints around Toby's arms and legs. Toby wrestled against them and kept saying, "No, please don't take me," as the dark form pulled him into the shadows of the cave behind him. The red light faded. Toby's screams did too.

My knees buckled, and I crumbled into a pile on the floor with relief.

I awoke in bed, my heart palpitating. My sheets were soaked in sweat, my chest heaving. *What a horrible dream. I'm not surprised after my experience at the funeral. My subconscious must have still been thinking about Toby dying without knowing Jesus.*

I saw Mike sitting at the foot of my bed, Indian style, his chin resting in the palm of one of his hands.

I sat up. "What's happening to me?"

"Your gift is gaining power. And God often uses your dreams to speak to you. You're being prepared for the coming battle."

I hoped I didn't have to battle anything like that creature in the cave I'd just dreamed about.

"Pray for God to rule over your dreams before you fall asleep."

"I can do that."

"You know that Toby's condemnation wasn't your fault, right?"

"Yes. But I still wish I could go back in time and talk to him about Jesus."

"I hope this gives you a deep passion to share your faith with as many people as God leads your way—before it's too late for them."

I know where Toby is—but what about Phillip? "Where is Toby's angel now?"

"He's been reassigned."

I wondered where. To another person? To another position in heaven? "Did he fail?"

"No. Toby's salvation was his own choice. But Phillip will grieve for a long time. He loved Toby the way I love you. He'll mourn like a big brother who's lost his little brother."

As Mike will weep for me, his little sister, when I die. I shook off the terrible mental picture that came to mind.

"Will he ever see Toby again?" I guessed the answer but still asked.

"No. Nor will Toby ever see God." He shuddered. "Total and eternal separation from God is one the most harrowing notions imaginable."

Now that God's presence was so strong in my life, I couldn't imagine not sensing it. *Without the Holy Spirit and His "still, small voice" in my mind, my life would be barren. As scary as this whole learning experience has been, I still would not change it for the world. I'll never see things the same again. And I'll be able to fight the enemy. And help others fight him.*

I lay back down and sank into my pillow. Mike sat beside me and took my hand.

"Don't you get bored just hanging around and watching me?"

He grinned. "Does a dog get bored sitting at its master's feet and following him from room to room?"

I'd watched Bev's Lab follow her everywhere she went. When Bev sat, she sat at her feet. She adored her. Of course, Mike wasn't my pet. But his illustration made sense.

"God asked me to watch over you. I don't resent it, and I never get bored." His face glowed as he tucked the blankets under my chin. "Now, get some rest. You'll need it for the battles that await you." Then he was gone.

God, make me stronger so I can live up to the gift You've given me. Help me not despise it but instead treasure it because it comes from You. Help me to not have any more bad dreams tonight. And most of all, I want to say I love You.

"I love you too."

God was talking back. I loved this. I'm not sure how I knew, nor do I think I could articulate it to another, unless they'd experience it themselves.

Why me?

"Because I chose you."

Will I get braver?

"With Me, nothing is impossible."

That sounded like a verse that was hanging in our church hallway in the classroom wing. So that could have been God speaking, or Him bringing that verse to my mind. Either way, He had given me an answer. *I'm scared.*

"I'll equip you."

I'll need it. Amen.

Chapter 16

WHEN I ENTERED my sister's house for my usual babysitting night, Tessa ran into the kitchen, crashed into my legs, and gave me a big squeeze. She turned her head up for me to kiss her, which I did.

"I missed you, Livvy," Tessa squeaked.

"I missed you, too, squirt." Diane had been sick last Thursday, so we'd missed a week.

My sister came down the stairs, wearing a red dress and matching heels. "Hey, Liv, how are you?"

"OK."

I wished I could share what I was going through with her. But since she was so much older than me, we weren't close enough for me to broach such an off-the-wall subject. I didn't know how she'd react.

After Diane and Brian left, Tessa took me to her bedroom to show me her latest sketches. My niece's crayon drawings were really lifelike. Sometimes she drew with pencil.

Tessa pointed to her newest picture, hanging on her pegboard. "It's Petey."

Sure enough, there was no mistaking Petey. "That's fantastic."

Tessa gave me her widest, toothless grin.

My eyes wandered over the other pictures hanging on her wall. One was of a zebra, one was a tree, and one was of her parents. I was stunned at the detail of their faces.

Suddenly an idea popped into my mind. "Can you draw an angel for me?"

I expected her to respond eagerly to my request, as she usually did when I asked her to draw something for me. Instead, she shuffled her colored pencils in her hands. Her smile disappeared and was replaced with a frown. "The last one I saw scared me."

Oh, no. Not Tessa. It was hard enough for me.

"I'm sorry, Tessa. Could you try just a quick sketch—if you want?"

I felt selfish asking her to do this just to further convince me I wasn't crazy. But I wanted to make sure I could explain it to her and help calm her fears. Maybe even teach her what I'd learned.

Tessa stared at the floor and then looked up at me. "OK. But can we throw it in the trash can after I finish?"

"Deal." *I'm almost afraid to see this.*

I sat on the floor and watched Tessa draw, using only her black pencil. As her hand flowed over the paper, she drew a cloaked figure with hollowed-out eyes, much like some of the demons I'd encountered lately.

"That's really good, Tess."

No smile. "Can we throw it out now?" Without even waiting for me to respond, Tessa crumpled the paper in her chubby little hands and headed toward the waste basket.

"Tess? Are you afraid?"

"Y-yes." She then chewed on her pencil eraser, staring past me as if deep in thought.

"Don't be scared. Your angel is bigger and stronger than any of the scary angels."

She looked back up at me and seemed to be digesting my comment.

"Do you believe me?" I asked.

She nodded.

"If you ever see one again, you pray and ask God for your angel to kill him, you hear me?"

She smiled thinly, then bobbed her head up and down, curls bouncing.

"Can we play now?"

"Let's play house."

I resisted the urge to suggest she draw a nice angel. "Sure. You be the mommy." I hopped onto her bed and stuck my thumb in my mouth and whimpered like a baby. Tessa chuckled and came over to stroke my hair.

That broke the ice after our gloomy exchange.

After playing house and hide-and-seek, we made paper boats and hats and then watched some TV. At eight we headed to Tessa's bedroom, where I followed her nightly ritual: a drink of water we brought up from the kitchen, then a story, and a hug.

"I'll pray tonight." I'd had a little practice lately, so it didn't seem so uncomfortable anymore. I crawled into bed beside her and pulled the covers up to my waist.

"How come? You never pray."

"Well, I guess I've been doing it more lately, so I'm more comfortable doing it out loud."

"That's good, Livvy. You shouldn't be shy about it."

She reached over and grabbed my hand and squeezed it as if offering her assurance that I should speak right up. I stared up at the dark ceiling.

I decided I'd add my own prayer before reciting Tessa's usual prayer. "Dear God, thank You for this day and the time tonight with Tessa. I ask You to protect her from the scary angel, and help her see the nice ones." Then I began the usual recitation, "As I lay me down to sleep, I pray the Lord my soul to keep. If I should die before I wake, I ask the Lord my soul to take. God, bless Tessa, her mommy and daddy, Petey, and—"

I spotted a glowing figure with the outline of a man to the right of Tessa's bed. The covers rustled as she turned in my direction. "Tessa? Is that him?"

"He's here!" Tessa sat up and clapped her hands, gazing at the glowing figure that now sharpened into an unmistakable angel.

"He sure is."

"You see him too?"

"Yes. He's beautiful. You're safe, sweetheart."

"Daniel, this is my Aunt Olivia," she said with such ease you'd have thought she'd just introduced me to one of her friends from school. *Well, they've obviously talked together if she knows his name.*

I stood to my feet. *Do I put my hand out for him to shake it?* He looked transparent, so I held back.

I tilted my head, cleared my throat, and said, "Pleased to make your acquaintance." I hoped that sounded respectful. I hadn't chatted with any angel as much as with Mike, but I didn't want to assume I could be so laid back with another one.

Tessa jumped up and down and giggled. We all joined in.

"Hi, my sweet Tessa." And at that moment his body turned solid. From hearing his laughter I could tell her angel had a very high-pitched voice— almost childlike. He appeared to be younger than Mike. I guessed him to be around fourteen or so. He was dressed in a white peasant shirt with black, billowing pants that covered his feet. His shoulder-length hair was the same blonde as Tessa's, with springy curls to match. One unruly curl dangled between his two emerald-green eyes. He brushed it aside and held out his hand to Tessa, who in turn ran and hugged him around his knees instead, like an old friend.

Mesmerized by this sight, I found myself speechless. Daniel saved me. "Nice to meet you, Olivia. It seems you and Tessa share a gift." He offered his hand, and I shook it. "It's quite common for it to run in families."

I finally found my voice. "R-really? D-do you know an angel named Mike?"

His smile broadened, showing the most perfectly white teeth I'd ever seen, which were all the more accentuated by his tan skin. "Why, yes, my friend Mike has told me so much about you."

Does that mean he told him good things? I always wondered when I heard that phrase. Obviously reading my thoughts, he added, "And yes, it's all good things."

What do I say to him? Then it came to me. "Thanks for watching over Tessa."

He bowed at the waist and waved his arm in front of him with a flourish. "My pleasure entirely." When he straightened, I faked a curtsy in return. He laughed lightly. I instantly felt at ease.

I heard the pitter-patter of Tessa's bare feet on the floor as she walked to her closet and pulled out an envelope, then handed it to Daniel. "I made this for you."

Daniel gasped in surprise and bent at the knees so he could look into Tessa's eyes. "My, I feel honored."

"Open it, open it!"

Daniel carefully removed the contents of the envelope. A piece of sketch paper appeared, folded like a letter. On the top was scrawled *to Daniel*. Below she had drawn large, puffy clouds, with a rainbow arching over them. On the cloud sat what was obviously Daniel, a crayon Daniel, to be exact. She drew him with wings, even though I had not yet seen them. *Must be he appears to her that way sometimes—and maybe so she knows he's an angel.* She had drawn him with the same clothes he had on tonight.

With the drawing still in his hand he enveloped Tessa with his willowy arms. "Thank you, Tess; I'll hang this on my harp."

Angels really have harps? Eh, why not? I guess they don't have refrigerators to hang artwork on.

"Now, you two go to bed. We don't want you falling asleep in school tomorrow, little girl."

"OK!" Tessa skipped around the bed to her side and dove under the covers.

"Well, it was nice meeting you." I then turned, expecting Tessa to say something. When I turned back around Daniel was gone.

"He does that sometimes," she said matter-of-factly. Mike did that too, so I chuckled to myself. Then she said, "Good night, Daniel," into the air of the room.

"I hope I can meet your angel friend, Mike, sometime."

"Me too!"

I tucked her in, turned on the nightlight, turned off the overhead lamp, and closed the door. Then I went downstairs and poked around the kitchen for something to eat.

As I settled in to watch one of my favorite TV shows, I heard Tessa crying in her bedroom. Then she screamed, "Livvy!"

I bounded up the stairs. *Oh, no, not a demon.* When I opened the door, the walls were covered in flies. Tessa was surrounded by them. She swatted at them with tears running down her reddened face.

"God, send Your angel." I said it out loud for Tessa's sake. She had to learn what I was learning.

Suddenly Daniel appeared, and blowing one long, hard breath, he dissipated the flies as if he were blowing a scattered pile of sugar off a table surface. Once they were all gone I sat on the bed and pulled Tessa into my arms. She hiccupped a few sniffles as she calmed down.

"You saw the flies, didn't you, Liv?"

"Yes."

"I'm glad."

I crawled into bed beside her and promised to stay there until she fell asleep. I sang one of her favorite Sunday school songs. Her breathing slowed as I sang.

"Mommy and Daddy told me I shouldn't keep mentioning angels. They said people would think I'm crazy. So I stopped. But then I didn't see my nice angel as often. A mean one came by a couple times. I didn't like him."

She turned on her side to face me. "What were the flies here for, Livvy?"

"Just to scare you. Sometimes the devil's little helpers do that kind of thing."

"I've heard about the devil in Sunday school. But they don't talk about nice angels that help you."

"What did you do when you saw the mean angel before? Were there flies then?"

"No. When I saw him I ran out of my room and slept with Mommy and Daddy. The next time I got Petey to sleep with me. But he kept growling, so I couldn't sleep very well."

"Did the bad angel do anything to you?"

"No. My nice angel kept him from hurting me, like tonight. Hey, how do you know an angel named Mike—the one you asked Daniel about?"

"I see angels too. All the time."

Her eyes widened. "Mean ones or nice ones?"

"Both."

"What do you do when you see the mean ones?"

"I ask God to send his nice angels to rescue me. And I pray out loud, telling the mean ones that I'm a child of God, covered by the blood shed during Christ's death on the cross."

Tessa tilted her head and looked into my eyes. "Are you borned again?"

"You mean 'born again'?"

"Yeah. I've heard about that in Sunday school. I want to be that. You are too, right? I saw how you prayed so bravely tonight both times. I knew you had to be. I want to be able to pray like that and tell the bad angels to go away!"

I smiled at Tessa's precious attempt to express her heart's desire.

Tessa was too young to understand a whole lot. But Jesus said He wants people to come to Him like little children.

I opened the Bible storybook on her bedside bookshelf and read her the story of the crucifixion and resurrection. I was certain she'd heard it in Sunday school, but it seemed to be appropriate tonight.

"That was better than any other story you've ever read me." Tessa squeezed her eyes shut and folded her hands. "Jesus, I want to be a Christian like Livvy. I want to be Your best friend."

What she said was so simple, yet so beautiful, I wanted to cry.

Brightly colored lights and little sparks darted all over the room as angels rejoiced over Tessa's prayer.

Tessa's face brightened as she watched the little lights dancing around.

I looked up and breathed a prayer of thanks.

We both fell asleep on her bed, and my sister touched me softly on the shoulder when she got home. I slipped quietly from beneath the covers, trying not to disturb Tessa, and went downstairs. Diane and I sat at the kitchen table to have a cup of tea.

Brian poked his head into the kitchen. "Good night, you two."

"Night," we replied in unison.

"So how did Tessa do tonight?"

"Well..."

Should I just blurt it out? Why not? Won't Diane be pleased?

"Tessa told me she wanted to become a Christian. So I prayed with her."

Diane walked around the table and threw her arms around me. "Thanks, Sis."

I was relieved that my sister wasn't upset that I'd had the privilege of witnessing this important step in her daughter's life. I hoped she didn't feel I'd robbed her of that moment with Tessa. But after the funeral and all, I guess I felt "now is the best time."

She danced a little jig in the middle of the kitchen and then stopped. "I have to tell Brian right away!" She walked over and hugged me again.

"I'll skip the tea tonight. I've got some homework."

"No problem. Thanks for babysitting." She gave me a peck on the cheek, then turned and ran to the stairs and up to her bedroom.

By the time I got home I realized my cheeks were aching from grinning the whole way home. I'd led my first person to the Lord. I'd met another angel tonight, done spiritual warfare, and I was in one piece. It was exhilarating.

Then it hit me. Now Tessa was a target like me.

Lord, help me be a good teacher for Tessa. Thank You for her salvation. Help me to be there for her when the warfare rages.

As I was getting dressed for school the next day, Diane called me on my cell.

"Hey, Liv. I found some disturbing pictures in Tessa's trash can this morning. Do you know anything about them?"

"Uh, yeah." I hesitated, wondering how much I should say. "Diane, Tessa sees angels—good and bad ones."

"She's told us that before."

"I do too."

"Really?"

From her skeptical tone of voice, I could tell she thought I was crazy. *Great.*

"I'm worried that Tessa will be like our cousin Kathryn, who hears voices and stuff."

"I thought I was crazy at first. But I'm not."

"How do you know for sure?"

"Mom made me see a psychologist." *I hope she doesn't send Tessa to one.*

"I could see Mom doing that."

"Yeah, it was really embarrassing having to see a doctor."

"What did he say?"

"Well, after interviewing me a few times, he convinced Mom that I wasn't crazy. Trust me, I prayed a lot."

"So you really think she is seeing angels?"

"Yes, Diane, it's not her imagination. I know the church we grew up in didn't talk much about the gift of discernment of spirits. But I promise to help her. Most people who have that spiritual gift think they're crazy. I don't want Tessa to grow up thinking that."

"Thank you, Liv—for everything."

"Oh my gosh, I have to call Kathryn and ask her if she sees angels!"

"Yes, you should!"

"I'll call her today after school."

Chapter 17

I SLIPPED INTO MY chair in Spanish class just as the bell rang. I pulled out my textbook and dropped my backpack on the floor beside me. Mrs. Gonzalez read to us from our textbook. I followed along as she read, having been given the page number by her to turn to.

I turned to my right and saw Andy paging through his textbook. Ever since our disastrous date last month, which felt like it happened years ago, I'd been trying desperately to avoid him. Even though we had to sit next to each other in Spanish class I no longer passed notes with him, nor giggled at his jokes during class, as I had before our horrible date. I tried to keep my eyes straight ahead and avoid him catching my stare.

When I looked in his direction—for whatever reason, I didn't know—he caught my eye.

Dang! I quickly looked down at my desk, embarrassed that he'd caught me looking his way. I wished Mike would come and distract me again. Why was I so attracted to this guy yet so repelled at our date? Or was I? It was tantalizing. I remembered the feeling of his lips on mine. Then his hands on my body. I'd come so close to being raped when Mike jumped in his alpha male dog form. Why was I so physically drawn to Andy?

Mrs. Gonzalez closed her textbook and set it on the desk behind her. "Today we are going to break up into pairs to work on your project for the Spanish fair, which is two weeks from Friday."

Oh, please don't pair me with Andy.

She read off the partners and paired me with Andy.

Really? Now this is just downright torture. I slammed my textbook shut.

Mrs. Gonzalez shot me a look over her reading glasses. "Is there a problem, Miss Stanton?"

"No." I slouched as low into my seat as I could, knowing I'd overreacted to our two names being announced together.

"Now, discuss your ideas for a project with your partner. Turn in your proposal at the end of class."

I was not about to move my seat to get any closer to Andy. I couldn't bear the thought of his scent.

Andy picked up his chair, slid it closer to mine, and sat beside me. I clenched my jaw. *That's close enough!*

When I looked up at him, he had his arms crossed over his chest and was smirking as if he was quite happy with the situation.

"You are the last person in the world I want to talk to right now," I shot at him.

"Are you sure? There must be some sinister dictator in the world who's lower on your list than me."

I had to admit, I loved his wit. "Don't be too sure."

"Look, I'm sorry about that night. But you did overreact a little, don't you think?"

Well, Mike overreacted the way I should have overreacted, to be truthful. "To what? The wild dog saving my life or you taking advantage of me?"

"I apologize for that. I wish I hadn't messed things up with you." He unfolded his arms.

Now he was baiting me.

Why did I still feel so drawn to him—so *undone* when he was so close to me? My conscience said *no*; my body said *yes*.

"We need to start on the assignment." As irritated as I was with the idea of working with him, I couldn't afford to fail this class assignment and pull my grade point average down. I pulled a spiral notebook from my backpack, ripped out a sheet of paper, and handed it to him. "You write down your ideas, and I'll write down mine. Then we can compare notes."

I could hardly concentrate with his body so close to mine. His cologne made me dizzy as I inhaled its earthy, musky scent. He hardly scribbled on his piece of paper, so I knew I had to come up with something. I jotted down a couple of Spanish recipes I knew how to prepare.

Finally we exchanged pages. His said, "Give me another chance?"

Can't he let it go?

I crumpled up the paper and threw it into the wastebasket behind my desk.

I glanced up at him and saw him grinning. "Let's just focus on the assignment."

"You still like me, don't you?" I felt his hand on my knee.

I jerked away. "I do like you. But I can't trust you."

His eyes flashed green. I wondered if he'd gotten new contacts. From what I could recall he had blue eyes.

"Do you have any ideas for our Spanish project?"

"Your lips look delicious."

I tried to ignore the queasy flutter in my stomach. "Do you want to cook some Spanish food for the fair?"

"I'd cook with you anytime." His eyes clung to me like magnets.

"Ten minutes," Mrs. Gonzalez shouted above the conversation in the room.

Andy leaned in. "Come over to my house Friday night for dinner. My parents will be home. Please?"

I wanted to punch him, but I also ached to kiss him. "I guess if your parents are going to be there, it'd be all right."

He touched my hand with his fingertip. "Great. I'll pick you up at six."

"Now can we focus on the assignment?"

We came up with some food ideas for the fair. When the bell rang I stuffed my textbook and spiral notebook into my backpack, then went to the front of the room and handed Mrs. Gonzalez our proposal. I rushed out into the crowded hallway.

Christina ran up beside me. "Hey, what's your hurry?"

I rolled my eyes. "I have to get away from Andy—and get to class."

She grabbed my elbow to slow me down. "Why?"

"He scares me. I know he's so wrong for me, but I find myself longing for him at the same time."

"Why does he scare you?"

"Well, let's just say he tried to push me a little further than I liked on our last date. It was awkward."

Christina paused. "And...you want to go out with him again?"

"He asked me to have dinner with him and his parents."

"That sounds interesting." She winked. I knew I shouldn't take advice—or rely on impressions from Christina. I tried to tell myself this date would be OK and was probably probing for Christina's approval regardless of the fact that I knew she was the last person to be taking dating advice from.

"His parents will be home. So it should be safe, right?"

"Yeah, sounds legit to me." I knew she'd say that.

We continued down the hallway and paused beside my locker. Vicki bumped into me. She flipped her perfectly curled hair. Her face had half a bottle of makeup on it. Her skirt was so short that if she bent over I was sure I'd see her bottom.

"You look tired, Liv. You sure you'll be able to make it through volleyball practice today?"

Why not? I'm always on my game every day.

"Oh, I'm totally stoked today."

Why would she say that?

"Coach said he's going to let me start during the game this Thursday."

What? I was the starting setter for the entire season. But Vicki had been begging Coach to let her start for a few games. My teammates had made sure I knew this whenever they heard her talking to Coach, asking for him to let her take my place more often.

Since our team was undefeated so far, scouts had started coming to our games. I had my heart set on the University of Delaware, which was known for its great volleyball program. If I could get a full ride from them, it would take a huge financial burden off my parents. Not only that—I'd be playing for one of the best teams in the country. I'd already sent in my application last month, and I was confident I'd be accepted.

"I'm sure you'll do fine," Christina whispered. "Don't let her shake you."

"See you at the net," Vicki cooed, then swaggered down the hallway.

Christina grasped my shoulder. "You're ten times better than her. The scouts will see that."

"Thanks. But I'm still nervous. Please pray for me, OK?"

Did God care if I played a good game of volleyball? Was that a selfish thing to pray about?

I had to call Kathryn! My "crazy" cousin. I'd almost forgotten. We'll see—I had my doubts that she was truly crazy.

I waited until that evening, after finishing my homework, to look up her phone number in my contact list on my phone. I'd only called her once before from what I could recollect. Would she be suspicious of me calling since I never did on a regular basis? Would she open up to me?

God, please give me the right words to say to Kathryn. Lord, let her be open.

I dialed her number. I counted the rings, almost hoping she wouldn't answer. On the third ring I heard, "Hello?"

"Hey—yeah—Kathryn, it's your cousin, Liv. Have I called at a bad time?"

I'd heard from my mom that she was living at home again after spending time in the behavioral sciences unit, so I was relieved to find her available.

"No, Liv, what's up? I haven't heard from you since we saw each other at the family reunion last June."

Did she suspect I was about to ask something crazy? She must be dumbfounded at me calling her so randomly.

"Listen, I know we don't talk that often, but I have a really important item I need to talk to you about."

There was a slight pause, then, "What's up?"

"Well. I know you've..." I paused to collect the right words "...been judged by some to be crazy." There was another brief pause, then an audible sigh.

I jumped in. "If you don't want to talk about it, it's OK. But...I think this may run in the family." I decided to just lay it all out there. "I'm seeing angels and demons."

"Oh—well—then yes, we do have something to talk about."

My shoulders dropped as the tension released. "Listen, Kathryn, I don't think you are crazy."

"Well, that's a first."

"When you hear voices, what are you hearing?"

"I see and hear spirits."

Bingo! "I see them too."

She let out a deep breath. "Has anyone told you that you are crazy?"

"My mom," I said in a sharp tone.

"Well, our moms were raised in the same church, same family. They didn't believe in that stuff. So when it happens, they just attribute it to something satanic or mental instability."

"I'm so sorry you've gone through what you have, Kathryn."

"Thank you. I've felt very alone in this until now."

"You're not alone. I understand. I am praying for you. Would you pray for me? My parents are making me see a psychiatrist. I don't want them to give me meds or put me in some behavior sciences unit at the hospital."

Her voice was methodic and confident. "Because *I* know I'm not crazy, I've been able to make it. I know what I see and hear. God knows."

Wow, she'd really learned to deal with this bravely. "Yes, He knows, and I pray that you will see this as a gift, not a curse. Call me anytime."

"Thank you," she replied. I heard more emotion in those two words than from any other time I'd heard them spoken.

"No problem."

"Hang in there, cuz. I've got you covered with prayer—and surrounded by God's angels."

"You can be sure your prayers were answered even before you prayed them," I said.

"Bye."

"Keep in touch, Liv. Later."

I sat in wonder, contemplating our conversation and the courage of my cousin. Would I be able to follow her example, or would I be a drooling mental patient eventually?

Chapter 18

ADRENALINE PUMPED THROUGH me as I shifted my weight from one foot to the other on the sidelines of the court, waiting for Coach to announce the starting lineup for the home game at our gym. We'd played this team before and beat them, so I figured we'd look pretty good tonight. If Coach picked Vicki to start, the scouts in the stands would attribute the win to her. Including the one from the university I wanted to attend.

I scanned the crowd on the bleachers. Sure enough. U of D Blue Hens hats and school colors caught my eye up in the top section to my left.

"Huddle up!" Coach shouted.

We all threw our warm-up balls to the team manager. She placed them in the mesh bag.

In the huddle Coach called out the other starting players. I twirled my fingers around the hair of my ponytail, awaiting the lineup. Finally he said, "Olivia, you're starting setter."

I stood up, cracking my knuckles half from nerves, half out of victory. Vicki shot me an icy stare. I'd pay for this somehow.

As we stood in a circle we put our hands into the middle and shouted, "One, two, three. Go, set, kill!" We jogged onto the court and got into our positions. I took my place by the net. Vicki plunked herself down on the bench beside Coach.

The game soon settled into a comfortable pace. I landed some great sets, resulting in great spikes that accumulated point after point, putting us far in the lead early in the game. I made some awesome saves that sent me flying onto the floor. The cheers from the crowd added to my sense of security about my impression on the scouts.

One of my teammates rolled the ball to me, and I waited for the whistle to serve. Just then Andy walked into the gym. From where I stood I could see he had my uniform number painted in white on his cheek. Vicki's eyes snapped in his direction. Then she turned and glared at me, nostrils flared. *I'm toast. Someone kill me now.*

The whistle blew. I bounced the ball three times, as was my routine. I hated knowing Andy was staring at me. I feared I'd lose concentration and blow my serve. I tossed the ball up and smacked it. It flew right into the net. Just as I feared.

My teammates gasped. I never missed a serve. Well, hardly ever.

Stinkin' Andy.

After a few high-fives from my teammates, I recovered my focus. One missed serve wouldn't ruin me.

Just then the ref blew his whistle, and Vicki rotated in. As we stood at the sideline, awaiting the scorekeeper to record our numbers, Vicki avoided my eyes. And instead of the friendly high-five we displayed as one player replaced another, she walked right by me, leaving my hand in the air. I jogged to the bench and sat down.

After Vicki fumbled two sets, Coach put me back in the game.

In the end we managed to win the match easily and maintain our undefeated status.

I lingered after the game to see what interaction may occur between Coach and the scouts.

A middle-aged gentleman in khaki pants and a blue shirt approached Coach. My heart leapt as I watched the man I'd spotted right before the game started. After shaking Coach's hand he glanced in my direction and nodded at me. Our eyes met.

Andy came up to me and gave me a hug. I recoiled. I was so engulfed in watching the body language of Coach and U of D guy that his interruption annoyed me.

Andy gave me an offended look. He then followed my eyes, realizing what I was absorbed in.

"Hey, sorry—"

I held my hand up. He got the message. But then he leaned over and whispered, "Sweet thing, they're negotiating your acquisition. How sexy…you being sought after by one of the best college teams in the country. That's hot."

As my heart hammered against my ribcage, I realized we had a date coming up. As always, Andy's voice dripped with seduction that made me lose concentration.

He placed a quick kiss on my cheek and headed in the direction of the exit.

I quickly scanned the room, looking for anyone who had observed that intimate interaction. I lucked out. Nobody seemed to notice. Most importantly, Vicki had huffed off to the locker room early, so she was nowhere in sight.

I didn't want Coach to see me lurking, so I slung my gym bag over my shoulder and walked toward the door leading to the parking lot. I lunged into the door, the chill of late fall hitting me in the face as I breathed in the refreshing air. My exhilaration was cut short as my body was slammed against the cold cement building. I gasped from the air being knocked out of my lungs. My eyes focused slowly, finding green eyes framed by blonde hair staring at me nose to nose.

Vicki. The chilled night air flared from her nostrils like a bull prepared to spear me with his horns.

"You watch your back, you—"

I hunched, ducked, and ran toward my car. Thankfully she didn't follow. She mumbled a few curse words, but my heavy breathing muted them. I rammed my keys into the lock, opened my car door and slung my bag into the backseat, and slammed the driver's side door, hitting the lock button immediately. I headed for home.

I felt like I'd just stomped on a hornet's nest. Someone was going to get stung. Guess who?

Chapter 19

I SAT IN THE kitchen, waiting for Andy to pick me up for dinner. I kept reminding myself that I'd be safe since his parents would be there.

"Andy has such a nice family," Mom said as she finished drying the last dish and putting it in the cupboard. I'd skipped dinner and held my appetite for my dinner at Andy's house.

Since she and Andy's mother had been best friends since high school, they probably wanted the two of us to get together so they could share grandchildren. Of course, if she knew about my first date with him, she'd change her mind.

I heard a honk and looked out the window. Andy's car sat at the curb. Apparently he wasn't going to come in and talk to my parents this time.

"See you, Mom." I grabbed my purse and headed to the front door.

"Don't get home too late."

"I'll be back at the usual time. Don't worry."

I walked to his car. He didn't get out to open my door like he did on our first date. I slid into the passenger seat.

"Hey, gorgeous." Andy leaned over the center console and lightly kissed me on the cheek. I flinched a bit, but I didn't think he noticed. He stomped on the gas pedal, making the car engine roar.

He shifted into drive and headed down the street toward his neighborhood, which was only a couple of miles from my house. The radio was so loud we couldn't really talk. I didn't know what to say anyway. I was relieved. I wanted to see how this date went. I still had doubts that Andy could change his ways.

I realized I'd never even asked for God's guidance in accepting this date, just like the previous date. And that was a disaster.

Oh, no!

When he pulled into his driveway I noticed his parents' car was not parked in the driveway. "Where are your folks?"

"They'll be here soon. Mom had to go to the grocery store to get some things for dinner."

I wondered if I should call my dad and have him pick me up. I decided to be cool and hope for the best, hoping his parents would be there, just as he'd promised.

I followed Andy into the house. The dining table wasn't set, and I didn't smell any food cooking.

I guessed I'd have to ignore the rumble in my stomach; it seemed that it would be a while before his mom started dinner.

Andy helped me out of my coat and threw it over the rocking chair in the living room, then led me to the sofa. "You want something to drink?"

"Sure. Thanks." I needed something to quench my dry mouth and give my hands something to do.

"I'll be right back." He went to the kitchen.

As I sat on the sofa, a flutter of nerves came over me, and I twirled my hair.

I hope his parents show up soon.

He came back holding two cans of beer.

"I don't drink." I'd never had an alcoholic beverage in my life.

His eyes opened wide. "Ever?"

"No.

"Why?"

"I just don't drink."

"I don't know any senior who *doesn't* drink." He set one beer down on the coffee table in front of me and snapped open the cap of the other.

"Do you have any lemonade or iced tea?"

He looked up to his left, as if mentally scanning the fridge. "Yeah, I think so." He returned to the kitchen. I listened to the clank of glasses, the clunking of ice cubes, and the sound of liquid being poured.

Andy entered the living room with a glass of iced tea, still holding his beer in the other hand. He handed me the tea.

"Thanks." I took a few big sips. It tasted a little sweeter than I usually made it, and it had a hint of some unfamiliar flavor. Could it be rum? I'd smelled it once before at one of my cousin's weddings.

Andy tossed back a few gulps of beer. "Want to listen to some music?"
"Sure."

Andy walked over to the entertainment center and turned on the radio. He tuned it to a soft-rock station. *Great.* I was a sucker for rock ballads. How did he know my weakness?

He sat beside me, our thighs touching. Feeling my hormones doing jumping jacks, and not liking how out of control I felt, I stood up. "Should we call your parents and find out if they will be here soon?"

"Sure."

I took another long sip of my tea, then set the glass on the coffee table. "Can I top off your drink?" Andy's voice echoed in my head.

The room seemed to lean to the left. I felt like I was looking at everything through one of those crazy mirrors you see at circuses that make everything out of proportion.

What's going on?

Mike shoved his way through the throngs of evil spirits crammed inside Andy's house. Every time he leaned into the black crowd they threw him back out onto the street in front of the house. He needed backup help.

That filthy spirit, Lagarre, had probably invaded the body of a young man who'd set his sights on violating Olivia. He'd seen it before. And this was one of Lagarre's favorite tactics.

Mike shouted words in angelic language.

The ground rumbled beneath him, signaling the arrival of his celestial comrades.

Gideon appeared above Christina's car as she pulled into Andy's driveway. He followed close behind her.

With his friend Gideon beside him now, Mike grew to twelve feet tall, towering above the car. Gideon did the same. Armor cascaded over their forms within seconds. Both angels withdrew flaming swords from behind their backs.

"Lagarre," Mike screamed, his sword held above his head. He had to save Olivia before it was too late. His close observance of a house with no parents—and the scent of some kind of chemical or substance in Olivia's drink—sent his angelic senses on fire. This boy, under the control of his evil archenemy, was hell-bent on defiling Olivia—or worse.

I slumped onto the couch, unable to hold my body in a sitting position. I felt paralyzed.

Oh, God! Save me. I'm helpless.

Andy scooped me into his arms and carried me down a narrow hallway to a bedroom. My body sagged in his grip. He dropped me on the bed. My teeth clanged together from the jolt.

A few sips of alcohol couldn't make me this numb. Maybe it was a drug he'd put in my drink.

I tried to lift my arm to slap him, but was powerless to control my limbs. Andy's voice was muffled. I couldn't tell what he was saying, but his voice was deep, his eyes were black, and his facial expression resembled a predator ready to kill its prey. I felt the weight of his body press me into the bed as he unbuttoned my jeans and slid them down to my ankles.

I tried to scream but could utter only a low moan.

My eyes fogged over as if I'd been swimming in chlorine for hours. I feared I was close to passing out.

Andy climbed on top of me, and his mouth devoured my lips. Andy's hands grabbed parts of my body nobody but my doctor had ever touched. His unblinking black eyes horrified me. Was I imagining it, or were they actually as black as night?

"Jesus!" I screamed inside my head.

A glowing light appeared behind his shoulder. *Mike!*

A knock on the window broke through my haze. "Andy?" *Christina's voice!*

He let out a string of expletives, then jumped off of me and raced out the bedroom door.

I heard the front door slam and voices arguing. It *was* Christina!

"Christina!" My lips formed the word but no sound escaped.

"Olivia?" I heard her call. She came into the room and scurried to my side. Cradling my head in her hands she mumbled, "Oh, God."

Thank God she showed up.

"You creep!" she screamed at Andy, who leaned against the doorjamb of the room. "What have you done to her?"

"I didn't do anything. She had too much to drink, I guess."

"Olivia does *not* drink!" she snapped at him.

"Just leave. Get out of my house!" he yelled back.

Christina ignored him. "Olivia, honey, are you with me?" She sounded like she was speaking in a tunnel. "I'm going to take you home."

"Thanks." The word came out slurred. I was relieved to be able to respond, even if it sounded ridiculous. Maybe God had heard my prayer for help. Christina's uncanny timing assured me He had.

My head ached, and my eyes rolled around, trying to focus, but failed. I gave in and closed my eyes.

Mike's and Gideon's large figures filled the room and sliced at Lagarre's hovering minions scattered around the room. They scurried away, disappearing through the walls and ceiling. As Mike's eyes burned into the back of Andy's head, a face appeared there, sneering back at him. When Christina entered the room, the apparition of Lagarre peeled away, leaving Andy's body. Both angels chased Lagarre out of the house. Once outside they cast their gaze all around and saw nothing.

"He'll be back," Mike mumbled, his swords drooping in his hands toward the ground.

Gideon grasped his shoulder. "I'll be there. Things will escalate. That's how Lagarre has always worked. But we'll summon all the warrior angels to assist us."

"Yes. We've chased him off temporarily, but it's time to utterly destroy him. Our next meeting will be our last." Mike placed his swords back in their sheaths and breathed deeply. He seethed with righteous anger.

"I must follow my Christina," Gideon murmured. Mike nodded in agreement. He would follow his Olivia.

They both observed as Christina struggled to carry Olivia to her car and fold her into the backseat of her white Toyota Camry.

Both angels sat inside the car, unbeknownst to the two girls.

I woke up in Christina's bed. She sat in a chair in the corner, reading a book. "What time is it?" I whispered, then coughed.

Wow, I can speak without slurring my words. My head felt clearer.

Christina put her book on the end table and came to the bedside. She glanced at her watch. "It's two a.m."

"My parents are going to kill me for being late. What happened?"

"Andy gave you a spiked drink. I know you don't drink, and darling, the way you were acting, it had to be drugged. Then he tried to rape you. When I found you lying on the bed you were in a...precarious position."

I looked at my clothes. Nothing was torn or missing. I hoped that meant he hadn't gotten very far before I lost consciousness. I recalled him taking off my jeans and his weight on me. Then I heard Christina hollering. I figured that was as far as it had gone. God had answered my feeble prayer. Again, I was embarrassed at how I'd trusted Andy and opened myself up to such a dangerous situation.

I sat up slowly, holding my throbbing head. A sudden wave of nausea made me bolt for Christina's bathroom. *Could a few sips of alcohol do this to me?* It had to be a date-rape type of drug. The sweet drink must have covered up the taste of the drug. Was that the bitter taste I'd mistaken as extra lemon or sugar?

After heaving up everything I'd eaten that day, I washed my face and went back into the bedroom and lay down on the bed. "How did you know I was in trouble?"

"I knew you were nervous about tonight, so I prayed for you this afternoon. While I was praying, I felt like something bad was going to happen, so I decided to go to Andy's and check on you. If everything was all right I'd make some excuse, like that I needed some homework information from you. When I got there, I saw Andy's car but no other car that could be his parents', and since they don't have a garage, I got scared, knowing they probably were not there."

She adjusted the pillow under my head and tucked her blanket in around me. "I knocked, but there was no answer. So I banged on all the windows. Finally Andy answered the door. I shoved past him, called out your name, and looked in every room until I found you."

"I'm glad you listened to the Holy Spirit's prompting."

"And I'm sorry I encouraged you to see Andy again."

"Your parents called me, asking if I knew where you were when you were late. I told them you're here and you're safe. I asked them if you could spend the night with me. Your mom seemed fine with it."

Relief flooded over me. I could rest and gather my senses before having to face my parents. "Can I borrow something to sleep in?"

"Sure." Christina opened a dresser drawer and pulled out some cute pink shorts and a gray shirt. As I rose from the bed to grab them, I stumbled. Christina steadied me, then helped me undress and put on the clothes.

I felt around beneath me to make sure I sat on the bed and didn't fall to the floor. I lay back down. Christina went back to reading her book. I wondered what I should tell my mom about what happened tonight. How much did I dare tell her? What would I say to Andy at school on Monday?

I wanted to ask my guardian angel to beat the snot out of Andy. I'm sure that wasn't biblical. But I was sure Mike was dying to deck him. Had he played a part in saving me tonight?

"Do you even have to wonder?" Mike whispered in my ear.

I closed my eyes. How could I ever doubt it?

"Liv?"

Yes?

"*Andy's body was occupied by a demonic force tonight. Remember the disembodied Nephilim spirit, Lagarre, that I told you about one time?*"

The one that goads you all the time and tries to detain you and kill your charges?

"*That's the one. I'm afraid he'll be back again—and that it will be a more intense attack than tonight.*"

I swallowed hard, wondering if he'd ever been successful in killing one of Mike's charges. Would he succeed in killing me?

Chapter 20

THE SECOND-TO-LAST BELL of the day rang, and I sprang from my chair in study hall last period and raced toward my locker, anxious to get out of the stuffy, windowless classroom and into my car to head home. I didn't have volleyball practice that day, and I was glad for the break.

"Olivia?"

I turned and saw Ty, our star football quarterback, jog up to me, wearing his letterman jacket.

"Hey, Ty. What's up?"

He let out a nervous sigh. "I want to do something really special for Eden to thank her for praying for me when I was hurt. It's taken me this long to get up the nerve."

How can Mr. Popular be so insecure when it comes to girls? Hoping he had only pure intentions when it came to my dear friend, I said, "Did you have something in mind?"

"I was thinking about having a private dinner for her at my house."

Warning flags went up in my brain. "How private?"

"My parents are going out Saturday night, so I was thinking—"

"Forget it." I flicked the padlock on my locker, wanting to strangle him. "Eden doesn't need some guy trying to get her alone and—"

"Actually, I was hoping you'd come too."

I glared at him. Was he suggesting what I thought? *What a perv!*

"I...I mean to help. I haven't a clue how to cook. And you're her friend, so you'd know what she likes to eat."

I was ashamed at my judgmental thoughts.

"Plus, I think you'd make a terrific chaperone. After all, I wouldn't want to do anything that might seem inappropriate."

I peered at him, trying to decide if I needed to reevaluate this guy. I'd never heard any rumors about him being a player. I guessed people just assumed that kind of thing when it came to someone like him. Was he being honest, or just backpedaling because he knew I didn't approve of what he was really after?

"I don't even know if she'd say yes. I'm not sure if she likes me."

My heart softened. *This guy is really legit. He's not arrogant. I think he is actually insecure in a way. Bizarre!*

Knowing how Eden felt about him, his insecurity made me want to giggle. But I couldn't tell him that. Let him win Eden over by being honorable. I didn't want to make it easy for him, knowing she had a crush on him. "Well, she *is* really picky about boys."

"I'm glad to hear that. I mean...I hope I can measure up."

There's nothing more attractive than a gorgeous guy who isn't impressed with himself.

"I might be willing to help you." I'd softened my tone. Hey, at least myself and two angels would be there to protect Eden.

A grin lit up his face. "Do you know how to cook?"

"Of course." I wasn't exactly a chef, but I could follow a recipe. And my mom had some good ones.

"Great. Are you free Saturday night?"

It wasn't like I had anyone planning a private dinner for me. "Sure."

"Thanks." He rolled his eyes. "You have no idea how much this means to me."

He had no idea how much this would mean to Eden.

"I'm going to call her right now." He started dialing as he walked down the hallway.

I had no doubt that she'd accept his invitation. I only wondered how soon she'd call to tell me about it. And what she'd tell me she wanted me to make for dinner when I asked her for her preference.

My cell phone rang three minutes later. It was Eden. I smiled as I answered.

"Ty asked me to dinner at his place! And he said you are going to cook for us!"

"Yep. I'll be there to keep him honest."

She squealed. "Liv, I'm so nervous."

"Don't worry. Be yourself. And pray. Don't be a fool like me and not consult God before going out with a guy."

"Andy?"

"Yeah. He's a creep." I didn't want to tell her all the details. It was bad enough that Christina knew.

"I'm sorry, Liv. I love you, girl."

"Love you too! Now, start thinking about what you want me to cook and let Ty know, and he and I will take care of it all."

"You're the best! Bye!"

"Later."

When I hung up, I felt excitement and anticipation about Eden's special date. I certainly wouldn't spy, but it would be fun watching them exchange shy glances at each other as I served them.

On Saturday morning I went shopping for all the things I needed to make Ty and Eden's dinner a success. Eden had requested my mother's three-cheese ravioli with white cream sauce, which she'd eaten at our place a few times. Mom offered to make the pasta for me. She even agreed to bake her famous cheesecake smothered in chocolate sauce and topped with strawberries.

While Mom worked on making the ravioli in the kitchen, I put a bunch of Eden's favorite songs on my iPod. I thought that would be a special touch, and Eden would be so happy I gathered all her songs for her special night. I sat at the kitchen table so I could help if Mom needed my assistance.

"Mom...about the other night at Andy's house..."

She put her hand up to stop me. "Christina's mother explained. Christina filled her in. I'm very disappointed in my friend's son."

"Yeah, me too."

Wow, gossip travels fast. At least I won't have my mom pushing me to go out with Andy again just because he's her friend's son.

"I'm glad you weren't hurt. But I'd sure like to—" She made a twisting motion with her hands as if she were wringing Andy's neck. She wiped her hand on a dishtowel. "I'm sorry, I had no idea that young man would get fresh with you...much less *drug* you."

"I hope this doesn't hurt your relationship with Andy's mom."

"Well, don't worry about that. I'll have a talk with her. She needs to know her son is preying on young girls. It's despicable."

"Thanks for helping make this dinner with Eden and Ty special."

"Oh, I'm happy to, after what you went through. I'm glad you'll be there. I don't know this Ty boy. At least you can be sure Eden is OK."

"Right, Mom. I feel the same way."

Mom shot me a rare smile. I smiled back.

"Could you check on the cheesecake, dear?" I loved hearing her use that endearing word and felt warm inside. This was how mothers and daughters should be. Talking, sharing, doing things side by side.

I hustled to the oven and grabbed the potholders. I turned on the light and peeked in to see that it looked perfectly done. Before taking it out I asked, "Mom, what do you think?"

She bent over and admired her perfect baking. "Looks marvelous."

I pulled it out, smelling the wonderful, sweet aroma rising from its warmth, and set it on the stovetop to cool. Later we would chill it in the refrigerator until right before I left for Ty's house.

At four o'clock I drove to Ty's place with a backseat full of brown paper bags and a covered glass pan of ravioli.

When I pulled up in front of his house I saw him in the front doorway, dressed in a blue sweater, khaki pants, and a tie. *Nice!*

As he strode across the yard toward my car he said, "Hey, let me give you a hand with that."

"Well, thanks."

After he helped bring in the bags of groceries, I peeked into the dining room and noticed he'd set out good china and candles in a crystal holder.

"Pulling out all the stops tonight, eh?"

He blushed. "I want everything to be perfect."

If I knew my friend she'd be more impressed with his character and manners than pretty dishes and tasty food.

I set my iPod into the docking station on the china cabinet shelf. "Do you mind?"

"Oh, not at all."

"I downloaded all her favorite songs." I grinned at his pleased expression, then gave him a knowing wink.

This was going to be a night to remember for my friend. A gorgeous guy, a fancy dinner, her favorite music playing. She deserved it. And down deep inside me, my romantic nature wanted to see this couple really hit it off.

I set sliced cheddar cheese and wheat crackers—one of Eden's favorite snacks—on a coffee table in the living room, then joined Ty in the kitchen. He'd already unpacked the paper bags and set everything on the counters. He gave me a quick overview of where to find everything in the vast kitchen.

Ty stood behind me as I turned the oven on. "I'm going to invite her into the backyard after desert. I have a surprise for her. I hung little white paper Japanese lanterns on the trees. So when we get to the sliding door, could you flick the switch so the little lights come on once we are outside?"

Sweet!

"Sure thing. Nice touch, Ty. I'm impressed." He shuffled his feet and glanced sideways, smiling. I was sure that he was pleased with himself and relieved at my glowing approval.

As I rinsed lettuce for a Caesar salad, Ty asked, "Has Eden ever dated anyone?"

"No one seriously." I picked up the bottle of olive oil and shook it at him. "So be tender with her. If you hurt her..." I put the bottle down on the table.

"I won't. I promise." His brow wrinkled as if embarrassed that I would even imply that he would.

I set the lettuce aside to drain and opened the box of croutons. "I'm sure you've broken plenty of girls' hearts."

He looked at me with his jaw tight. "You think I've been around? Truth is, I've never even kissed a girl."

My mouth dropped open. *He can't be serious. If he is, I seriously adore this guy. Is he too good to be real?*

"It's true." He pulled one hand out of his pants pocket and held it out, palm up.

"Thanks for telling me that."

OK, you can stop the interrogation now, Olivia. Go easy on him.

I began to chop the lettuce, then shot him a wide grin. "You know, I think this evening *is* going to be perfect." His shoulders dropped as some tension released. I decided I needed to encourage him so he wouldn't be so nervous that he'd fumble and spill something tonight. I wanted him to be himself in front of Eden.

"I sure hope so." Ty fiddled with his tie.

His fidgeting was adorable. "Don't worry. You look terrific."

The doorbell rang. Ty stiffened, smoothed his hair, then headed for the foyer. Resisting the urge to peek, I finished the salad and put the ingredients for the white sauce into a pan on the stove.

As I stirred the sauce Mike appeared beside me. "So, you're a chef now, huh?"

"I can fake it when I need to." I pointed to the loaf of Italian bread on the butcher-block island. "Since you're in human form, think you could slice that for me?"

I put a large pot of hot water on the stove and began to boil it for the ravioli, then turned to Mike.

His eyebrows arched. "Unless you plan to slice off a finger, that's hardly in my job description. I'm your guardian, not your servant."

I gasped, afraid I'd overstepped some boundary and offended him. But then he chuckled, and I sighed with relief.

"Mmmm...smells terrific, whatever it is." He moved toward the stove, stuck his finger in the sauce, and popped it in his mouth.

"So do you angels eat?"

"We don't need to, but we can."

As I sawed the crusty loaf into half-inch chunks, I heard Ty say from the dining room, which was next to the kitchen, "Would you like something to drink?"

Just in case Ty or Eden walked in, I glanced around to see if Mike was still there. He'd disappeared.

"Sure," Eden replied.

"Do you like sparkling cider?"

"I've never had it, but it sounds good."

Before Ty came into the kitchen I grabbed two goblets from the china cabinet. While he waited in the doorway I put pre-sliced lemons on the rims and poured the cider. Ty took the glasses and mouthed, "Thanks," then took them out to Eden in the living room.

"Who's this?" I heard her ask.

"I see you've met my new puppy."

I didn't know he had a puppy! Where had it been while we were unpacking? The garage?

That would go over with Eden for sure! I glanced into the living room and saw Ty nestling a little black ball of fur in his neck, then kiss the tip of its nose. "This is Twinkle. She's a French bulldog." He held her out toward Eden.

When the puppy rested in her hands, she looked like she would melt. She hugged Twinkle to her chest, then she received a soft lick on her cheek. The pup's little tail wagged faster the more Eden giggled.

"Are you ready for dinner?"

"Whenever you are."

That was my cue. I tossed a dishtowel over my forearm to look official and brought the salad and bread to them in the dining room, holding the large tray like an experienced server at a fancy restaurant.

"I'm here to serve you, *mademoiselle*," I said in my best attempt at a French accent.

She chuckled.

Ty pulled out a chair for Eden. After she sat, he handed her a linen napkin, which she laid on her lap.

Eden fluttered her eyelashes. "Thank you, Ty."

I set the salad bowl on the tea cart beside the dining table, then placed the bread basket between them.

"Thanks, Olivia," they both said.

"My pleasure." I punched the play button on the iPod, and soft music filled the room. Behind Ty's back I winked at Eden, tipped my head toward Ty, and mouthed, "I like him!" She stifled a smile. After wishing the couple *Bon appétit*, I returned to the kitchen.

Mike stood at the stove, stirring the sauce. Beside him stood a fierce-looking warrior angel dressed in bear skins. His cloak was fastened to his neck with a bear claw. It was Eden's angel!

Mike spun around from where he was stirring my sauce. "Olivia, this is Cabriel, Eden's guardian angel."

The warrior removed his helmet shaped like a bear's head. "My name rhymes with Gabriel, but I'm no archangel. Nice to see you again." He sort of grunted when he spoke and flicked his eyes back and forth from me to the floor.

Of course he'd be here. He came with Eden!

"Pleased to see you again."

I took the spoon from Mike. "I thought you weren't supposed to assist me with menial tasks."

He shrugged. "I didn't want it to burn. Besides, this stuff smells...heavenly."

Mike and Cabriel laughed, and I joined in as I checked my large pot with water that was boiling the ravioli.

"Besides," Mike added, "I've already scoped out the periphery of the property. No evil lurks here. All three of you have drenched this night in prayer, so tonight should be serene and safe. An evening to enjoy, not battle."

Boy, was that a relief.

Cabriel took up a position in the doorway between the kitchen and the dining room, where he could keep an eye on Eden but also watch me and Mike.

When I announced, "The ravioli is ready," Cabriel lifted the heavy pan and poured it over a strainer in the sink.

This was fun! In my wildest dreams I'd never imagined I could be making dinner with the help of two angels. The thought made me shake my head and giggle.

After greasing a baking sheet I placed the cooked ravioli on the pan and put it in the preheated oven.

Just like Mom's recipe said, the pasta turned golden brown in about four minutes. I drizzled some butter over the ravioli, then covered it with cream sauce. It looked and smelled delicious. I wished I had eaten before coming tonight, but I was too excited and nervous so I forgot. My stomach rumbled. Hopefully there'd be some leftovers.

Holding the platter of sauce-covered ravioli, I headed toward the dining room. In the doorway, I nearly dropped the plate when I saw a tall, thin angel standing at the head of the table. His dark face was painted like an African warrior with white and red dye. His chest was bare, and a leopard skin encircled his midsection. He held a spear in his right hand, pointed end up.

"That's Suriel," Mike said from behind me. "Ty's angel."

Suriel pulled back his lips to smile at me, exposing a set of brilliant white teeth. A laugh rose from deep within his chest and erupted from his mouth. It was contagious, and the other angels joined him.

I tried not to tremble as I served the main course to Ty and Eden. I didn't want to spill anything. I wanted everything to go smoothly. And seeing this new angel caught me off guard.

"Wow, Olivia," Eden said. "This looks amazing. I didn't know you were such a great cook."

I let out a nervous laugh. I hoped Eden would think my nervousness was the result of her compliment and not the sight of the imposing angelic being standing guard behind Ty.

I took the half-empty salad bowl and the two salad plates back to the kitchen. I paused just inside the doorway when I heard Ty say, "Eden, I really appreciate you praying for me at the football game. Do you do that often? Pray, I mean?"

I peeked around the corner of the doorway.

I love that he starts with a spiritual topic.

"Actually, I do." Eden helped herself to the ravioli. "But I'd never prayed for someone to be healed before."

"Well, it sure seems to have worked." Ty filled his plate, and the two lovebirds sat in silence, glancing at each other shyly across the table. They were so cute together.

Eden sliced a ravioli in half with her fork. "I was honored to pray for you. But I was kinda surprised that you invited me to come here for dinner. I mean, you never even spoke to me in school before that night at the football game."

Ty wiped his mouth with his napkin. "I was too nervous to approach you."

Eden swallowed, then wiped her lips with her napkin. "You were?"

"I've had a crush on you since first-grade Sunday school class."

"Why didn't you say something before?" Eden asked in a breathy tone.

"You're the pastor's daughter. I figured I couldn't possibly be good enough for you."

Eden laughed. "I figured you'd never notice me since you're the most popular guy in school. You must have girls flocking to your door."

"Yeah, but not the kind of girls I *want* to be with." Ty locked eyes with Eden. They didn't flinch for several moments.

My heart fluttered. I was eavesdropping. Not cool. Mike tapped me on my shoulder. When I looked back he had a reprimanding look. *"You shouldn't be spying."*

You're right. Feeling a bit ashamed, I left the romantic scene in the dining room. "Hey, wait a minute. You guardian angels eavesdrop all the time."

Mike's cheeks reddened a little. "And to be honest, it's a little uncomfortable sometimes. But we're not human beings. So we don't get embarrassed about the same things you do. Besides, we have a divine purpose."

I took the cheesecake out of the refrigerator. "Do you think Eden can be happy with Ty?"

"I sense his heart is pure," Cabriel said.

"Me too." I looked in the drawers for a cake cutter. "But she's been hurt so much." Eden's angel would know the details of her sexual abuse.

Suriel appeared in the doorway, still holding the spear in his right hand. "I've fought long and hard to preserve that young man's purity." His deep voice rumbled. "You wouldn't believe all the young ladies who've thrown themselves at him. But he has a strong spiritual foundation and a devotion to our Father. His mother prayed fervently for his purity since the day he started middle school. Her prayers have kept me quite busy."

That reminded me to add my own prayers to the effort. *Lord, let Eden trust again. Help her to heal from her uncle's inappropriate touching and open herself up to a pure touch. And make Ty behave himself tonight. If he doesn't, launch Suriel's spear at him!*

Giggling to myself, I brought out two plates of cheesecake.

"Oh my," Eden said. "That looks amazing. But I don't think I could eat another bite."

"Me either," Ty said. "I ate way too much of that awesome ravioli. And salad. And bread."

"I'm glad you liked it so much." I set the desserts on the sideboard and picked up the dinner plates. "No sweat. Eat it later if you want."

"Would you like to see our backyard?" Ty asked Eden. That was my cue.

"There's a two-person swing under a rose trellis out there. The flowers have faded, but there's a bright green vine around the arbor."

"It sounds lovely."

Ty came around the table to pull out her chair.

"Thank you." Eden looked at the floor, a smile exploding on her face.

Ty placed his hand on her back, directing her toward the back door. She didn't flinch.

Thank You, Lord!

"Let me get your jacket." Ty went to the foyer to get her coat.

When Ty was out of the room, Eden did a little shuffle dance as we exchanged smiles.

She tried to compose herself before Ty entered the room.

He held out her coat so she could place her arms in the sleeves. As he adjusted it on her shoulders, his fingers brushed her neck. Eden smiled. I sensed no tenseness there.

Ty slid open the door, and the two went into the backyard. I flicked the switch, and the lanterns glowed.

After closing the back door, Ty reached for Eden's hand. She laced her fingers in his. Their two angels smiled as they followed the couple outside.

I wanted to laugh and dance and sing to heaven. My friend had prayed for someone else's physical healing, and in the process she'd received emotional healing for herself.

I tackled the dirty dishes.

"I wish you could give me at least a little hint of when my perfect guy will show up."

Mike picked up a dishtowel. "It will happen in God's perfect timing. I don't want you to be distracted by those kinds of thoughts, but I understand why they are on your mind now."

When all the dishes were washed, dried, and put where they belonged, Mike gave me a reassuring look. "You really want to know what's going on out there, don't you?

"Yeah, I do.

"It wouldn't be eavesdropping if you went out to see if they'd like some cheesecake now."

"Great idea!" I rushed into the dining room, picked up the two plates, and headed for the back door. Just then, Eden's favorite song began to play. I set down one plate so I could turn the volume up on my iPod, enabling Eden to hear it outside. Then I grabbed the desserts and headed toward the backyard.

Ty and Eden sat close together in the swing, their two angels standing guard behind them. I stopped in the doorway, enjoying the beautiful sight.

"Tonight was really sweet," Eden said.

"I can't believe I waited so long to ask you to dinner. What do you say we make up for lost time?" Ty took hold of the tips of her fingers and stood with her. He put his hands on both sides of her face and tilted her head up. He stared into her eyes. Eden gazed longingly into his. He cupped her face and slowly moved his lips to hers, barely grazing them. Eden wrapped her arms around his neck. He ran his lips along her jaw until they reached the curve of her ear.

"Is this OK?" he whispered. I could barely hear him, but was glad I heard him ask permission.

A smile played across her lips. "You have no idea how OK this is."

"I've never kissed a girl before, so I hope I don't disappoint."

"I've never kissed a boy before. So we're even."

Now I was inside, gazing from the patio door out of sight.

Foreheads touching, they laughed at their mutual awkwardness.

"I don't think they want dessert now," Mike whispered in my ear.

"You're right. But I'm starving. I'm headed for the leftovers!"

I sat at the kitchen table and gobbled down ravioli.

Mike sat across from me, his chin in his hands. "You did a really nice thing tonight."

"Thanks. Want to pass the cheesecake?"

He slid the pie plate toward me. "You should slow down."

"I can't. For me, eating is equivalent to taking a cold shower. It's my new way to stop thinking about 'the one.'"

Mike shook his head. "He'll come. Sooner than you think!"

"When?"

"Can't say."

"Urgh!" I threw my napkin at him.

Chapter 21

THE AIR PULSED with rhythmic club sounds as bodies undulated to the music. I danced with Christina and Eden while colored lights played on the wooden gym floor. I didn't mind not having a date. It was actually kind of fun just goofing around dancing with my girlfriends. We'd heard about this new teen dance club and decided to check it out.

As soon as a slow dance began, Ty whisked Eden away. Christina and I just danced together. Amid all the sweat-covered bodies around me I spotted Andy following a beautiful gothic-type girl in a floor-length white gown. They crossed the dance floor, headed toward a door with a sign over it, saying No Admittance.

Two dark figures, both clothed in black hoodies with silver baseball hats and shoes, followed them. They weren't dressed like any students I knew from school. Curiosity made me follow the two figures as they followed the girl and Andy. I told Christiana I was headed to the restroom.

The girl opened the door, took Andy's hand, and dragged him inside. The two strange guys snuck in just before the door closed.

Who was this girl? I hoped one of the guys in black and silver was her boyfriend and they were going to catch them together making out or something. Or was one a jealous boyfriend and about to beat up Andy for sneaking into a closet with his girl? This I had to see!

I turned the knob and pushed the door a few inches. The room was so dark I couldn't see a thing, especially after being in a room full of lights. I heard loud voices not too far away. I couldn't make out the words. At least three voices were interacting.

I crept inside, careful not to make any noise that would reveal my presence. The large closet was one that must have been used by a janitor to store equipment. Once my eyes adjusted to the dark, I could see buckets, mops, old light bulbs, and shelving filled with various kinds of tools and equipment. A soft glow of light emanated from another room adjoining the closet.

I peered around a cement pillar and saw Andy's wrists chained to a rafter, his hands raised above his head. The girl in white paced around him like a cat stalking a mouse. In her left hand she held a golden whip. Andy's chest heaved. His eyes were wide in terror. Neither said anything.

Just behind Andy I caught a glimpse of a head of blond hair and a face with translucent blue eyes. It looked like Mike, but his chest and upper arms were covered in scars. I'd never seen my strong champion look so battered. He approached Andy from behind, flaming sword in hand. His lips curled in a sneer.

The two black-cloaked figures stood silently to either side of Andy, their legs spread and fists clasped behind their backs.

Andy's mouth opened wide, revealing a double row of pointed teeth. I clamped my hand over my mouth to stifle a scream. He looked more demonic than human. What was he?

Mike dropped his sword at his side. "Seraphina," he hollered, "take him out."

The girl in white cracked her whip. "This is your kill."

Was he going to kill Andy? Was he going to kill a spirit possessing Andy?

Mike raised his large blade. It radiated light. "I'll send you straight to the abyss!"

Mike circled Andy, his grasp on his sword growing tighter and his veins on his face protruding.

"You can no longer possess this boy. You will never again attack my charge using his body."

Mike's going to kill Lagarre! But how?

Andy's eyes rolled back in his head. His head thrashed back and forth, straining at the chains around his chest, feet, and hands.

I inched forward, trying to get a better look at the scene. I stumbled over a string of electrical cords. When I straightened, Mike, Seraphina, and the two boys in black stared at me, mouths slackened.

The blond boy yelled, "Who's there?"

The brunette asked, "Can she see us, Mike?"

I cleared my throat and in a quivery voice said, "Yes, I can see you."

Oh, no. How will they take this?

The short boy snarled, "You'd better get out of here."

Mike stepped forward and stood between me and Andy. "Let her be. I want her to see this." He puffed his chest out as if to punctuate his insistence of my presence.

"No way. Get this girl out of—"

Andy howled and lunged toward Mike, straining against his shackles. He lashed at Mike with nails and teeth that resembled metal blades.

I backed up and tripped on a bucket, collapsing on the floor with a thud. My lower back felt bruised, and I rubbed it as I clamored to stand up.

Why do I have to be so clumsy? How embarrassing.

Seraphina swirled her whip, catching Andy around the waist. He yelped and crashed to the ground.

The taller boy lunged at Andy and jabbed a knife blade into his chest. Bluish-green liquid gushed from the jagged gash.

Wow, is that the color of demon blood?

Andy's body rolled, flailing and gurgling as he held his hand over his bleeding chest. After a few moments of writhing and moaning, Andy's body went limp.

Is he dead?

Seraphina grazed her whip softly across Mike's wound, and it closed, leaving no scar behind.

That's no normal whip. She seems to be able to control whether it wounds or not.

Mike stood over Andy, raised his own leg, and smashed it into Andy's already wounded chest. "Go straight to the abyss, Lagarre!"

Mike was facing away from me, but I could see that he'd sprinkled something on Andy's body. *What is that?*

Andy's body convulsed violently, then went limp.

I stepped closer. Not a trace of blood remained on his chest or on the floor.

Where did the blood go?

Seraphina and the boys in black vanished.

Mike bent over Andy, his wings hanging limp against his body. "Lagarre will never return. The Lord of All gave me authority to end this feud once and for all."

Why couldn't he end his life earlier? Had there been a purpose in his lingering? Maybe for me to learn my final lesson in discernment when it came to boys?

I clamored to Andy's side and held his head in my hands, his body limp and eyes closed. Would he be OK when I saw him in school on Monday? *He'll sure need the weekend to recover from this.*

Mike tucked something tiny into a pouch on his waist. "He won't bother you anymore."

What a relief. But I was more concerned that Andy would be all right at that moment.

I gently set Andy's head back on the floor, then raised my eyes to scan Mike's body. "Why are you so scarred?"

"I incur many wounds in my battles for you—and others. I usually hide them when you see me." He fluffed out his wings and curled them around his body to cover the scars.

Come to think of it, when he appears in human form he's usually covered in a long-sleeved shirt and jeans. Tonight he was shirtless and was wearing a tunic-type skirt. Golden shin guards covered his legs, and his chest glistened with a matching golden breast plate.

"I'm so sorry I caused those."

The corner of Mike's mouth turned up. "I consider them badges of honor."

My eyes misted. What sacrifices he had made for me, ones I'd witnessed, and surely many in my past.

Andy began to stir and groan.

Mike nodded in Andy's direction. "We need to go before he wakes up."

"I can't just leave him here. Won't he need medical help?"

"He'll be OK. He'll assume he blacked out and feel a bit disoriented. He won't remember what happened."

"So he won't remember trying to rape me either?"

"No."

That was a relief since I'd have to face him in school. Perhaps it would cut out the awkwardness in seeing each other.

"Is Andy a 'good guy' now?" My usual conflicted feelings for Andy began to stir in my stomach.

"Give him some time." Mike read my mind. "Don't rush into being too 'familiar' with him for a while."

"You're trying to say he's not 'the one'?"

Mike nodded slowly, his head cocked to one side. "Try to concentrate on your spiritual walk right now, your friends, and school. OK?"

"You're right. And I trust you, Mike." I stepped forward and threw my arms around his shoulders, practically bouncing off his chest it was so solid. Then with my hands remaining on his shoulders, I traced my index finger on my right hand across a scar on his left side that led from his collarbone to the middle of his bicep.

"Me?" I cringed.

"No." His eyes stared at the floor. "Lagarre," he growled.

"But that's over now, right?" I dropped my arms to my sides.

Mike lifted his gaze and looked me in the eyes. "Not really. He has cohorts that would love to carry out his revenge, as well as avenge the death of one of their own. Lagarre's son, for one."

I peered into his liquid-crystal blue eyes. His brow furrowed in worry.

"When the time comes and I'm able to pray you through a battle, I'll be there for you," I stated.

The concept sounded rather backward, since he was the one that was supposed to help me. But, then again, weren't we beings with the same Creator, fighting the same battle? I wasn't sure how that concept would play itself out, but I had a feeling I'd end up in a dual battle with this creature, someday—one way or another, side by side—and we'd equally cover each other's backs. Goose bumps rose on my arms. I knew prayer was my best weapon. That would be some heavy-duty praying. Or would more be required?

"Sister in battle?" He offered his hand as if to shake mine, but instead grasped my forearm in a shake I'd seen guys do in movies involving brotherhood or battalion comrades. I returned his grasp and squeezed his lean, muscular wrist since that was as far as my small hands could reach.

My eyes fastened on the tiny pouch at his side. Before I could ask him about it, his form was gone.

I blinked in the darkness, looking for a slice of light coming from the door.

I had no desire to dance. I walked out of the storage room, meandered through the crowd, and headed toward the parking lot. I'd see if Christina was outside since I could not spot her among the throng inside.

Christina came running down the steps behind me, yelling my name.

I turned around.

"We've been looking all over for you. Where have you been?"

"Settling a little score with Andy."

Christina's face brightened. "Did your guardian angel bust his butt for attacking you that night?"

I smirked and shot one eyebrow upward. "Totally."

"Awesome. What happened?"

"It wasn't really Andy who attacked me that night. A spirit possessed him—one that Mike, my angel, knows well. They've had run-ins before. But Mike assured me I'd never have to worry about this creepy spirit again. God gave Mike the authority to send his enemy straight to a place called the abyss. I guess it's a place they can't escape. "

Christina placed her hands on her hips and wagged her head back and forth. "Wow. Wish I could've seen that."

"I did. It was scary. Especially when four angels, including Mike, caught me spying on them during the whole exorcism thingy they did."

She leaned in. "Four angels? Cool."

It was sort of awesome watching those angels surround Andy.

"I don't feel like hanging out tonight. Is that OK?"

"Sure, no problem." Christina waved her hand as if to say, "Go."

"See you at school tomorrow." I hugged Christina, who then turned to go back inside.

I scrounged into my purse for my keys as I walked to my car. I opened the door and slid in, but before I even got the keys into the ignition Mike appeared in the passenger seat in human form, wearing his red, long-sleeved shirt and jeans.

Ahh...that's better. I didn't care for the scarred, armored Mike. I felt like a close friend had just popped in to hang with me.

I leaned across the console and wrapped my arms around him. He returned my hug with a squeeze, then disappeared, leaving my arms hanging limp in my lap.

I slapped the seat where he'd sat. "Why'd you do that?" I growled.

I heard a belly laugh coming from somewhere. I wasn't sure of the location.

"Ha!" I said, expelling all the air from my lungs. His laughter broke through the stress that had lingered from the scene I'd just witnessed at the dance. I was thankful that Mike had put me at ease in his light-hearted way, which I'd become used to.

As I drove home, I felt the tension in my shoulders peel away with each mile, although I still hoped that Lagarre was gone for good. But I wondered if his companions would return for revenge. Was tonight an end of a battle or the start of a new one?

Chapter 22

A RAPPING NOISE ON my bedroom door jerked me awake at eight thirty.

There should be a rule against waking anybody before nine on a Saturday morning!

The door knob clicked as it opened, and Christina's face peered at me.

"Hey, Christina," I said in a drowsy voice, hoping to make her feel guilty for waking me up. She knew I hated getting awakened early on Saturday mornings.

"Eden just called. She told me her dad is trying to get some teens to come help at the homeless shelter today."

Not today. Not after last night and that whole ninja angels scene.

I squinted at Christina, then flopped my head back onto my pillow. "You're kidding me, right?"

I vaguely remembered Pastor mentioning that last Sunday. No way was I going to a place like that. And I surely never thought Christina to be the type that would light up at that idea. Then again, she *was* the risk-taker. And she had all that "new Christian" energy and drive.

"I want to go. Will you go with me?"

I was glad to hear Christina's excitement about serving the Lord, and I didn't want to diminish it. "I'll think about it."

"Great! I'll start finding some clothes for you!"

"Wait!" I groaned as she began rummaging through my drawers, looking for something for me to wear.

I sat on the edge of the bed, staring at my feet dangling near the floor. The idea of getting close to dirty, smelly homeless people made me shudder. Yeah, I'd just watched four angels beat up a demon in a storage closet and watched it ooze weird-colored blood the night before. But homeless people? They scared me more. I didn't know if they were good or evil. At least with demons and angels it was pretty obvious. Were they homeless because they were drug dealers, drunks, or deadbeats?

That's pretty harsh. How judgmental!

I didn't want to think about it. So I decided to get up. I pulled on sweat pants, a hoodie, and sneakers I'd left on the bathroom floor the night before, totally ignoring Christina's creation of a wardrobe. When I came out of the bathroom I saw Mike sitting on the edge of my bed.

"You should go to the shelter with Christina. And no, Christina can't see or hear me."

Of course he knew what I was thinking.

I'm really not into this. I ran a brush through my hair.

Guardian angels could be a bother sometimes. *"It will help Christina grow in her faith,"* Mike chirped with an opened-mouthed grin. He put his hands over his head, with his thumbs and middle fingers touching to make the shape of a halo. "And it will help you get over your fear of homeless people."

I'm not afraid. Just not interested.

Christina turned around and looked me up and down, then tossed the clothing in her hands on my bed. "I'm going to go downstairs and make some toast. Do you mind?"

"S-sure." I waved her out the door.

After I heard Christina's feet land at the foot of the stairs, Mike continued. "Why aren't you interested in helping homeless people?"

I wasn't ready for a lecture this early.

I leaned against my dresser and crossed my arms. "If you've been with me my whole life, you should know."

He rested his arms on his knees. "Are you talking about that trip to Philly when you were nine?"

I walked into the bathroom and brushed my teeth and applied some light makeup so I'd look more awake than I felt.

Every time I saw a homeless person, I thought about the day my mom took me to Philadelphia. Even now, the scene was as vivid in my mind as when it happened.

We went to an art museum, the Liberty Bell, and Independence Hall. At the end of the day we ordered Philly cheesesteak sandwiches in the train station. After eating half of mine I put the rest in the wrapper and walked with Mom toward our departure area.

When we reached the platform I saw a wrinkly man crouched in a corner, wearing a torn, stained jacket and scuffed, holey shoes. His white beard was stained with brownish-yellow streaks. When we got close he grabbed my arm.

I screamed.

Mom pulled me away. "How dare you touch my daughter!" I'd never heard my mother talk like that to anyone. It scared me.

"I'm sorry," he said in a scratchy voice. "I didn't mean to frighten the girl."

"Then why did you grab her?" She stared at the man like he was a rattlesnake about to strike.

"It's just that…I'm so hungry. I haven't eaten in three days."

I wanted to give him the rest of my sandwich, but I was too terrified to move.

"Come on, Olivia. Let's get away from his stench." Mom jerked my arm so hard I dropped the sandwich. "Get a job," she screamed over her shoulder.

While she dragged me away from the man, I turned and saw him struggle to his feet and pick up the sandwich I left behind. He was missing a leg.

I turned to watch the train, but I couldn't block the image of that man from my mind. He was alone, with no one to help him. What if my daddy lost his job? And his leg? Would he have to sit in a cold train station, begging little girls for half a sandwich?

As the noisy train came to a halt I reached into my coat pocket and grabbed the change Mom had given me for spending money that day. I dribbled it onto the sidewalk behind me, hoping the homeless man would find it, knowing Mom wouldn't hear it over the noise of the screaming brakes that filled the subway station.

"I'd think that experience would make you want to help people in need," Mike said, interrupting my memory.

I placed my toothbrush back in its holder on my sink and spit. I wiped my mouth on the towel hanging by the sink and said, "It did, at first. But on the train ride back Mom kept talking about people who didn't want to help themselves. She went on and on about how hard my dad worked and how he'd never ask for a handout. She told me not to give any money to homeless people because they'd just spend it on drugs and beer."

"Not everyone who's homeless is lazy. Most want to work and would if they could find jobs. In most cases, life circumstances or the actions of others have brought them to this point."

I couldn't argue with him. But I was still scared to go to the mission. "Look, plenty of other people help at the mission. Why do I need to?"

"There are far more homeless people at shelters than those volunteering to help." He tilted his head. "Probably because so many have the same misconceptions and fears you do."

A wave of guilt ran over me. I had a roof over my head and a warm bed, and my belly was pretty much always full.

A Bible verse came to my mind. *Jesus said, "Whenever you did to one of these things, to someone overlooked or ignored, that was me—you did it to me.*" I grinned at Mike. "You put that Scripture in my head, didn't you?"

"Uh, no, that would be the Holy Spirit. It's Matthew 25:40. You memorized it at camp two summers ago out of *The Message.* That new, modern version of the Bible they had there. Everything you put in your mind can be pulled out when you need it."

I thought about the verse. Basically Jesus was telling His disciples that whenever they helped people in need they were helping Him. I closed my eyes and asked God to forgive my selfishness. When I opened them, there stood the old man from the train, his piercing blue eyes staring at me. I gasped and stepped back.

After a flash of light he stood on two legs instead of one this time. His tattered green clothes turned into a three-piece white suit, and his hair became a long, blond mane. White wings spread out from behind him. His wrinkles faded. The only thing unchanged was his beautiful, ice-blue eyes.

"Mike?" I knew it was him. He had used a powerful, creative way to demonstrate how the man could have been an angel in disguise.

"Remember Hebrews 13:2. You learned it at camp that same week. 'Be ready with a meal or a bed when it's needed. Why, some have extended hospitality to angels without ever knowing it!'"

"That was you at the train station?"

"I gave your cheesesteak and coins to a real homeless man that day."

I felt like someone had just leaned a warm pillow against my heart. *My sweet, generous angel.*

God, You created a wonderful being. Thank You for sending him to help a homeless person that day so long ago. I want to do that too.

"I'm glad I dropped that sandwich—and the coins." Apparently I'd had a faith test in my childhood—and passed.

"I still have a few of the coins as a memento." He reached into his pants pocket and pulled out three quarters. "That was a precious moment. Your heart was soft even back then."

I stared at the coins in his palm. I couldn't believe he'd kept them all these years. "I'm still scared to go to the mission."

"That's OK. It's in terrifying moments that you see Jesus the clearest."

I knew he was right. I'd go, knowing God would make me strong. And Christ would work through me.

"Hey, where's that leather pouch you had on you that night at the dance club?" I asked.

Mike's expression went sullen. He rubbed his chin. "Umm—it's a secret weapon." He avoided my gaze.

"For what?"

Mike disappeared. Instead of being annoyed at his sudden exit, yet again, I clamored to the bedroom door and yelled down the stairway so Christina could hear me in the kitchen. "I'm coming down in a second."

Shoot! I hope I didn't wake Mom and Dad up.

I shut off my bathroom light and quickly made my bed, then shut my bedroom door behind me and walked down the hallway, treading lightly so it didn't creak loudly just in case Mom and Dad were still asleep—doubtful. I tiptoed down the stairs and entered the kitchen. Christina was spreading peanut butter on her toast.

"I can't wait. This is going to be so much fun." She licked the peanut butter off the knife and set it on the plate with a *clink*.

"Yeah. Fun." I grabbed my purse off the hook near the back door in the kitchen.

Christina handed me two pieces of toast with peanut butter and jelly between them. She'd wrapped the sandwich in a napkin for me. I'd eat it on the way.

"Let's go!" Christina grabbed her purse and keys off the kitchen table, and we went out the front door and got into her car, which was parked at the curb in front of my house. We both slipped in and shut the doors. Christina held her peanut butter toast in her mouth while she put her purse in the seat behind us and turned the ignition.

There was no turning back now.

Christina pulled her car into the church parking lot at ten. My stomach did a flip-flop. I was really going to have to be around homeless people.

You can do this. I tried to believe my own pep talk as we got out of Christina's Camry.

Five men gathered around a table in the lot filled with coffee pots. They were drinking from foam cups just outside the entrance to the church.

Seven middle-aged ladies stood in a circle by the front of the bus, wearing pleated pants and floral button-up shirts. I felt out of place in my black T-shirt, distressed jeans, and scuffed-up sneakers.

Christina and I were the only teens I saw. Everyone else looked to be at least thirty. I guessed most teens had other things they'd prefer to do on Saturdays. I'd been guilty of the same thing. But I suddenly felt as if God were smiling at me and Christina like a proud Father.

Eden's dad waved to me from the church steps. I waved back. Gee, I'd never seen him in jeans, a sweatshirt, and sneakers before. He looked—normal. I guessed I figured pastors wore suits every day of the week. It would look really tacky going into a shelter dressed like that anyway. I was no longer ashamed at how I was dressed. Who knows— maybe I'd blend in better having not tried too hard to look anything but comfortable.

Eden came out of the front door of the church and hurried over to us from across the parking lot. "I was worried you weren't coming. It's almost time to get on board."

As we approached the bus the ladies greeted us with wide smiles.

An older man wearing a red baseball cap, who looked to be in his sixties, opened the bus door from the outside, then boarded the bus and sat in the driver's seat. He waved us in.

"All aboard," Pastor shouted. He stood at the bus door as we all got on. As Christina and I passed him, he said, "Thank you both for coming."

"I'm scared but excited," I replied.

He laid his hand on the center of my back and gave me a reassuring rub. "You'll do great!"

Somehow I believed him.

Christina shook his hand and followed me up the stairs into the bus.

I walked to the back and took a seat. Christina and Eden sat in the seats in front of me.

As we rode to the shelter, people's conversations were garbled by the roar of the engine. As I did most mornings when riding the school bus, I stared out the window and watched the cars go by.

I wondered how many homeless people would be there. Would they smell? Would I be able to keep from wrinkling my nose at the stench? What would I say to them?

God, help me do a good job today. Help me encourage at least one person.

Our ride progressed from the country setting where our church was to a four-lane highway, then through congested areas cluttered with row houses and industrial buildings. We came to a stop in front of a red brick building with graffiti on the front and a yellow awning over the front door with words printed in black: Water Street Mission. A chalkboard on a pedestal at the curb read "Soup kitchen today at noon."

I started to twirl my hair and nibble on a nail as I spotted several people in tattered clothing and dirty faces leaning against the outside of the building.

Would they be nice?

Just smile at every single one that catches your eye.

Pastor led us to the front door, where he greeted a man in a green wool sweater with shoulder-length, unkempt, gray-and-brown hair. He gave us one of the warmest smiles I'd ever seen. His blue eyes sparkled almost like Mike's. "I'm Mac. I'm so pleased you all have come to serve lunch today."

He shook everyone's hand. When he shook mine his calluses rubbed against my soft skin. This guy must be a hard worker.

Mac led us to a large, cheery kitchen that smelled of freshly made bread and chicken noodle soup. So far nothing seemed scary.

Mac gestured toward two round ladies in bright floral aprons and hairnets, one bent over a large sink, the other slicing a loaf of bread. "This is Millie and Barb."

They greeted us with rosy-cheeked smiles bearing deep laugh lines.

"I'm Millie," the taller one said as she wiped her hands on her apron and smoothed gray hairs from her forehead. "We're honored to have you with us today." She folded her hands across her full belly. "You'll be meeting a variety of folks today. Don't let them frighten you. Just remember they are hurting people, and you're soothing some of their pain by filling their stomachs. Offer a smile. That's more love than most of them get in a week."

I could smile. That wouldn't be hard. But what if one of them spoke to me? What would I say?

Millie walked us to a long counter with stacks of trays, Styrofoam bowls, plastic silverware, loaves of white bread, and a vat of steaming soup. "I know some of you have done this before, but any who are new— one of you can hand out the trays; two can give out the bowls, napkins, and silverware; and two can hand out the bread and spoon soup into bowls. The rest of you can help with clean-up by clearing tables and throwing out trash, then wiping them clean for the next folks. If you need anything, come find me here in the kitchen area."

Eden's dad gave each of us a task based on the arrangement Millie had given. Since we were new, Christina and I were assigned to clean up the dining area. Eden got to spoon out the soup with her dad. I would've preferred handing out bowls or bread so I could hide behind the counter. I had no desire to be out there mingling with the homeless people. But I knew God had me in this position for a reason. Maybe He'd send a special person for me to encourage. So I stood by one of the folding tables set up in three rows across the dining area with folding chairs surrounding them.

Christina stood beside me with a bucket and two washcloths in her hands. She set it on the floor by the wall so no one would trip over it. We exchanged glances as we waited for Mac to open the door for the people to enter. Christina elbowed me in the side. "Here we go. We'll stick together." Maybe she could sense my fear.

When Mac unlocked the door the first person who entered had a dirty white beard, wore dark green clothing, and used crutches because he only had one leg. I winced inside. It was like I was standing in that train station again with my mother. Then I remembered Mike's disguise, and the memory fled. It could be an angel. Or just a nice old man. Or Mike!

It's him.

I heard Jesus' words reverberate in my spirit. It was no mistake that God sent this person through the door first, knowing I would need the right perspective from the get-go.

He hobbled over to where I stood by one of the tables.

I grinned. "Hi, Mi-—I mean, sir." I caught myself, still caught up in the mental vision of Mike turning into a homeless person. Maybe it *was* him.

"Hello, miss." He winked. I guessed he didn't want me to use his name when other people were close enough to listen.

I led him to a table and helped him sit down, holding his plate and cup for him as he got comfortable. "Thanks for being here," I whispered. I waited to see if the old man would look at me like I was loopy.

"I thought you could use a cheerleader today." *It was Mike!*

Christina approached. "Can I bring you some soup and bread, sir?"

I straightened. "Actually, this is..." I looked to Mike, wondering what to say. "...a friend of mine."

Mike stuck out his hand. "Captain Michael, at your service."

She shook it and shot me a questioning look. Either she wondered if this was my angel, Mike, or she was surprised I'd jumped in so quickly to introduce this man to her so enthusiastically.

"Um...he's a war hero," I said. *Well, he is.*

I shot an exaggerated wink at Christina, and she gave me an "I gotcha" look.

"Pleased to meet you," Christina said. She shot me another look as she walked away.

Mike smirked. "Fancy wording there, Liv."

"Well, you *are* a war hero. You saved my dad in the spiritual war. And me—several times."

"Quite true."

I returned to the soup line to help a lady with a walker who was having a hard time holding her tray. "I'll help you with that."

She looked out from behind cloudy eyes surrounded by sagging eyelids. "Thank you, dear."

Eden handed me two cookies wrapped in cellophane. "That gentleman forgot his cookies." She pointed in the direction of Mike.

"I can take that to him." I shoved them in my hoodie pocket and led the lady to a table nearest to the food so she would not have to walk far. I put the tray down, then folded up her walker for her as she balanced herself on the folding chair. I placed it against the wall by the table, then put my arm around her to help her get seated. A pungent smell hit my nostrils.

Ignore it, Liv!

Once she was settled I helped place her napkin on her lap. She looked up at me, and there were pools of tears on her lower eyelids. I gulped. Why was she crying? All I did was help her carry her food and seat her.

Maybe you're the first person to ever lift a finger for her. Have you thought of that?

In a shaky voice she said, "Thank you for your kindness."

Feeling my own eyes mist over, I swallowed and replied, "You're very welcome. Enjoy your meal. I'll be here if you need anything." I patted her shoulder softly as she turned to plunge her spoon into her soup.

How could something I dreaded so much touch me so deeply and cause me happiness I'd never felt before? I felt euphoric.

That's what it feels like when you are serving another, selflessly, in My name.

I turned around to check on Mike, but as I did I noticed people pouring through the door and taking seats faster than they had since we started. I had no time to chat with Mike. There were so many others. They were of all colors and personalities. Some young, some old. A couple of them talked to each other, but most stood staring straight ahead, waiting their turn in line.

See them as I see them. Don't see the clothing, or the faces. See the hearts. Each is a special individual created by Me. I love each one as deeply as I love you.

Some left, and as they did I gathered trash and wiped down the tables where they had been. They began to fill the tables quickly, so Christina and I sped up our pace to keep up.

I passed Mike at one point, wondering if he had eaten anything. I'd never seen him eat anything before, not even when he helped me make those yummy goodies for Eden's date with Ty. He'd only tasted my sauce.

"I'm getting such a kick out of watching you and Christina doing such a great job." He stood up and pushed in his chair as if to show me he was leaving. He stopped, looked behind him, then turned back to me. "Hey, look at that girl over there."

I glanced in the direction he'd just scanned and saw a teenage girl approaching the table where Mike had been. When I turned back around I didn't see my guardian angel anywhere. His table and food were left untouched.

It had been so comforting knowing Mike was there. Would I be OK without him around?

With Me, nothing is impossible.

I trust You, God. I meant it.

The girl wore torn jeans, but I doubted hers were distressed to be fashionable. Her short black hair had a white streak alongside long bangs. She slurped soup with her head low, letting her hair fall over her face. She sat alone, away from the others.

I grabbed Mike's tray and took it back to the kitchen.

Barb, one of the aproned ladies, was stooped over a large sink, washing huge, stainless steel pots. I could not find Millie, so I tapped on her shoulder. She turned around and wiped her hands on her apron and smiled widely. "What can I do for you, sweetie?"

"I'm sorry to interrupt. This tray of food was uneaten. What should I do with it?"

"Oh!" She gestured for me to follow her as if she had a secret to show me. Her round figure wobbled between shelving on either side of a long hallway in the back area of the kitchen. She reached down and pulled out a brown paper bag. "We'll save that for my pets at home. We can't reserve the food once it's been served."

She grabbed the tray and placed the bread and cookies into the bag, then produced a Ziploc bag and proceeded to dump the uneaten soup into it.

"How nice. Nothing goes to waste. What kind of pets do you have?"

"Oh, just about anything that comes around looking for a handout. Cats, dogs, birds." She chuckled. "They're my family. My husband died of cancer five years ago. All my kids are grown and moved away. All I've got are my animals and the people here at the mission. And I love them all."

"I'm so sorry to hear about your husband. And that is so sweet how you take care of strays. I used to do that when I was growing up."

"Aw, dear girl, we are kindred spirits, now, aren't we?" She held my one hand and clasped it between both of hers. "Thanks for serving today. I hope you find joy in sharing this little time with those that others try to ignore."

"I'm so glad I came. I've already been blessed by the people here. All of them."

"I better get back to my pots!"

I turned back and returned to the sink, listening to Barb's pantyhose swishing as she followed.

Millie was in the kitchen, opening bags of bread at the counter that looked out over the dining area.

"Millie, I know it's busy, but can I take about five minutes to sit and talk with one of the people out there?" I asked.

She reached out and touched my elbow. "Why, of course, dear. I'll cover for you."

She handed me a chocolate-chip cookie wrapped in cellophane from a shelf above her and smiled. "Go on. That one"—she pointed to the girl I was referring to—"needs some cheer."

My eyes widened in amazement.

How'd she read my mind? I bet she's very good at spotting ones who need special help. She's been doing this for quite a while.

Christina was cleaning up the table next to the one I was headed to. I sat across from the girl and held out the cookie. She grabbed it and mumbled, "Thanks."

"I'm Olivia. Over there is my friend Christina." I turned and pointed at her. Christina waved in our direction. "What's your name?"

She peered up, only one eye visible from beneath the long bangs. "Angel."

I almost choked. Surely this wasn't another of Mike's disguises. "How old are you?"

"Seventeen," she said as she chewed a chunk of bread.

"Is this your first time here?"

"Nah." She took another sip of soup, then broke off a chunk of bread and dunked it in her bowl.

Apparently this girl didn't want to share anything about her personal life. Obviously she did not want to talk to a stranger. Instead of making her feel singled out I said, "Hey, you're the first teenager I've seen here today, so I thought I'd say hi."

Then I went with a safe question. "You got a favorite band?"

"Devil's Opposition."

Christina glanced at me with a grin as she passed in front of me, a stack of plates piled in her arms. She stopped. "Did you say *Devil's Opposition?*"

Angel looked up at Christina and set down her spoon. "Yeah. You like them?"

"I *love* them. They're playing at a music festival in the area this April. It's free."

"Really?" she asked with a note of sarcasm.

"A church is sponsoring it."

Uh-oh. Hope that doesn't chase her away.

Angel pushed her hair out of her face. "I thought the only music Christians listened to was organ music."

"Gosh, no," I said. "There are as many kinds of Christian music as what you hear on the radio. You should come to the festival."

She shrugged. "Sounds cool."

I pointed to Eden. "The girl serving soup can give you all the details." Then I added, "We'll both be there, so if you go, try to find us. We'll have staff T-shirts on."

She finally cracked a smile.

"Well, I hope we see you at the festival. I have to get back to clearing tables. Millie has been filling in for me. Bye."

Angel waved at me, then picked up her spoon and bent over her soup bowl again.

I grabbed a few trays people had left after finishing their lunch and took them to the kitchen to be washed. When I came out I saw Angel standing near the serving line, talking to Eden, who handed her a brochure from her purse on the floor behind where she'd been working. The girl shoved it into the back pocket of her jeans and moved toward the exit.

God, I hope she comes to the concert. Help her find You there.

I cleaned up Angel's tray and trash, then headed to the kitchen and picked up a new washcloth to wipe down some tables since mine was getting very soiled. When I returned to the dining area Angel was gone.

As more people crowded the dining room, Christina and I hustled to keep up. We didn't talk to any other people, except to say hello and offer a smile, because there were so many of them. No other teenagers showed up. But a few little children accompanied some of the young women who came in. I caught their eyes and smiled at them all and made sure they had cookies when I passed by their tables attending to my task.

When I boarded the bus that afternoon I felt a sense of satisfaction.

I'd conquered my fear of homeless people. God let me see them through His eyes.

Christina plopped down on the seat in front of me, her face beaming. "That was great. We really helped people today, didn't we?"

"Yeah, we did. I'm glad you invited me to come along."

"Me too."

As Eden joined Christina, I thanked God for stretching my faith.

Then I wondered, What would He do to stretch my faith next?

Chapter 23

I NEEDED TO BE at the festival in a half hour.

I dressed quickly, threw my hair into a ponytail, dusted on some makeup, and bolted toward the door to the garage.

"Don't you want some breakfast?" Mom asked as I grabbed my backpack.

"No time."

She handed me a piece of toast with some peanut butter on it. I popped it into my mouth to hold it as I grabbed my purse and keys and headed to my car.

Mike sat in the passenger seat. "Ready for today?"

"Yes... and no," I said through a mouthful of bread and peanut butter.

"I'll be with you every step of the way. Did you put on your armor this morning?"

"No. I woke up late."

"Why not take some time to talk to your heavenly Father now?" Mike vanished.

As I drove, I talked with the Maker of the universe. I recalled a Sunday school song I memorized as a kid based on the Bible verses in Ephesians 6:13–17, which talk about the armor of God. I pictured myself putting on an actual suit of armor as I thought of each phrase of the song. I mentally shod my feet with the preparation of peace. I took up my sword of the Spirit and my shield of faith. I put on my breastplate of righteousness and the helmet of salvation. I prayed for God to protect me. By the time I pulled into the parking lot at the festival grounds, I felt ready for battle.

I took a spot beside where Eden was parked. She leaned against the hood of her car, her arms folded and her foot tapping. Eden was always early. I was chronically late.

I got out of my Honda and gave her a serious look. "We've got to pray hard today. The devil is going to do whatever he can to stop what God wants to do here."

"I know. We've already had four cameras stop working and a speaker blow out."

I put a hand on each of Eden's shoulders and prayed, "Father, empower us with Your Holy Spirit to do the job we need to do today. Protect us from evil. Thwart the schemes of the enemy to cause confusion and distraction so the message of the music and the speakers is heard by those who attend."

Eden's tense muscles loosened a little, and she uncrossed her arms.

After I said, "Amen," I removed my hands from Eden's shoulders.

Eden heaved a sigh. "'I'd say you'll do your best by filling your minds and meditating on things true, noble, . . . ' right (Phil. 4:8)? I just read that in my Bible this morning, but I guess I forgot it already."

"I know what you mean." I decided to focus on my job for the day. First thing I had to do was find Samantha and find out who I needed to report to. Samantha had left me a voicemail on my cell phone last week to let me know what my assignment would be. I was really looking forward to shooting T-shirts into the crowd and operating a camera.

Women under a tent to the right of the stage prepared hot dogs and hamburgers on grills by the concession stand. I was instantly hungry and hoped I got a break at some point to sample their cooking. I pitied them standing over hot coals on such a scorching day. In Maryland, April could feel like the middle of summer occasionally. I'd heard on the radio that it was forecast to reach ninety degrees. I already felt sweat trickling down the center of my back.

My cousin Samantha approached us. "Hi, girls. I'm glad you're here." She gave us our staff T-shirts and all-access passes. "Wear these at all times."

We put the T-shirts on over our clothes and hung the lanyards around our necks. I felt so official. I hoped I'd get to meet some of the band members or speakers.

Samantha checked the clipboard in her hand, running her finger along the print. "Olivia, you'll be on camera one, stage right." She handed me a blue sheet of paper. "Here's the schedule for when I need you onstage. Jake will fill in for you on camera when you come on stage for hype crew."

The page showed what times all the bands would be performing. The hype crew would be launching T-shirts and water balloons between each act.

"Eden, you're on camera two." Samantha pointed toward stage left. "That guy standing by the Porta-Potties will direct you to your spot and give you a quick tutorial."

"See you guys later." Eden gave me a thumbs-up and jogged off.

Samantha turned to me. "Pastor James wants to gather some people together to pray before the gates open. You want to join us?"

"Definitely."

We walked behind the stage area toward a patch of grass where about twenty people stood around a man I'd seen at the concert at Samantha's church back before Greg died. It was Pastor James. I remembered him closing the concert in prayer.

We all joined hands.

"Heavenly Father," Pastor James began, "we're here today to implement Your plans and purposes for those who attend this festival. Thank You for everyone who volunteered their time and talents to pull this off. We ask for Your angels to encamp around this fairground."

I was glad to know he realized that angels would be there. I had no doubt they would be.

"May You be glorified, and may lives be changed as a result of this event. Amen."

Various voices echoed, "Amen." We unclasped hands and headed off to our areas of assignment.

As I approached stage right I felt a tap on my shoulder. I turned and saw a short man with brown hair and freckles, wearing a headset and holding a camera. "Olivia?"

"Yes."

"Hi, I'm Glenn. I'm in charge of the camera crew."

"Great." We shook hands and walked toward my station.

"Your job is to follow the lead singer. The other cameras will be covering other areas of the stage, and the mobile ones will be onstage getting close-ups." He pointed to a small brown trailer to the right side of the stage. "I'll be in there, mixing the camera images and projecting them onto the large screen on the left side of the stage."

I was excited to think of seeing my shots projected up there soon.

We climbed a ladder onto one of the film towers, and he had me sit behind the camera. From my high perch I scanned the grounds, taking in the merchandise tents, security guards, and concession stands. I loved the bird's-eye view.

Glenn reviewed all the camera buttons and made sure I knew how everything worked. It was really very easy. Then he handed me a headset.

I placed it on my head and adjusted the mouthpiece in front of my lips. "I used a headset like this when I worked in the drive-thru at McDonald's one summer."

"Terrific. It's the same idea. So the whole crew can communicate. Samantha says you have a good eye, so I'm sure you'll do great."

"I'll do my very best."

"Staying with the lead singer can be hard sometimes. They jump around and run a lot."

"I got this. I'll keep up with him."

"I know you will." He gave me a pat on the shoulder.

"Thanks, Glenn." I watched as he shimmied down the ladder.

I hoped I wouldn't have any problems. At least I knew where Glenn would be if I needed him.

"The view is breathtaking from above, isn't it?" Mike stood beside me, covered in fish-scale armor from head to toe. He wore a silver breastplate with a lion's head on it. I sure felt safe with my "knight in shining heavenly armor" beside me.

Mike pointed at the crowd starting to come through the entrance. Most had tattoos, piercings, and strange hair colors. "Beautiful, aren't they?"

Through Mike's eyes I saw each of these individuals as a precious soul treasured by God, much like my experience at the shelter. And I was part of an extraordinary event that would reach out to people who were often ignored, even rejected by the church. They were coming to hear their favorite bands, but they would get to hear about God and hopefully have their lives changed forever.

I looked toward heaven and gave thanks and praise to the great Creator who made all this possible.

"Take *another* look," Mike said.

When I scanned the crowd again I saw hundreds of angels in full armor, doubling the size of the crowd. There was an angel for every single person. *Of course.*

Mike disappeared. The drummer took the stage and started a slow, driving beat on his kick drum. The crowd screamed in anticipation.

I fixed my eyes on the microphone in the center of the stage and checked the focus on my lens.

Security guards encircled what would soon be the mosh pit.

Sheesh, I guess it gets pretty wild in there. Hope there's no blood or broken bones today.

A guitar chord blasted. The bass player entered the stage, wearing a black T-shirt and jeans. His long, blond hair had a red streak down one side. My camera was right on him. I didn't recognize the band, but I was excited for the music to kick in.

A tall man with blond dreadlocks that hung to his elbows ran in, screaming out a note I thought could shatter glass, and held it for about fifteen seconds. The audience yelled louder. I fixed my eyes and camera on him as he jumped to the drummer's rhythm.

That's the lead singer! Got him!

My foot started to tap, but I stopped when I realized that it made the platform under the camera shake.

Dreadlock guy screamed, "How are you all out there?"

Everyone yelled and applauded.

"We're Sacred Sabbath, and we're here to shake up your world today!" The colorful audience began to crowd the stage, their arms in the air, clapping or thrusting their fists to the beat. I wasn't really that into hard-core metal bands, so I'd never heard these guys. But I loved any kind of music. Even if it wasn't my taste I could take one day of it.

Greg would have loved this festival.

As the band played their opening song several people in the area that I could observe mouthed the lyrics. I couldn't understand a word.

After the first number the lead singer said, "Every member of this band is a Christian. God has radically changed our lives, and He can change yours too."

Many people clapped and whistled.

After five songs a slim guy with frizzy dark hair tapped me on the shoulder. "I'm Jake."

My heart sank. I was having such a good time, I didn't want to leave. But it must be time for the hype crew to take the stage soon.

When he reached out to shake my hand I saw a tattoo of a cross on his right forearm.

I love that.

"I'm Olivia." I tried not to stare at the tiny crystal stud in his pierced nose.

Does it hurt when he blows his nose?

As I slid out of my seat I noticed a cloud of dust brewing inside the mosh pit. Security guards rushed toward the commotion. Wondering if a fight might be breaking out, I prayed, *Lord, don't let anyone get hurt.*

Five armored angels that looked like ancient Vikings descended into the pit and swept away five demons. I watched as they were thrown, one by one, into an open black hole in the area above the stage. All of the demons had horns on their heads and tattoos that looked like bleeding wings on their shirtless backs.

I breathed a sigh of relief, said good-bye to my replacement, then climbed down the ladder. I pushed through the crowd to the security gate that led to the backstage area where Samantha was. The guards let me through when they saw the all-access pass hanging around my neck.

I found Samantha pulling T-shirts, wrapped in rubber bands, out of a box. They were shaped into balls that could be shot from a large slingshot.

"Hey, Liv. After we launch the first couple of shirts, hand me some water balloons, OK?"

"Right." I looked into the box beside the shirts and found some balloons already filled with water. I picked up the box, ready to follow Samantha on stage.

"By the way, we've had over five thousand people come through the gates today—and we have not even gotten to our headline band yet, scheduled for tonight at seven o'clock. I'm so stoked!"

Giddy, I replied, "That's awesome."

After the band finished playing they marched off the stage. When they'd passed us, Samantha said, "Follow me."

The second my foot hit the stage my nerves quivered. I'd never been in front of so many people.

Samantha stepped up to the mic. "Anybody want a free T-shirt?"

Hundreds of arms raised high and the crowd roared.

I giggled as I handed the T-shirt launcher to Samantha. *This is going to be a blast! Especially when we get to the water balloons.*

Samantha launched five shirts into the audience. Then it was time for the balloons.

People jumped when the bulging balloons sailed toward them. Everyone who got soaked cheered their appreciation for the water that cooled them off in the open field under a blazing hot sun. I giggled. We were definitely succeeding at getting the crowd pumped up for the next band.

As I handed more T-shirts to Samantha I saw Eden striding though the chaotic crowd as calmly as if she were gliding through a peaceful forest. Her lips were moving. Her guardian angel, Cabriel, followed close behind her.

That's cool. We might need him today.

Eden stopped to talk to a girl wearing a tight red T-shirt and jeans. She put her arm around her shoulder and they bowed their heads. Eden was no doubt praying over her.

How amazing to see the transformation in my friend.

Christina strode among the crowd too. Her angel, Gideon, walked right beside her. He pointed to a corner of the field where a small group of people huddled together, praying. Christina headed right toward them. I knew she'd eagerly join them.

This event needs all the prayer it can get.

Samantha launched another balloon. It landed on the head of a muscular guy with tattoos and a shaved head. He yelled and cursed loudly, throwing his water bottle at the stage. It landed in the mosh pit.

Three armored angels flashed to the spot where the young man stood, leaving blue streaks of light in their path. A green snake slithered out from behind the angry guy and wrapped itself around one of the angels. The angel jerked his arms outward, bursting the snake into dozens of green pieces.

Way to go, warrior!

The crowd quieted and turned in his direction. The angry guy huffed off toward the merchandise tent.

When Samantha had run out of T-shirts and balloons, we exited the stage. "You did a great job, Liv."

"Thanks. It was fun."

"I didn't think the balloons would get someone ticked off."

"Me neither."

"I think we should stick with T-shirts from now on."

"Good idea." I checked my watch. "I need to get back to my camera."

"OK. I'll see you again in two hours."

I returned to my perch. After Jake left I took the seat and directed the camera toward center stage, waiting for the next band to begin. I was glad to be back at my station. I loved filming the lead singer and listening to the band play.

Goose bumps rose on my forearms when I spotted two burly, bearded angels standing in front of the stage. I looked into my lens and zoomed in. They had ruddy complexions. They faced the crowd, arms folded across their chests.

I pitied the demon that tried to mess with them! They were the biggest, scariest-looking angels I'd ever seen.

They remained in place during the entire song set. Their presence seemed to have a calming effect on the crowd. They must be specifically trained for this sort of thing. No fights broke out. They must be the backup angels that Mike had mentioned before, not guardians, but ones called in as reinforcements. Perhaps someone had prayed them in after the breakout in the mosh pit and the angry guy who got hit in the head with the balloon. I had no doubt that Eden and Christina knew *exactly* how to pray today.

Before the band left the stage, Jake returned. "Samantha says she'd like you to join her backstage to pray with the speaker before he goes on."

"Thanks." I wondered why she'd called on *me*, but I was honored.

I found Samantha backstage. When she saw me from a distance, she pointed at a middle-aged blond man chatting with one of the band members from a band that had performed before the one playing now. Her voice came through my earpiece. "Olivia, that's our speaker. Please tell him I'm going to introduce him in about fifteen minutes and will escort him to the stage when it is time. Then pray with him. I was going to join you, but they need me here backstage. Can you handle this one on your own?"

"You got it." I walked up to him. "Mr. Lutz?" I'd seen his picture and name on the concert poster. He clutched his Bible to his chest as if drawing strength from it.

"Yes?"

"I'm Olivia. My cousin Samantha will be here shortly to escort you to the stage. In the meantime, I'd like to pray with you."

"I'd appreciate that." A trace of distress crossed his face. "Most of the music festivals I've spoken at are attended mainly by Christians. I've never stood in front of a crowd like this." He wrung his hands. "I'm not sure I'll be able to hold their attention."

I put my hand on his shoulder as we bowed our heads and closed our eyes. I felt power transfer from me to him. Like part of my strength left me and entered him. "Lord, calm this man's heart and nerves. Speak through him today. Control the crowd, and limit any distractions that might keep these people from hearing Your word for them."

I opened my eyes and spotted a cloud of huge bats heading straight for us, darkening the sky. I held out my hand toward the demonic assault, grasping for the power that could only come from God's authority given to me.

Mike appeared and put one hand on my back and the other on top of my head. I felt a heaviness from his hand, and I knew the power of God was being dropped into me at a time I needed it. I shuddered, wondering what kind of evil I would face.

Another angel appeared behind Mr. Lutz and encircled him with mighty wings.

I had no idea what to say, so I just said, "Jesus," over and over.

A blue beam of light shot out of my raised hand. I turned my palm and shot the beam from my palm at the bat-like creatures. Mike and Mr. Lutz's angel did the same. More blue lights shot from the hands of additional angels surrounding me, just as I raised my hand. The beams joined, forming a force field that sent the bat-like demons flying backward.

Cool. This is new. I feel like some superhero in a movie right now.

A dome of light appeared around the stage and extended over the entire festival grounds. All demons within the circle of light were sucked out of the illuminated orb and into a slice of space that opened again, just above the stage. I let my hands fall to my sides. My throat constricted from tears of joy, relief, and wonder.

Mr. Lutz hugged me and whispered, "Thank you." He clutched his Bible to his chest and directed his attention toward the stage where Samantha was walking up to the microphone.

My cousin shouted, "Put your hands together for national speaker and best-selling author Mr. Bill Lutz!"

The crowd applauded enthusiastically as he walked up the steps. Since I didn't need to work the camera during his talk, I joined the audience. Christina, Ty, and Eden found me and Eden tapped me on the shoulder. We stood together, waiting for Mr. Lutz's talk to begin.

As Mr. Lutz spoke to the throng, a few people walked away. Some talked among themselves. One tall boy with a Mohawk who was standing near the stage shouted, "I didn't come to get preached at."

A murmur arose. All eyes turned to Mr. Lutz to see his response.

"Hey, buddy, you don't have to stay if you don't want to. But I'm just going to talk to you, not preach." His tone was soft and sincere.

God, silence him! I prayed regarding the guy that yelled out.

The two burly angels still in front of the stage covered the heckler's mouth. He turned and walked toward the concession tent.

I let out a sigh of relief. *Thanks, God. That was quick.*

After breaking the tension with a few jokes, Mr. Lutz opened his Bible and read Luke 18:16. "People brought the babies to Jesus, hoping he might touch them. When the disciples saw it, they shooed them off. Jesus called them back. 'Let these children alone. Don't get between them and me. These children are the kingdom's pride and joy. Mark this: Unless you accept God's kingdom in the simplicity of a child, you'll never get in.'"

Bill shut his Bible and set it on the platform at his feet. "At the time this passage was written, children were to be seen and not heard. But God made a point of saying that young people are the kingdom's pride and joy." Bill's voice wavered as he was overcome with emotion.

The crowd quieted. The hecklers stopped. More faces turned toward Bill than when he'd begun speaking.

"I speak at high schools all over the country. I've met young people who feel unloved, unaccepted, and unimportant. But Jesus loves every one of you—no matter who you are or what you've done."

This is a good message. Anyone could relate. Great way to connect with the audience, Bill.

"Your parents may be divorced. Maybe you just broke up with a boyfriend or girlfriend. Perhaps you had a fight with your parents before you came here. Or you're pregnant. You might be waiting for the next high to escape a life you're unhappy with. Perhaps someone you love just died. I want you to know that it's no mistake that you're here today. God cares about you so much that He came to Earth two thousand years ago to live as a human. And to show us how much He loved us, He died so that we can have a relationship with Him here on Earth, and also after death."

Go, Bill!

"Do you know, beyond a shadow of a doubt, where you would be if you died in a car crash on your way home from the festival tonight?"

Someone shouted, "I'd be partying with my friends in hell."

A few in the crowd laughed.

They have no idea how serious of a question that was.

"That's what a lot of people think. Or perhaps you believe there's a heavenly scale that will weigh the good things and bad things you've done, and that as long as the good is more than the bad God will let you into heaven. But God doesn't require a certain measure of good deeds. He offers the gift of everlasting life for free. All you have to do is accept it."

Lord, let every individual hear him out.

Bill reached into his pants pocket, pulled out a twenty-dollar bill, and held it out over the heads of the people standing near the stage. "Who wants this twenty?"

A hand ascended from the crowd near the stage and grabbed at it. Bill released it. The crowd laughed.

"I gave that to you as a free gift." He looked at the young man who'd taken the bill. "You didn't have to do anything to get that money. You didn't have to impress me. I held it out, and you took it. God offers Himself to you that way. All you have to do is reach out and accept His gift of Jesus Christ. He'll wipe away all the bad things you've ever done. And He'll forgive all of your failures in the future."

Oh Lord, empower Bill's words. Continue to speak through him.

"God wants to heal you from drugs, alcohol, suicidal thoughts, cutting, rejection, pain. Don't live life alone. Jesus wants to be your friend. He walked this earth for thirty-three years. He can relate to what you are going through. Imagine a God that would become human. And die for you. He loves you *that* much."

A girl dressed in a black t-shirt and ripped jeans stumbled through the crowd toward the stage. "There is no God," she shouted.

I stood on my tiptoes and recognized Angel, the girl I'd met at the shelter.

Lord, give Mr. Lutz the words to say to Angel. Make Your presence known in spite of this distraction.

Someone hit my head from behind. I thudded to the ground, landing on my side.

I scrambled to my feet, looking around to see who'd done it. My head swam, and I wondered if I'd black out. *Mike, where are you?*

My guardian angel appeared as if he'd been launched by a great force. "Lagarre's son is here to avenge the banishment of his father. His disembodied Nephilim spirit is here to try to kill you, and attempt to bring this concert to a halt."

I thought about the fight at the dance. And the story Mike told me about Lagarre's Nephilim son. Half angel, half demon. I needed to pray for Mike. I was sure he was in the midst of a battle. Had Lagarre's son been the one who'd knocked me to the ground? He wanted to kill me, just like his father had.

I shoved through the crowd, searching for Christina, Eden, and Ty, swerving from the blow to my skull. I needed more prayer warriors to join me. If Lagarre's son and his cohorts were about to descend on this place, I needed my friends and fellow warriors by my side. Every life present was at stake.

"Young lady," Mr. Lutz said to Angel, who stood boldly right in front of the stage. "Please come up here."

A hush fell over the crowd, and they parted for the girl.

As she inched toward the stage, I saw Ty's head rising above all the others. Christina and Eden stood beside him. I nudged, squeezed, and wiggled my way in their direction.

I grabbed Ty's shirt and Eden's arm and pulled them close. "Pray," I whispered. "Something big is going down. Mike's under attack. And something just hit *me!*"

Eden's lips began to move. Her eyes were still open and alert.

Ty and Christina bowed their heads. We all joined hands and prayed silently. I kept my eyes open as I prayed so I could observe what was going on in front of me and pray accordingly.

In the background I heard Mr. Lutz say, "Young lady, do you know that Jesus loves you?" He kneeled down closer to her face. Angel stood inches away from the speaker.

"Go to hell!"

The crowd chattered.

"I love you," Mr. Lutz said softly.

"No you don't." She spat at his face. Everyone gasped.

Mr. Lutz blinked, then pulled a handkerchief out of his pocket and wiped his cheek. He calmly put the cloth back in his pocket. "I still love you. And so does God."

Angel's mouth gaped open. "If Jesus loves me, then how come—"

Shouts from across the field interrupted her question.

Ty looked over the heads of the crowd. "A fight is breaking out. Keep praying." All of our mouths moved silently. Several police officers pressed toward the commotion with billy clubs raised, yelling into their walkie-talkies.

"Ty, hoist me up on your shoulders!" I knew he could hold my weight with no problem.

As I regained a bird's-eye view I looked back at the stage and saw Angel on her knees, sobbing. Several people wearing staff T-shirts surrounded her, laying hands on her and praying. God's love was being demonstrated despite the tumult raging around us.

My eyes turned toward the sky. A dark cloud hung there. The bright, sunny day disappeared. Thunder and lightning came from the cloud and penetrated the force field I'd seen earlier when praying for Mr. Lutz.

I couldn't get to Mike, and he couldn't get to me. It's what I had feared. One day we'd be in a battle, fighting for each other. He in the angelic realm, me fighting through prayer.

I'd heard that when two or more are gathered in God's name, He is there. *We need God's presence to overwhelm this piece of ground now.*

I spotted a head of blonde curls toward the back of the crowd. My niece, Tessa, sat on her father's shoulders. Those curls and Brian's muscles were unmistakable. Tessa's head was tilted up, and her chubby little arms were lifted above her head. I choked up. Even my little niece knew how to pray in the Spirit. She probably observed the angelic realm today as I had. Brian had made sure to be here, no doubt, to support this concert with prayer. Plus, Tessa loved loud music.

A glint of copper hair caught my eye.

Daniel! Tessa's angel.

Wings sprang from behind him, unfolding like the enormous feathers of a peacock. He threw his arms wide, tilted his chin toward the sky, and closed his eyes.

To the right of Brian and Tessa I saw Bev, her hands raised and her lips moving in silent prayer. I chuckled. I never thought to even tell her about the festival because I doubted she'd actually come. *I hope she brought earplugs!* She had put aside her personal taste in music to pray for the individuals who attended this festival. The fringe crowd. Knowing Bev's special burden for young adults and teens, it made sense that she'd be here.

I looked up again when I heard a roar from above and saw the cloud warp and twist. Flashes of blue lightning exploded from within it. It dissipated into a mist, then evaporated.

Police officers and security guards escorted two handcuffed men to the exit.

"Don't stop praying," I said to my friends. I knew Mike was still battling.

Mr. Lutz walked up to the microphone. "If you've been hurt by life like this precious girl, I invite you to come to the foot of the stage. We have people here who will pray for you to experience God's love, which is pure and free and knows no bounds. Even if you're mad at God, I want you to come anyway."

Band members and people in staff T-shirts lined up in the front of the stage, looking out at the crowd, having left their posts. A few audience members inched up toward the front and talked to the staff in hushed voices. Within a few minutes more than a hundred people stood in front of Mr. Lutz, their arms raised. The sight of the staff members taking time for this most important moment humbled me.

Thank You, Lord! Mr. Lutz hadn't just talked about love; he'd demonstrated it with his loving attitude toward Angel, even when she lashed out in hatred.

Pastor James came on stage, sat at the keyboard, and played a praise song that blanketed the grounds through the sound system.

Open my spiritual eyes, Lord, so I know if there is anything else I need to pray for.

As I prayed, hundreds more people, surrounded by angels, moved toward the stage. Volunteers laid their hands on people's heads. One angel wrapped an arm around a young girl who'd come forward for prayer. Angels enveloped each individual with their wings.

Mike stood in a grove of thin white pine trees just behind the stage, every fiber of his being on alert for an attack from the half-bloods who'd been harassing him for thousands of years. This time he knew they were hellbent on detaining him long enough to kill Olivia.

The atmosphere around him began to vibrate, faster and faster like the wings of a hummingbird, as if the universe were about to shake itself apart. Then it did. Four demons hit him from behind and pinned him to the ground on his back, spread-eagle, leaning their forms on each of his limbs. Mike groaned, trying to roll to his side, his eyes focused on his saber. Strong, bony fingers pried away until the shield popped out of his hand and spun away. He thrashed, throwing his head to his other side, just in time to feel his sword leave his grasp. It flew in the air and whirled out of sight.

He wondered where his backups were. Would he be rendered helpless as the evil forces hunted and killed his precious charge?

He struggled for freedom, but the pressure bearing on his limbs threatened to break him into a thousand pieces. Inside his head he screamed, *Father, I beseech You for rescue forces!*

The demons threw back the hoods hiding their faces, exposing their identity. They glared at him. Mike recognized Agathar, Lagarre's son, and his gang of half-bloods. He'd been battling them since the Flood. Their eyes flashed yellow, the pupils as thin as those of a snake. Their faces appeared human-like aside from the curled, red, ram-like horns that rose from behind their skulls. Their green-black wings jutted from their backs.

"This battle won't end with my demise, and you know it," Mike growled through clenched teeth. He squinted at the light of their eyes, which stabbed at his own.

All four threw back their heads and cackled while crushing him further under their grasp.

Agathar came almost nose-to-nose with Mike, the stench of his breath nearly unbearable, causing Mike to gag on the stale, dark air. "We've got you outnumbered," he snarled. "Where are your angel buddies now?" He cocked his head to the side and let out a maniacal laugh. Green drool slid off his chin.

As Mike turned his head to keep from getting spittle on his face, he saw his shield and sword lying just out of his reach.

Where were his reinforcements? Why the delay?

"After we finish you off we'll tear apart your sweet Olivia." Agathar pulled his lips back into a devilish grin, exposing two rows of mangled teeth as sharp as swords. "We won't just kill her. We'll dismantle her, body and soul, painfully slow, until she destroys herself and everyone around her, disgracing the character of—"his face twisted in disgust— "Him." The other three spat black tar at the acknowledgment of the Creator.

Mike's heart hammered against his chest at the thought of what some of Agathar's other minions might be doing to Olivia at this very moment. "Then I guess you'd hate for me to mention His Son, Jes-—"

Agathar's slimy hand slammed into Mike's lips, causing his head to throb mercilessly. "Don't say that...*name*."

If he couldn't speak the name of Jesus, Mike knew he wouldn't have the power to protect Olivia. Then again, he hadn't always been able to save his charges' lives. Sometimes the Father had told him it was time for someone to leave the earth. Other times he'd been confined for so long due to lack of prayer on the part of his charge that the enemy succeeded in destroying the life under his guardianship. He couldn't bear the thought of life without Olivia. She was growing stronger and bolder each day. Could this gaggle of devils possibly know what a world-changer this girl had the potential to be? It was the only reason he could imagine for them being so ruthless this time. Oh, yes, they'd tempted and tried to obliterate some of his other charges, but somehow this time was different. In some way Olivia was unique. Chosen. Rare.

"Father!" Mike shouted with every ounce of strength he could muster. As if a hot blade had sliced through soft butter, a hole ripped open the atmosphere behind his tormentors. A crackle of energy burst as blue streaks snaked out, shimmering from Gideon's sword as he stormed toward him. Like azure lightning, the bolts slithered up his arm and covered his entire body. As Gideon thrust his free arm in and grabbed Mike's forearm, the light transferred from him to Mike, climbing gradually, enveloping his whole body as well.

For a split second, the demons' attention was diverted. Mike wriggled his arm from the grasp of one monster and reached into a leather pouch hanging from his belt. He drew out a tiny glass vial and clenched it in his fist.

Light emanated from the sword on the ground near him, making the vial's pearl stopper flicker.

Agathar gasped and recoiled in fear, releasing his hold on Mike. His companions vanished into thin air.

With the lithe movement of a panther, Mike strode toward Agathar. His opponent retreated back one step for every one of Mike's forward strides.

Mike extended his arm, clenching the glistening vial, revealing its red-liquid contents. "That's right," Mike growled. "It's the blood of Jesus!"

With a plaintive whimper, Agathar crossed his hands in front of his face. He fell to his knees, his head hanging low.

Mike towered over him. He placed his foot on Agathar's shoulder. "I've been carrying this blood for two thousand years. A handful of my comrades were there when Jesus was taken from the cross. They gathered every drop of His blood they could before it fell to the ground."

"So you're…one of *them?*"

"That's right." Mike squared his shoulders, standing straight and tall. "I'm a blood bearer."

Mike's foe choked out a fetid scream. His skin dripped off his bones, melting into a puddle of bubbling green-and-red blood. Steam rose from the stinking pile of offal at his feet.

With a sudden flash of light, the mass vanished. Mike's foot fell to the grass.

Mike turned to Gideon. Gideon placed his hand over Mike's fingers, which still clutched the vial, and guided them toward the leather pouch. Mike's grasp slackened, and the object returned to its holding place. "It's the only thing that works with certain half-bloods. Sons and grandsons of the ones bound in chains."

Gideon nodded. "So I've learned."

"I had to bind Agathar for good, just as I did his father. He'll now join him in the abyss."

"Yes," Gideon's eyes widened with understanding.

Mike recalled the swine begging Jesus not to send them to the abyss. They knew full well that if sentenced to this holding point while awaiting their final banishment in hell for eternity, they could no longer scour the Earth thirsty for another body to inhabit. Their kind only found satisfaction with possession. And severe oppression.

"Olivia!" He ached with pain at the thought that he may be too late to save her from lingering half-blood spirits that may still be in the vicinity. "I must go!"

"Go! And I'll rejoin Christina."

"I'm back," I heard Mike whisper in my ear as I stood facing the stage.

"What happened?"

"Lagarre's son, Agathar, returned to avenge his father's demise."

"I knew you'd been detained. I felt the vacuum."

"I'm so sorry, Olivia."

"How'd you defeat him?"

"Suddenly, as quickly as he came, Agathar disappeared."

"Because of prayer?"

"Yes."

My friends and I had formed a circle of prayer that had changed the course in the heavenly realm. *Awesome!*

I felt a tap on my shoulder. "Is someone looking for these?" I turned and saw Suriel, Ty's angel, holding a sword in one hand, a shield in the other. The tip of his spear jutted up from behind his left shoulder.

Mike materialized enough for me to see him—just an apparition. He took the saber from Suriel and returned it to the sheath on his back. The shield vanished. "Thank you, my friend."

Suriel responded with deep, rumbling laughter.

Both angels turned toward the stage. I followed their gazes and saw hundreds of people praying.

"What a beautiful sight." Mike sighed.

Eden touched my arm. I hugged her and Ty. I was so lucky to have these strong Christian friends at my side.

Suriel rested his hand on Ty's shoulder, and Cabriel stood beside Eden. Neither of my friends gave any indication that they knew their angels were there.

I wondered if Ty would ever have the pleasure of seeing his wonderful guardian angel. Maybe I'd tell him about Suriel someday.

Christina stepped into our group, Gideon towering above her, his hand on her shoulder where her hand rested, covering hers. I smiled at her. She winked back. I knew Christina could sense him but was not convinced she could really see him yet.

I thanked God for allowing me to be involved in such a wonderful event, and for giving me the privilege of personally contributing, both physically and spiritually. I prayed for those who would walk out of there the same as when they entered, both Christian and non-Christian. I prayed that this event would be seared into their memories and that a seed would be planted so they would respond to God's love and acceptance.

Suddenly I realized that those making decisions to follow God today were targets. The battle had only begun for them. It seemed that as God's kingdom was growing on Earth, the hounds of hell would only heighten their attack.

I had another battle still facing me. An appointment at Dr. Stein's office on Monday. My heart sank. Would this meeting lead me closer to "not crazy" category or right into a straitjacket?

Chapter 24

D R. STEIN HAD talked only to Mom today. I was left sitting in the waiting room.

What horrible things was she saying about me?

I had to have faith that God could deliver me from being committed to a mental institution.

Mom entered the waiting room with her chin held high as if she'd convinced Dr. Stein I was crazy. I was confused. She'd begun to soften with me over the last few weeks. But she still seemed determined to push counseling on me.

As Mom and I drove home in the car, I gathered my nerve to ask, "So, what did you and Dr. Stein talk about?"

I fidgeted with my hair as I awaited her response.

She drew in a deep breath and blew it out. "Liv, listen, I want to be sure this is not something genetic. You seeing things...hearing things..."

"Does Dr. Stein think I'm crazy?"

"Not exactly, but he'd like to do some tests."

I leaned forward, "Like what?"

"I don't know exactly. He said he'd get back to me this week."

Thanks, Mom. That's vague. Are they going to give me a lobotomy? Shock me with electricity? Shoot me up with drugs?

I was better off acting calm, confirming that my metal state was stable. "Mom, I'm fine. Please don't do this to me."

"I need time to think."

I slammed back into the seat behind me and crossed my arms, refraining from any retort. "Mom, I'll prove that I am mentally stable any way I can. Trust me. Please."

The rest of the drive was silent.

Your faith is being tested, God assured me.

The minute we got home I raced up to my room. With a running leap I landed facedown on my bed, my arms sprawled in front of me.

I heard a shuffle behind me. There was Mike, sitting in the beanbag chair in the corner of my room.

"I'm about to be sent to the loony bin. Mom says they want to do some 'tests' on me. What the *heck* does that mean?"

"Oh, I have a surprise up my sleeve." Mike made a military salute.

"I can't wait!" I knew he had creative ways of intervening. How I hoped this would be one of those times.

There was a knock on my door.

"Who are you talking to, dear?" Mom must have been listening from outside my door.

"No one."

Dang!

"I heard you speaking to someone. Please open your door."

Whatever.

I hopped off the bed and opened the door.

Mom stood with her lips pursed and her arms crossed. "The visit with Dr. Stein certainly was timely. You're talking to someone again. I'm very concerned." Her tone wasn't rude this time but concerned. She tossed an envelope on the dresser beside the door. "You may have some interesting news in there." She shut my door.

My mother gasped on the other side of the door. Then she burst into my room, eyes wide. She slammed the door behind her and leaned on it. Her chest heaved up and down.

What the heck? She looks like she's seen a ghost!

"I just saw...I don't know what."

I glanced over my shoulder at the beanbag chair. Mike winked at me.

Way to go, Mike. That was no ghost. It was an angel.

"What did you see?" I feigned a calm, concerned tone.

I'd never seen Mom so *undone* like this. She was always the picture of composure. Her eyes darted all around the room. She rubbed her eyes. "Something bright white and shimmery that looked like a man—just standing in the hallway as I left your room."

I stifled a giggle. "What do you think it was?"

"I-I don't know."

I feared saying the next words. "Did he look angelic?"

Mom came over and we both sat on the bed together.

I laid my hand on her thigh. "It's OK, Mom. I've seen him. You are *not* crazy. Neither am I."

Mom was breathing rhythmically as if trying to keep from passing out. "Oh, my gosh. It's gotten to me too." She clasped one hand over her mouth.

"No, Mom, it hasn't. You're just seeing what I see. I prayed that somehow you wouldn't think I was crazy. Never in a million years did I think you'd see an angel. But I hope now you'll understand what I've been going through."

"I'm going to my room." Mom stared in front of her like a zombie, probably trying to process what was happening. She stepped out into the hallway after peeking around as if to make sure *he* wasn't out there. I heard her footsteps echo down the hallway.

I jumped on my bed like it was a trampoline, the way my mother scolded me for as a kid. *Yes!*

Mike joined me on the bed, his face radiating amusement. We jumped in unison for several minutes, stifling our giggles to try to avoid attention from my mother.

"That was sweet! Great timing."

"Glad you liked my creativity—and my timing."

"You're awesome!"

We stopped bouncing and stood facing each other. "Couldn't you have done that sooner?"

"Didn't have permission to. It was a faith-building process I had to let you experience."

"Who was the shimmery guy?"

"Her guardian angel, Touriel."

Love it! "Well, tell him I said thank you."

"I will."

I jumped onto the floor and grabbed the envelope off the dresser that my mom had placed there. When I saw University of Delaware in the return address, I ripped it open and yanked out the page within.

After the greeting, I read, "Congratulations on your acceptance to the University of Delaware."

"I'm in," I squealed. "Now all I have to do is wait for a call from the athletic department to see if they want me to play volleyball." I knew the tuition would be a burden on Mom and Dad, so I hoped for a scholarship.

"I'm sure you'll hear from them. You're an excellent player." Since Mike knew about "the one," I took reassurance that he was right on this matter as well.

I tossed the letter and envelope back on the dresser.

Mike returned to the beanbag chair, picked up my Bible, and began to read it.

"Don't you know all that stuff already?" I sat beside him on the floor.

"Yes—and no. We angels still ponder the mysteries of God. We love to hear and read the Word. To us it's a living, breathing revelation of God.

We love to worship God. And we'll do it for all eternity, alongside you humans."

I looked forward to that day. No school, no parents, no bullies like Vicki.

"I'm sorry you have to babysit me."

"You know, if it weren't for the Fall, I wouldn't have to be babysitting you."

"Gee, I never thought of that. You weren't originally created to do this guardian thing, were you? I'm so sorry."

"It's my pleasure. If it's the Father's will, then I take joy in the task of protecting you."

"Someday in heaven things will be different, huh? I mean, we'll be similar, right? Kind of like it was originally intended. Two different creations, yet unseparated by realms."

"Yeah. The Bible says you Christians will judge angels."

"Really?"

I doubt I'll ever feel worthy to judge angels.

"Before the Fall we were not that different. We were created as different beings, but there wasn't a veil between us.

"I look forward to being in heaven with you."

"I do too. I can't wait to hang out with you there, where we won't have to do any spiritual battle."

"But there's going to be a larger war before that, isn't there? I've read about Armageddon in Revelation."

"I'm afraid so. The enemy will unleash every scheme in his bag of tricks during the last days. Are you ready if this war happens in your lifetime?"

"I pray that I would be. Will Lagarre's son be back?"

"No. But his nasty friends may be." Mike disappeared.

I figured the ancient grudge wouldn't be over. They'd be back—one way or another.

I couldn't wait to talk to my mother at breakfast. I wondered if she'd tell my dad about what she saw. Her worst fear had come true. I wasn't crazy. Or she was as crazy as me. I relished the thought of her chewing on that thought.

My cell phone rang. Christina.

"Sorry to bother you so late."

"No problem. What's up?"

"I was in a car wreck last night."

"Are you OK?"

"Yes. But my car is probably totaled."

"What happened?"

"Some girl hit me from behind on Mainline Boulevard. She'd been tailgating me for miles. She kept looking down. I bet she was texting. My car spun in a full circle, then landed on the sidewalk in front of that new shopping center across from the mall. Luckily, there weren't many cars on the road. No one was hurt."

"Thank God!"

"When my car came to a stop, this guy appeared at my driver's side window. He told me his name was Gideon."

I knew it. I knew she'd see him.

"He helped me get the door open so I could get out since it was stuck. Cars were coming at my car in each direction. As soon as he got me out of there, two cars smashed into mine. He stayed with me while I phoned the police and got the other driver's insurance information. When the cops arrived I turned to look for him so I could thank him. But he'd vanished. He never said good-bye or anything. But I felt like I'd known him my whole life."

Memories of my night on that back road when Mike came to my aid rushed back.

"Liv, I think that guy might have been…an angel."

"Why do you think that?"

"I prayed that God would let me see angels like you do. Up until now, I'd only seen demons. I wanted to see good spirits too."

My friend saw spirits before becoming a Christian. It only made sense that God would redeem that gift and turn it into a discernment of spirits.

"At the festival I felt an invisible hand on my shoulder. Do you think that was him too?"

"I know it was."

"How?"

"I saw him."

I tiptoed down the stairs, hoping to grab a midnight snack, but heard Mom and Dad talking in the den. I sat on the bottom stairs, listening.

"…I saw something. I know I'm not crazy," Mom said.

"No, dear, you surely are not."

"So…do you think our daughter sees things?"

"I'll never forget that night she saw something choking me. She prayed. It left."

A short silence followed, and I heard the crinkle of newspaper that Dad must be folding.

"We need to tell her we believe her," Dad said.

I closed my eyes and dropped my head on my knees in relief.

I rose and made a loud clamor in the kitchen, hoping they'd call me in. Sure enough, Dad spoke up. "Olivia, can you come in here?"

"Sure, Dad." I grabbed the bag of pretzels out of the cabinet above the microwave and brought them with me.

I walked into the den and sat on the floor, leaning against the TV stand with the bag of pretzels between my legs, which were crossed.

I bit off a chunk of the pretzel and waited for my dad to speak.

He removed his glasses and set them on the hearth behind his reading chair, then leaned forward, entwining his fingers into a fist, resting them on his knees. Mom closed her book on her lap and folded her hands on it. I swallowed the pretzel and didn't take another bite, knowing the crunching would reverberate in my head so loudly I wouldn't be able to hear Dad speak.

"Look, Liv. We've been a little too quick to jump to conclusions. About the things you see." He rubbed his palms together, then held them out toward me. "We're sorry."

I glanced at Mom to see her reaction, and she gently nodded her head in agreement. For Mom that was a stretch. I don't think she'd ever directly apologized for anything that I could remember.

I let out a sigh as I stared at the floor. "You know, it really hurt that you didn't believe me."

"I can imagine. And we are truly sorry," Dad said.

"Thanks. I forgive you." I grabbed my pretzel bag and rose. "Good night."

"Night," both said in unison.

"Oh, Liv, one more thing." Dad rose from his chair. "Your mother mentioned you received a letter from the University of Delaware today. What's the news?"

"I was accepted!"

Dad clapped his hands together once. "That's wonderful."

"Congratulations," Mom said. She dipped her head and looked up at me with her smile, which I knew meant she was pleased.

"I'll hear soon about whether I'll get a scholarship for volleyball."

"We'll pray that you do, Goldilocks." Dad held his arms out for me to fall into. I readily complied.

Mom stood as well and held out her arms. Inside I was stunned but tried to keep my surprise from showing, hugging her in return. "You'll get that scholarship, I just know it," she whispered.

I turned and left the room, put the pretzels away in the kitchen cupboard, then headed to bed.

I wasn't very patient, but I had to sit tight and wait for that call from the university athletic department. If I didn't get the scholarship, I wouldn't be able to afford to go to U of D. I'd have to go to a local community college. My dream had always been to play for U of D. I'd watched their team play since I started volleyball in junior high. Of course, every other fantastic player around the country was dreaming the same dream.

Christina, Ty, and Eden were planning on attending U of D. They'd decided way back as freshman that we'd all attend the same university and stay close to home. If I didn't get my scholarship I wouldn't be able to be with my friends next year. My heart sank at the thought.

I sat at the kitchen table, staring at the phone. The athletic department at U of D had called yesterday and set up an appointment for the volleyball coach to call me at four o'clock today. It was three fifty-five.

Eden, Christina, and Ty had also been accepted to U of D. Ty had gotten a football scholarship. He'd said he was sure I'd get one too. But I wasn't so sure. My coach had gotten a few calls from U of D over the last couple of months. I took that as a promising sign.

Eden sat across the table from me. "Breathe."

"I'm nervous."

Eden reached over and put her hand on mine to silence my finger tapping. "And remember to speak slowly. You tend to talk fast when you're nervous."

I'd never noticed that. "I'll do that."

The phone rang. I looked at caller ID. It said Athletic Department.

"Aren't you going to pick it up?

"I don't want to seem too anxious."

I answered on the third ring.

"This is Coach Spencer for the University of Delaware volleyball team." I gulped. "Hello, sir."

Should I have called him sir? Was that too formal?

"Your team had an impressive record this past fall."

"Yes, sir." I did it again. Oh, well. Better to be too formal than sound disrespectful, right?

"I've attended some of your games, Ms. Stanton, and you're quick on your feet. A consistent setter and aggressive at the net. A good all-around player. I'd like to offer you a spot on our Blue Hens volleyball team."

I looked at Eden and clenched my free hand to keep from screaming into the phone. "I'd be proud to join the team, sir."

He didn't say anything about a scholarship yet.

"We are prepared to offer you a full scholarship."

I gave Eden a thumbs-up. She started dancing around the kitchen. I waved at her to stop so she wouldn't distract me. "That's wonderful, Coach."

"You'll need to keep your grades up to stay eligible for the scholarship."

"No worries there. I've gotten almost straight A's all through high school."

"I know. I've seen your transcripts."

"I'll be able to handle it."

"I'll have my secretary mail you a packet of information. We start practicing before classes start. I'll let you know what day we begin when time gets closer."

"I can't wait."

After I hung up, I jumped up and down, chanting, "I'm going to U of D. I'm going to U of D."

Eden gave me a hug. "I'm so proud of you."

I picked up the receiver and dialed Christina's cell phone. "I have two words for you: full ride."

She gasped. "That's awesome."

"Thanks." I was ecstatic that we'd all be at the same school next year.

I couldn't wait to tell Mom and Dad when they got home from work.

After Eden left I heard my mom come in from the garage. I met her with a smile, reaching for the brown grocery-store bags in her hands.

"Guess what?" I set the bags on the counter.

She placed her purse next the bags. "What?"

"I got the scholarship!"

"I'm *so* happy for you." She smiled broadly, which was unusual for Mom, so I knew she was very happy. And probably relieved that the tuition would not put a strain on their budget.

"Your father will be pleased also. Can you help me carry in the rest of the sacks in the trunk?"

My excitement faded at the quick change of subject. "Sure." I followed her into the garage and grabbed two of the four bags in the trunk.

That's about as excited as Mom gets. Be happy with that.

By the time we finished putting everything away Dad came home.

"Hello, girls." He set his shoulder bag on the floor by the door and looked at me.

"I got a call from Coach at U of D today. *Full ride!*" I jumped up and down, pumping my fists in the air.

"I'd been praying about that phone call all day." He held out his arms. "Come here, honey." We hugged, and Dad gave me three squeezes, meaning "I love you," just like he used to do when I was a little girl. "This calls for a celebration. Let's all go out for dinner."

"Not cooking sounds great to me." Mom let out a short laugh.

"Where do you want to go?" Dad asked me.

"Tortellini's." It was my favorite Italian restaurant, and we went there every year on my birthday.

Dad planted a kiss on Mom's cheek. She placed her hand tenderly on his cheek and stared into his eyes for five seconds.

I didn't get to observe many moments like these between the two of them. I felt that Mom was lightening up. And I hoped her new attitude was also improving their marriage.

I was light-headed with happiness over the scholarship, Mom being nicer lately, and getting to pig out on my favorite food.

Thank You, God!

Out of the corner of my eye I saw Mike's apparition sitting at our kitchen table. There was a glint in his eye. I knew that look. He had something up his sleeve.

Chapter 25

ON PROM NIGHT I stood at my bathroom mirror, running a curling iron through my hair—something I never did. I figured I'd look more formal that way. I'd always dreamed about this night. I imagined myself in a sparkly dress, my hair in a fancy updo, and a hot date that picked me up in a limo.

I didn't have a date, an updo, a sparkly dress, or a limo, but Christina convinced me to go anyway since she didn't have a date either. She said there'd probably be some guys there without dates who would be willing to dance with us. If not, we'd still find a way to make the most of this memorable night.

My dad told me yesterday he'd gone to prom with his sister. I'm sure he was trying to help me feel better about not having someone who'd asked me to prom. And since I didn't have a brother to go with, I guessed going with a girlfriend was better than missing the whole event.

Besides, I wanted to see Eden and Ty together. Just watching them smiling and dancing would make my night.

The prom committee had chosen a Roaring Twenties theme. I'd found a great flapper dress at a thrift store that fit me perfectly. I put it on, then added a string of long, fake pearls I'd picked up to go with it.

I put on some mascara, blush, and a shade of lipstick that was bolder than usual, with a hint of red, then ran my fingers through my curls and patted them into place and spritzed on a bit of hairspray.

I slipped on my white flats. If I danced at all, at least I wouldn't twist my ankle.

For a final touch I pulled on some long white gloves that came with the dress.

As I stood in front of the full-length mirror on my bathroom door, I was pleased with my appearance. But I couldn't help wondering why no one would ask me to the prom. *Am I that boring?*

I heard feet thundering up the stairwell. Christina burst into the room and spun around in her dark green dress with a fringy hem. It was dazzling against her red hair.

"You look amazing," I blurted out.

"And look at you. The picture of simple elegance."

I squared my shoulders in satisfaction.

Christina snatched her cell phone out of the small sequined purse that matched her dress, then put her arm around me and flashed a photo of the two of us. I did the same with my phone. Holding the phone and pressing the camera button was awkward with those thick gloves. But at least I'd have something to remember all the fuss I went through getting dressed and putting on makeup.

We put our phones back in our purses and descended the stairs. Mom and Dad were in the backyard, planting some new bushes they'd just purchased. I opened the screen door off the kitchen. "I'm headed out." I lifted my gloved hand in the air.

Dad stood. "Hold on a minute. You're not going anywhere until I get a picture." He started removing his gardening gloves.

I groaned. Usually I hated having my picture taken. But the eager look on Dad's face made me shrug in agreement.

Mom set her gardening shovel on the ground. "I'll get the camera!" She ran across the yard and stopped in front of me. "You look lovely."

I couldn't remember the last time Mom gave me a compliment. I choked back tears. "Thanks." My voice quivered.

She slipped past me and headed upstairs.

The screen door slammed behind me. I spun around just in time to see my dad staring at me with tears in his eyes. I'd only seen him cry once before, at my grandmother's funeral.

"You're...gorgeous." He placed his hands on my shoulders and kissed me on the cheek.

I blinked back my own tears and gave him a bear hug.

"Oh, I almost forgot." Dad whisked past me and opened the refrigerator door. He pulled out a clear plastic box with flowers inside.

"You got me a corsage?"

"Sorry. I couldn't resist." He popped open the top and gently lifted out the arrangement of white carnations and baby's breath.

My heart fluttered at his sweetness. I looked down at my dress, looking for a place for him to pin it.

"Don't worry. This is the kind you put on your wrist."

I held out my arm and he slid the corsage over my hand.

"Thank you, Daddy."

He grinned at the intimate name for him that I hadn't used since I was six. "You'll be the most stunning girl there tonight."

I stood on my toes and kissed his cheek.

Mom rushed in, camera in hand.

I looked around for Christina. Where had she gone? I rounded the corner of the kitchen and peeked out the living room window. I saw her waiting in the car, adding some last touches to her makeup.

"How about we pose by the old oak tree?" Dad suggested.

"Perfect," Mom responded.

Dad grasped my hand and led me out the back door to the largest tree in our yard.

If I ever got married I hoped I'd find a guy who was as perfect a husband and father as my dad. I wrapped my arm around him and he rested his arm over my shoulders.

Mom pointed the camera at us and counted, "One, two, three."

Right before the flash, Dad pecked me on the cheek.

I exploded in laughter. My parents joined in. I wanted to savor this moment and sear it into my memory. Date or no date, it was a special night—if only for this.

"I better go." I gave Dad a one-armed squeeze, then gave Mom a hug too. When I drew back, I saw a haze in her eyes. Could it be tears? I couldn't remember ever seeing my mom cry.

I jogged out to Christina's car. As I got close I heard thumping music. When I opened the door the decibel level stung my ear. There was no use trying to have a conversation. Thankfully it was only a ten-minute drive to the school gym.

As Christina drove, I wondered if anyone would ask me to dance. How humiliating it would be if no one did.

After she pulled into a parking spot Christina cut the engine. Mercifully, her music went quiet. But I heard a loud thumping of bass coming from inside the gym. My heart twitched.

I lowered the visor and checked my makeup.

"You couldn't look any better," Christina said.

My sweet friend. I flipped the visor back up and stepped out of the car. Despite not having a date, I felt a surge of anticipation. If no one asked me to dance, I'd dance alone or with Christina. And boy, was I going to make the best of it. I could hardly wait to hit the dance floor.

Christina linked arms with me, and we strutted toward the entrance.

As soon as the door opened I was hit with a wall of music, voices, and flashing lights. *Awesome!*

I tapped Christina's shoulder. "I'll be right back." Not knowing if she heard me over the beat of the speakers, I pointed toward the restrooms. She nodded.

I wove my way through the throng of dancing bodies filling the gymnasium, awed by the atmosphere created by the prom committee. I felt like I was on a movie set in the 1920s.

When I opened the bathroom door a blow hit me in the stomach. I fell to the floor, gasping for air. The room spun around me.

I heard peals of laughter. A head of blonde hair blurred into my vision. Vicki towered above me. Three other girls stood just behind her, all staring at me, hands on their hips. I squinted, trying to identify the other individuals. But with my impaired vision, I couldn't make out their faces.

I rolled onto my side in an attempt to turn away from any further blows that may come, hoping to protect my face if they kicked at me again. A foot slammed into the small of my back. I swallowed the vomit rising in my throat. I clutched at the pearls around my neck, hoping the string wouldn't break. I held my gloves to my chest, trying to keep them unsoiled by the girl's shoes.

What does my dress look like?

Hopefully there wouldn't be a huge footprint on it.

Vicki spat on my face. The thick liquid rolled down my cheeks. I couldn't even gather the strength to wipe it away. *What did I do?*

"I heard you went out with Andy."

I blinked at the two images of Vicki in my limited field of vision.

She crouched over me. "Did you think I'd never find out?" She laced her fingers around my neck, twisting the necklace in her fingers until it was so tight it pinched at the skin beneath it.

"I'm sorry," I managed in a raspy tone.

"Me and my girls here are gonna beat you up, you sneaky whore. Get ready for an ER visit."

Just then, one of the chaperones entered. She stared wide-eyed at me. "What's going on in here?" Vicki and her friends darted into the bathroom stalls.

"Are you all right?"

"I'll...yeah...I'll be fine." I managed to rise to a sitting position, my head spinning.

The lady helped me stand. "You be careful, dear. If you need anyone, I'll be right next to the punch bowl tonight."

I was in too much pain to talk, so I ignored her.

As I left the restroom, I heard the woman yell, "Girls? Get out here this instant!"

Without bothering to use the restroom I stumbled to the exit, holding my stomach, and limped down the hallway back to the gym. I felt for my corsage to see if it still held its position on my wrist. It was OK!

Halfway down the hall I felt a surge of warmth envelop me. I looked up and saw Mike's beautiful face. He was wearing a black tuxedo. He touched my cheeks, brushing away my tears...and Vicki's spittle. In an instant all my aches and pains vanished. He brushed his fingers over my corsage, then tugged at my gloves to make sure they came up to my elbow. He walked around me, inspecting my dress. "Good as new."

I collapsed into his arms, sobbing. He felt solid. Strong. "Are you in human form?"

"You need more protection than I can give you in my angelic form."

"Can other people see you?"

"Yes." He stroked my hair as my dad had done so often in my child-hood. "Nobody will touch you tonight."

"When did you get here?"

"Uh...I'm always here."

As I took several deep breaths, I realized I had a bodyguard. And a prom date. *This is great!*

He offered me his arm, and I snuggled my hand around his elbow. He prodded me toward the entrance to the gym, and I followed.

What will my friends say? And how will I explain who he is?

Vicki came out of the bathroom with her friends, laughing. She almost ran into Mike. Their laughter stopped when they saw him. Vicki nar-rowed her eyes in obvious jealousy.

"Hello, miss," Mike said politely. "Are you a friend of my beautiful date?"

Vicki's eyes widened, and she stammered for a minute. Then she stormed off with her friends.

"Thanks, Mike." I nudged his shoulder. We laughed.

Mike walked into the gym like he owned the place. He greeted my classmates as if they were old friends, and they returned his familiarity with confused looks. I'm sure they wondered who the strange, handsome guy was and where he came from. No doubt the girls were jealous. I was giddy with pride.

Mike drew me to the center of the dance floor, then turned me around to face him. With respectful distance, he led our bodies in a beautiful swaying motion.

With my eyes closed, I imagined the stares we were getting. I was sure many people wondered if I'd invited a date from out of town, since no one had ever seen him before.

I tucked my head into his muscular chest, but glanced up once and spotted Christina, watching us wide-eyed. I'm sure she had a million questions about how I'd landed this ravishing dance partner.

Mike led our steps smoothly, with no hint of awkwardness. Our dancing was flawlessly fluid.

I heard a familiar voice from behind me. I turned and saw Eden and Ty dancing. She winked at me. *She knew!* I was glad.

When the song ended, the DJ switched to a thumping hip-hop tune. I froze. I could sway to a slow dance, but when it came to cutting loose, I became self-conscious and usually found an excuse to get some punch or chat with someone. But then I remembered how determined I was to have *fun* tonight.

Mike tilted his face down. His eyes burned into mine. *"Watch this!"*

What do I do?

"Just sway to the beat and let me provide the moves."

Mike flew around with me in his arms. I could barely keep up with him. I hoped I wasn't making a complete fool of myself.

In mid-song, Mike paused and whipped off his jacket in one fluid motion. I laughed. He gave me a cocky look, then threw his jacket at me. I caught it, wondering what he was doing.

To my amazement, he started break-dancing! The crowd formed a circle around him. He was incredible.

Who knew that angels could break-dance?

One of the students walked into the circle and tapped Mike on the shoulder. He stopped. The guy did some of his own break-dancing moves. Then Mike scored some moves that put his competitor to shame.

When the battle ended everyone clapped. Mike gave his opponent a strong handshake.

The rest of the night Mike worked the room, nodding and greeting each person who passed by. Each one stared in wonder at his gorgeous face. One girl gazed at him for so long she bumped into her date and fumbled to keep from falling over. I snorted.

Everyone loved him!

Many people clapped him on the back and fawned over his dance moves. He flashed his wide grin and graciously thanked each individual.

Vicki and her three friends lurked in a dark corner, whispering things in one another's ears. I was sure they were stewing about my great come-back and my amazing date.

When people asked where he was from, Mike just said he was from "out of town." He called me an "old friend."

He complimented each of the girls who stopped by on either her hair or dress. He greeted the guys with, "Good evening. I hope you are having a splendid time."

That sounded kind of formal. But this was a twenties-themed dance, after all.

During one of the songs, Ty and Eden inched their way toward us. When the music stopped Ty extended his hand to Mike. "Welcome to our prom. I'm Ty." He wrapped his arm around Eden's shoulders. "This is Eden."

Mike clasped his hand, then gently shook Eden's. "Pleased to meet you."

"So, how did you learn to dance like that?"

I didn't hear Mike's reply, because Eden leaned in and whispered in my ear, "You little devil."

I put my lips close to her ear and replied, "Devils don't dance with angels."

She threw back her head and laughed.

The satisfied look on Ty's face told me Mike must have come up with another one of his vague yet true excuses.

"I've heard a lot of good things about you two." Mike tilted his head and winked.

Eden's eyes sparkled. "I've heard a lot about you too."

Mike shot me a crooked smile.

Ty's forehead wrinkled. Eden and I exchanged glances, enjoying our private joke.

Several people invited Mike and me to after-parties, but Mike said that he'd promised my father he would have me home at a decent hour. At first I was surprised by the lie. Then I realized he wasn't talking about my earthly father.

Christina poked my arm. I spun around, dragging Mike with me since our arms were locked. She'd been dancing with so many guys all night I'd only been able to offer an occasional wave. She kept winking at me and giving me a thumbs-up.

Her eyes focused in on Mike. "Have I seen you somewhere before?"

"Perhaps."

After a few moments of awkward silence, her expression turned from concern to acknowledgment to excitement.

She shook Mike's hand. "I couldn't have picked a better date for Olivia."

"You're very kind." I loved his formal, genteel, Southern tone.

"Guess I'll see you around, huh?" Christina flashed him a knowing grin.

He bowed to her in response.

I cracked up at the way Christina was toying with Mike. And the way he teased her right back.

Mike cringed inwardly each time he said a word. He found it easy to talk with Olivia when they were alone together. But whenever he opened his mouth among her friends, formal speech came out.

It was awkward having a bunch of teenage girls stare at him like a piece of meat. Things hadn't changed much in thousands of years. Humans always looked at the outward appearance, lusting in their hearts.

Regardless, he was glad to have been able to step in and rescue Olivia from broken bones and a crushed spirit. Being seen by her friends unnerved him at first, but dancing to the music excited him. He loved to dance. Especially in the presence of the heavenly Father. It was all about expressing joy and worship.

However, he'd had to turn away when he observed dancers moving in provocative ways. Why did they think that was dancing? His face flushed in embarrassment for them.

I had to snap my fingers to get Mike's attention. When he came out of his deep thoughts he said, "I'll go pull the car around front." After clearing his throat, he adjusted his tie and buttoned his jacket, then exited the gym door, walking with that slight swagger of his.

"Wow, aren't you lucky." Christina jabbed her elbow in my side.

I let out the laugh that had been bubbling up inside me all night. "You could say that."

We both slid through the exit door. The cool evening air blasted our faces.

I looked for Mike's shiny red Camaro. I couldn't wait to ride in it.

Ty and Eden appeared beside us. "Classy guy, Liv," Ty said. "Where'd you find him?"

"He's heaven-sent for sure," I cooed.

Eden placed her head on Ty's shoulder. "I'll explain later."

As the four of us stood outside the school, chatting about Mike's incredible dancing techniques, I felt a sudden pain in the back of my head. I whipped around and saw Vicki holding a clump of my hair. Her eyes were wild with anger.

"You think you're so special," she screamed like a rabid raccoon.

I wanted to rake my fingernails down her face. But I refused to stoop to her level.

As I moved my head around to see who might be able to help, I saw Eden and Christina staring at me. Ty's fists were clenched as he glared at Vicki.

"Ty, don't." I wasn't sure why I said that. Every fiber of my being wanted to see Vicki in ultimate humiliation.

"You're crazy," I said to her. Then I grasped her hand, trying to relieve the pressure of hair being ripped from my scalp.

Vicki yanked harder at the wad of hair, but stopped when we heard a loud roar of a car engine.

Startled, Vicki let go. I ran behind Ty. He placed a protective arm around me, clasping me safely behind him.

Mike's car screeched up to the curb, ran through a mud puddle, and showered dirty water all over Vicki. Dripping in mud, she shook with rage.

I had to put my hand over my mouth to keep from laughing.

The small crowd that had gathered, probably hoping for a catfight, scattered.

Mike jumped out of his Camaro. "I'm sorry, Vicki." He reached into the backseat and pulled out a large towel with red beach umbrellas all over it. He tried to put it around her shoulders, but she ripped it out of his hands and huffed off, disappearing into the gym with it.

"Nice timing." Ty smiled broadly. "And nice ride."

"Thanks."

Mike gave me the once-over. I'm sure I looked dreadful. My hair was a tangled mess. No doubt my mascara was smeared from the tears that had escaped from my eyes.

Mike pulled a white handkerchief from the chest pocket of his suit coat. He dabbed at the gunk under my eyes. Eden gently smoothed my hair from behind.

Mike put the handkerchief back, fixed his crystal eyes on mine, then put his hands on my shoulders. "Good as new."

I sniffed, breathed deeply, and gave him a side smile. "Thank you." I leaned my forehead against his strong chest for a moment. He rubbed my back.

I feel like I have my own superhero.

"See you Monday, Liv," I heard Eden say from behind me.

I spun around and threw my arms around her, then stood on tiptoe and gave Ty a peck on the cheek. When I withdrew, he blushed.

"Don't let this one out of your sight, Eden."

She linked her arm in his and tilted her head up to him. "I don't intend to."

He leaned down and planted a quick kiss on her cheek.

Christina leaned close to me and whispered, "I knew we'd find a way to make this prom memorable. I just didn't realize how memorable." She giggled, then hugged me before turning and walking away from us.

Ty and Eden laughed as they sauntered to the parking lot in search of Ty's car.

Relief overwhelmed me. Ty had come close to punching a girl. Thanks to Mike's perfect timing, he had avoided doing something he probably would have regretted.

Mike grasped my hand, guiding me over the mud puddle beside the car.

"I don't recall it raining today," I said as I thudded into the passenger seat.

"Me either. Weird." Mike winked.

Chapter 26

O N GRADUATION NIGHT we seniors gathered behind the stage in the gym and put on our caps and gowns. At six o'clock we lined up in the hallway in alphabetical order with "Pomp and Circumstance" playing over the sound system.

My heart raced. I teared up. I'd been looking forward to this moment for four years. I'd never be in high school again. Well, I wasn't mourning that so much as I was looking forward to my future and all the things awaiting me in college next fall. Besides, I always cried when I heard this song, no matter who was graduating. Just like I cried during every wedding processional.

Since my last name started with S, I was near the end of the line. The guy I was going to walk down the aisle with was the quiet type. We'd hardly exchanged two words all year. He sat next to me in freshman-year algebra. That was all I could recall.

When it was our turn to join the procession I scanned the room, looking for my family. When I found Tessa, she waved at me. Dad smiled. That always put me at ease.

I blinked at the cameras flashing at us from different parts of the gym. Sweat trickled down my back from the heavy robe.

The trip down the aisle felt like it took forever. I was relieved when we were all told to be seated.

The principal started talking, but my thoughts about Mike, my friends—the whole year—clouded my mind. I didn't catch a word he said.

No one knew who was going to be valedictorian, but five people were in the running, including Eden and Ty.

I tried not to fidget as our guest speaker addressed the class. I just wanted to get my diploma and run, not listen to the mayor drone on about our future and changing the world.

I couldn't help but peek at Tessa every few seconds. She climbed from one lap to another among my family. Whenever she caught my eye she made a silent clapping motion. I tried not to laugh.

At the entrance to the gym, an usher handed a program to a blond guy in a black tailored suit and tie. It was Mike! And he looked amazing.

He slid into the back row. Several girls stared at him. He looked hot.

When the mayor finally finished talking, people applauded and our principal returned to the podium. "We will now present the diplomas to our graduates."

We all stood, moving in line as names were called.

My pulse quickened as I got closer to the podium. I always hated being in front of crowds, except for the time I got to shoot T-shirts and water balloons at the festival.

"Olivia Stanton." I grabbed the diploma, waited for Mr. Klein to move my tassel, then went to the back of the line. That was it. I was officially a graduate.

After all the names were called Mr. Klein said, "Congratulations to you all."

The applause went on for a full minute. We all continued to stand.

"And now it's time to announce our valedictorian."

Eden and I exchanged glances, and I winked at her.

"Mr. Tyler Hudson, please come forward." It was sort of funny to hear him called by his full name.

I clapped hard as Ty stepped toward the foot of the stage and shook Mr. Klein's hand, then leaned forward slightly as our principal placed a sash around his neck. Ty moved to the podium.

I glanced at Eden. She was dabbing at her eyes with a tissue.

Smart girl. I never thought to hide some tissues in my robe.

"I didn't prepare a long speech. But I do have a few people I want to thank. Mom and Dad." He glanced in their direction. "Thanks for all those late nights helping me with homework and for always coming to my football games."

I thought of how close Ty came to dying on that football field this past fall. Most of these people had been at that game, and everyone had at least heard about it.

"I want to thank all the teachers for their patience and help when I needed it."

Several people clapped, then more joined in.

"Most of all, I'd like to thank God. If not for Him, I would not be here."

My eyes misted. How wonderful to see the most popular guy in school share his faith so openly.

"Thank you for this honor."

The crowd stood, applauding. Ty took his place among the class. Many students slapped him on the back or high-fived him as he worked his way back to his seat.

When the room quieted, Mr. Klein spoke into the microphone. "And now for our salutatorian."

I had no idea who this would be.

"Would Miss Eden Jones please come forward?"

My heart leapt with joy, and tears flowed. I clapped as loudly as I could.

Eden looked around as if she thought Mr. Klein was mistaken. The girl beside her reached for her diploma to hold it. Eden rose and made her way to the podium. Mr. Klein gave her a hug, wrapped the honorary sash around her neck, then motioned for her to move to the podium.

I wondered if she had prepared a speech. She hadn't mentioned anything to me, and if she'd known she would have told me. I prayed for God to give her the words to speak.

She pulled a piece of paper from the pocket of her robe. She *was* prepared! My humble friend must have suspected she might be honored but had kept it to herself.

As the cheering died down Eden read from the paper. "Fellow students, faculty, and family. I have the difficult task of trying to say something that will keep your interest and, hopefully, be meaningful to you. I decided to give you a little advice that I've been raised with."

Eden spoke with such clarity and confidence. I felt proud to be her friend.

"Do what makes you happy. Don't let yourself be miserable in any aspect of your life. Only you know what you have a passion for, so don't rely on other people to make the major decisions in your life. Live in the place you want to live, marry the person you truly love, work at a job you enjoy. Give yourself plenty of reasons to wake up in the morning."

I glanced at Ty. He was doing what guys do when they cry and try to hide it: he acted as if he was scratching his nose, when, in fact, he was dabbing at the tears there.

"Put your heart into everything you do. You can accomplish things if you're passionate about what you're doing."

I had a passion for God. As for my career in life, I hadn't really decided yet.

"Don't let anyone make you feel worthless. Not everyone is going to like you. That doesn't mean you're inferior to anyone else. Always remember, you are a wonderful person."

To hear the absence of self-loathing in Eden's speech showed evidence of God's healing in her life after the horrible abuse.

"Always have compassion for other people. You never know what someone is going through. Henry Longfellow said, 'Every man has his secret sorrows which the world knows not; and often times we call a man cold when he is only sad.' No matter how strong we think we are, there's going to come a point in time when we need to be held and comforted. And there's nothing wrong with that. Just be sure to offer to other people what you want to be offered back to you. There is no such thing as being too kind."

How true. I wanted to be "too kind." What a great thing to strive for!

"Life can be hard, and sometimes you'll feel like giving up. You may feel alone and abandoned. But bad things happen to everybody. That's why we have to reach out to each other. Don't turn your back on someone in need. You never know when you'll want a shoulder to cry on.

"Smile a lot, laugh a lot, and be nice to everyone you meet. Above all, love your life. It's the only one you've got. My fellow graduates, I wish you the best of luck. And most of all, thank You, God."

Everyone stood and clapped. I used the sleeve of my robe as a tissue.

Mr. Klein returned to the microphone. "I'd like to ask for a moment of silence for two students who are not with us tonight. Toby McCarty and Greg Monahan."

We all bowed our heads for thirty seconds in remembrance of our departed friends.

How I wished they were here.

"Pomp and Circumstance" played again, and we began our recession. Once we were out in front of the school, we tossed our hats in the air and cheered.

I sliced through the sea of graduation robes to find Eden and Ty. Christina was already hugging them.

I threw my arms around Eden. "Great speech. You deserve the best of everything. I love you."

"I love you too, dear friend." She wouldn't let go of me.

Ty tapped her shoulder. "I think you need to let go so Olivia can breathe."

I embraced Ty, then did the same to Christina.

"I'm so glad we'll be together next fall. You guys are the best friends in the world." All of them smiled back at me.

Grabbing her stomach, Christina said, "I'm starving. Let's head down to the cafeteria and get something to eat."

As we walked across the lawn I felt a hand on my arm. I turned and saw Mike looking into my eyes as if to say, *"Aren't you going to wave me over?"* Ty, Christina, and Eden stared at him.

Could they see him again like at the dance? The expressions on their faces hinted that they did.

"You remember Mike, right?" I motioned for him to come closer.

Ty held out his hand toward Mike. "Good to see you again, man."

"Congratulations on your award and speech." He returned Ty's shake.

Christina nudged Ty to the side and stepped in, her willowy hand extended to Mike. "Well, I'm Olivia's *best* friend. So how come it took so long for us to meet?" She shot me a look that seemed like a warm challenge. She winked.

"Yeah, you never introduced me to him to me either, until the dance," Eden said with a twinkle in her eye.

I looked into Mike's eyes, searching for any hint of caution. He seemed totally fine with my friends seeing and talking with him and inclined his head slightly as if to assure me all was well. I could only blink quickly a few times as a nervous response.

"I've known Olivia for some time, actually, but we've only just recently been reunited."

Not one of my friends challenged his answer, to my surprise. But I could imagine that Eden and Christina were jumping up and down on the inside, knowing who he actually was.

Christina shrugged. "Well, we all look forward to getting to know you better."

Ty and Eden responded in unison, "Yeah."

Will Mike begin appearing in human form to my friends more often now? Why?

"Let's go." Mike put his arm around my shoulder in a familial way and squeezed me slightly. "You all must be starving."

I left out a heavy sigh at the convenient escape from a conversation that caught me speechless.

Christina and Eden exchanged a glance, their eyes wide, smirking at each other as they shared a similar look of pleasant surprise and amusement at Mike's second bodily appearance. Ty squinted and stared at Mike as if he was about to play a big-brother role in approving of this guy I was with...or something manly-like of that sort. How could I blame him? Actually, I found it adorable. At least I had nothing to worry about. Mike would never disappoint.

As we entered the cafeteria my family approached us. Mom, Dad, Brian, Diane, and Tessa all hugged me, then shook my friends' hands and offered them all congratulations. They all responded with their thank yous.

"Hey, where's your friend Mike?" Christina asked.

Darn it, I just turned my back. Now where is he?

"Oh, he has a way of disappearing sometimes." I was relieved I didn't have to figure out how to explain Mike to my family. "He, um, must have left to find the restroom."

Eden and Christina snorted. Ty eyeballed them both, wrinkling his brow in confusion. Perhaps he felt left out of the inside joke we were all sharing.

Ty, Eden, and Christina scattered to find their parents and relatives.

Tessa handed me a rose.

I bent over and grasped the bloom and kissed her on the forehead. "Thanks, squirt." I picked her up and swung her around as she giggled. I buried my nose in the petals and inhaled the aroma. Then I smelled fresh-brewed coffee and decided to go in search of it.

After setting Tessa back down, I said, "That coffee smells heavenly. I'm going to grab a cup. Anyone else want some?"

"I'll take some," Dad replied.

No one else made a peep, so I hurried to the table where the large coffee thermoses sat.

With such a loud hum in the cafeteria due to all the people in conversation, it was difficult to talk to anyone. My family and I stood and nibbled on cookies, drank punch, and sipped coffee until Brian and Diane said they had to go home to get Tessa to bed. They gave me a good-bye hug and left me standing with my parents.

Dad put his arm around me. "Congratulations, my little angel." I giggled inside at the new pet name. Would I live up to it?

"Thanks." As I leaned my head on his shoulder I scanned the crowd, thinking I may never see some of my classmates after this night. My heart sank at the thought, but at least my closest friends would be in my life come fall when we'd all be starting college. No doubt we'd hang out often.

"Congratulations, Olivia," Mom said as she leaned in to peck me on the cheek. "Have you seen Andy's mother?"

I'd caught sight of him and his parents out of the corner of my eye a few moments earlier and had been intentionally keeping my glances away from that direction. I pointed. "Over there."

"I'll be right back, you two." And off she went, weaving through the crowd.

Dad and I found some folding chairs against the wall and sat down.

"I love to watch people," Dad commented, then wiped his napkin over his face, crunched it in his hand, and stuffed it into his empty coffee cup in his other hand. I remembered other times Dad and I had done the same thing at the mall. We could sit for almost a half hour in silence, watching people. I'm not sure why we found it so fascinating.

Finally Dad stood up. "I'll find your Mom so we can leave. Are you ready?"

Annoyed that Mike had never returned but at the same time relieved, I said, "Yeah, sure." Dad went off in search of Mom.

Ty, Eden, and Christina found me again.

"Let's all keep in touch this summer, OK?" Christina said as she sat down next to me. Eden and Ty sat down on the other side of me.

"Of course. We better," Eden responded.

"Hey, did you guys get that job at Rehoboth Beach?" I asked Ty and Eden.

"Yeah, we both found a job at Grotto's." I knew the pizza shop well as a famous landmark restaurant on the boardwalk. Everyone at school looked for jobs at the beach for the summer. The ones who didn't find them worked locally at fast-food restaurants or retail chain stores. I never liked the beach much, so I never sought employment there.

My heart sank at first, but I reassured myself that it would be only eight weeks until I saw them again.

"How about you, Christina?" I asked.

"I'm going to stay in town and volunteer more often at the homeless shelter. Plus help my aunt at her floral shop, as I usually do."

Yes! I'll have someone to hang out with.

"Maybe I'll join you at the mission." I was shocked when that slipped out of my mouth. I hadn't actively looked for a job yet, but her choice sounded like one God would be pleased with. It could help me overcome my fear of homeless people, and instead of just making money, I'd be making a difference in people's lives.

"Awesome, Liv!"

I knew when I told my parents about my plans, they'd wholeheartedly support me. And hopefully help me with gas money. During past summers they had given me a generous allowance, so I didn't have to work. Instead, I spent time babysitting for Tessa occasionally while Diane taught swimming lessons at the local YMCA. It was enough to provide some spending money for me. Other than that, I buried my nose in as many novels as possible, which I loved because I never got time to read much during the school year with all my homework and volleyball.

When the season was over, I always snuck in a book or two, which I relished.

I choked back a sob. "I love you guys." I looked at each one, pausing a second as my eyes fell on them.

Ty got up and leaned over to hug me as I sat in my chair.

When I turned to Eden she brushed a tear off the end of her nose. I stood up and threw my arms around her again. After a few moments I released her, and she hooked her arm around Ty's. "Gotta get home. Mom's throwing a graduation party for my immediate family. Just a small dinner." Then she looked up at Ty. "You're coming with me. I insisted." Ty gave her a half smile that would make any girl melt.

"What happened to that Mike guy?" Ty asked.

My mind raced for another excuse. I didn't want to lie. "He had to leave early."

Blank expressions gazed back at me.

"Too bad. I would have liked to have talked to him more. Eden says he's a good guy," Christina said.

Thanks, Eden.

My eyes darted in her direction and her smile met mine. There was no need for words.

As I watched them walk away, I prayed fall would come fast so we could all be together again.

"That leaves the two of us," Christina chirped. "And Mike." She giggled.

"I'm sure he's here, of course. And will continue to be," I replied.

I wondered where he was and how often I'd see him. Would I see him less often now that I was out of high school? Would I see him more because college had to be as treacherous to navigate as high school—if not harder?

"I'm going home. I got invited to a few graduation parties, but I know they are going to be wild—people sneaking alcohol in and everyone getting smashed. No, thanks," Christina exclaimed.

"Same here. Thought I'd skip those too."

"See you around." Christina stood and grabbed her diploma off the seat beside her. We embraced one more time.

"If not we have to be sure to at least all get together when Ty and Eden return from the beach."

"Good idea! A pre-college and 'good-bye, summer' party."

"For sure."

Christina disappeared into the swarm of bodies still crowding the gymnasium.

Dad approached me with Mom as I headed toward the exit. I waved at a few classmates as I passed them on my way out, wishing them a great summer. As we left the building I breathed in the fresh spring air and stopped midway down the stairs leading out to the parking lot and turned back to gaze at my school. *This is it. My life begins now.* Well, not really, but that's how I felt.

As we approached our car Mom said, "I hear Andy is going to U of D next year. Did you hear?"

My pulse began to race.

Oh, no! Can't I get away from this guy?

We slipped into the car and shut our doors. Dad started the car and turned on the air-conditioning.

"I hadn't heard." I almost choked on the words. My mouth went dry.

"He asked me to give you this." She held a single red rose wrapped in cellophane, which she pointed in my direction. I'm sure he knew that if he gave it to me I would have crushed it to pieces in front of him if no one had been watching.

"Thanks," I mumbled, and gingerly took the gift from her and laid it on the seat beside me. I slowly nudged it away until it was leaning against the opposite backseat door.

I felt a hand on my shoulder.

Mike? Oh, thank God.

"I'm here."

I'll still be seeing you, right?

"Nothing will change."

Andy—

"I've got you covered."

He's going to be at U of D. What if he stalks me again? Or attacks me? He's relentless.

"So am I. I'll be there."

Never leave me.

"I won't. I'm always right here. Only a prayer away."

Chapter 27

COUPLE OF WEEKS before my first day of college classes I drove from my dorm to the campus sports complex for the beginning of volleyball camp.

My pulse sped up a bit as I walked toward the gym.

How will I measure up to the other players? Will they like me? Will my nerves take over today and make me look like a loser?

The *thunking* of balls hitting walls and the squeaking of sneakers hit my ears as I entered.

Several girls were warming up, doing stretches and practicing serves. I watched for a few moments before setting my duffle bag on the bottom bleacher. These were the best players on their high school teams. I'd have to prove my skills. But I also wanted them to like me as a person.

At freshman orientation I'd met a few girls who said they played, but I didn't see any of them yet.

I shed my heavy sweatshirt, then moved to the wall by the net and did some leg and arm stretches, shooting smiles at the girls who passed by.

"Five more minutes," Coach Spencer yelled from the other side of the net. "Then we'll huddle up for introductions."

I was a little nervous to meet Coach. Would we hit it off? Would he be extra stern with the newbies or gentle so we'd relax? I'd seen pictures of him in the college catalog, and he looked exactly the same. He hunched over a bit when he walked and kept shoving his round glasses up his nose.

"Hi."

I glanced at a tall girl who started doing stretches next to me.

"I'm Jessica."

"Olivia."

"You nervous?"

"A little. But I'm also excited."

"Can you believe we're going to be playing for one of the best volleyball teams in the country?" Jessica's eyes twinkled as she tied her long, straight red hair into a ponytail.

I sat on the bleacher and tightened the laces of my sneakers. "I feel humbled to be in the same gym with these girls."

"I think all freshmen feel intimidated. You'll do great."

Strangely, her words made my nerves settle a bit.

The whistle blew. "Huddle up!"

The sound of bouncing balls ceased, and the fifteen girls walked to the middle of the gym, where Coach stood, exchanging glances and smiles along the way. I waved to the two girls I recognized from orientation. I couldn't remember their names. I'd have to look at the roster and pictures Coach had taped to the wall near the door to the locker room.

"It's a privilege to work with you all. You are some of the best volleyball players in the country, and you're playing on one of the best teams in the country. But this is a new year, and we've got to keep the winning streak going. We play hard, and we play fair. We're good winners. But we need to be good losers as well."

I liked that. Being a good loser builds character.

"This week is our time to bond, learn each other's skills, and start to formulate a strategy for this year." Coach turned to the tall brunette girl on his left.

"I'm Brittany. I'm a senior, and I was the team captain last year. I want you all to introduce yourselves. Tell us where you're from and what position you play. Let's start with the freshmen." She glanced my way.

"I'm Olivia Stanton. I'm from Rising Sun, Maryland. I'm a setter." I offered a big smile.

The introductions went quickly, and I knew I'd never remember all the names. Thank goodness for that roster on the wall, so I could glance at it whenever I needed to.

Coach shouted out the first drill. "Setters, spread out over the two nets. Newbies, team up with one of our present setters."

I was about to share a court with some girls I'd watched on ESPN for the past four years. I hoped I wouldn't embarrass myself the first day.

I must have had adrenaline racing through my body, because I did really well, setting up some great spikes. I got several compliments from teammates and the coach. That settled my nerves, and I began to have fun.

The seasoned players were all kind and helpful, except for one tall blonde hitter who never once glanced in my direction. I figured she was probably threatened by the "new blood." I decided to go out of my way to win her over as soon as I had the opportunity.

I had so much fun, practice seemed to soar by. I couldn't wait until tomorrow. It was refreshing to play with such seasoned players.

On my way out I looked at the roster and found the name of the tall blonde hitter: Anya.

I waved at Jessica, grabbed my gym bag, and headed to my dorm. Rounding a corner in the hallway I ran into Anya. The collision pushed her back against the wall. "Sorry." I laughed nervously.

"No problem." She shifted her backpack into place. "You did well today. But you need to work on your form."

"Thanks. I'll try to do better."

Irritation rose in me. I would have accepted that suggestion from Coach. Coming from Miss I'm-Better-Than-You who'd snubbed me the entire practice was humiliating. Being nice to her was going to be a real challenge. Her eyes and her voice were equally icy.

Anya flipped her long hair and continued down the hallway.

I stormed out the door and headed down the elm-tree-lined path to the myriad buildings I'd have to begin thinking of as home. Tears of frustration crept up. I stuffed them.

It's only the first day. Things will get better.

As I headed onto the Green in the center of the campus, I saw three guys in soccer uniforms about twenty feet in front of me. They must have finished practice and were heading somewhere to hang out together. They looked hot. I wondered if they might be going to the food court at Trabant University Center. If so, maybe I'd go over there myself.

I tried to check them out without getting caught staring. One of them had wavy blond hair exactly like Mike's. I snuck behind some bushes that were just tall enough to hide my face so I could observe them secretly.

As the blond guy walked along the pathway, his stride looked so much like Mike's, my heart leaped. Could the other two hotties see him?

His companions slapped the object of my pursuit on the arm and then went in the direction of Memorial Hall.

So they can see him! Maybe they're all three angels. In soccer uniforms?

Blond Guy entered Morris Library, a large brick building with white colonial trim. I waited a moment, then followed him inside.

A week from now this place would be bustling with students, but today it was practically empty. It smelled musty, but the smell of books made me inhale deeply. I loved that smell.

The librarian looked up at me from the front desk. "Can I help you?"

"No, thanks. I'm just touring the building."

Since the aisles all went the same direction, I could scan each one as I strolled along. After passing several rows of books, I saw him. I stopped so suddenly I almost tripped myself.

His back was turned to me, and he was paging through a book. I took a deep breath and walked in his direction. When I was about a foot from him, I said, "Excuse me."

He looked up, and I exploded in relief. "Mike! It *is* you."

Confusion shrouded his face. "Excuse me?"

"Real funny, Mike. What are you doing here?"

He stuck out his hand, "Sorry, but my name's not Mike. I'm Leo Palmer."

I couldn't figure out why Mike was playing this charade. "I'm from Rising Sun, Maryland."

"Really? What part?" I decided to play along for a while. Maybe there was someone in the library Mike didn't want to reveal himself to. But why? There'd been countless times he'd let me see him when no one else could.

"Do you know Sullivan Street on the west side?"

"That's only a few miles from where I live." The guy who had filled my gas tank that dark night almost a year ago lived on Sullivan Street. That guy was Mike. Wasn't it?

"So what's your name?" He shut the book he was holding and tucked it under his arm.

I looked up at his face. His expression was guarded. This really was a stranger.

"I'm Olivia. Sorry for acting so stupid, but you look just like this guy I knew back home. In fact, he could be your twin."

I wished he would suddenly laugh and confess to being the guardian angel I knew. But his expression didn't change.

Leo opened the book he'd been reading. On the binding was one word: *Angels.* I tilted my head. "Are you interested in angels?"

He flashed me the same smile I'd become so familiar with. "I am."

Coincidence?

The skin on my forearms prickled. *Was it some kind of sign?*

"Would you like to get some coffee?"

I was relieved he'd invited me to join him and didn't just walk away thinking I was some freak.

"Sure."

Leo slid the book back onto the library shelf.

We headed down the aisle toward the exit. I wondered what Leo thought about me. Did he wonder if I'd cooked up a pathetic pickup line to start a conversation with him? Or did he think I was a crazed lunatic?

When we got outside the building, we walked toward the food court.

Leo chatted, flashing that brilliant smile. I couldn't help being attracted to him. Leo was a flesh-and-bones version of Mike. I grinned. How brilliant of my guardian angel to take the form of a real person, a guy he knew I'd be attracted to someday.

Fluttering with anticipation, I glanced at Leo, then immediately looked at the ground as I felt heat rise from my neck to my face.

As we approached the cafe he opened the glass door for me. What a gentleman!

When we entered the room, a girl shouted, "Hi, Leo!"

I followed the voice, and my eyes came to rest on Anya. She was sitting at a booth with two of my new teammates.

Great. The one girl who hated me seemed very familiar with my new human angel. No doubt she was very attracted to him. Her face glowed until she saw me standing beside him.

Leo waved, then gestured toward me. "Anya, this is Olivia. She and I just found out we're from the same hometown."

Anya's expression darkened further. "Oh, that's interesting." She drew out the last word. She stuck her nose up in the air and stared me down. I felt like a weak animal about to be hunted by a stealthy beast. I smiled at her, waved at the other volleyball players, then walked up to the counter to place my order.

Oblivious to anything that just passed between Anya and I, Leo shouted, "I'll catch up with you later, Anya, OK?"

Leo stood so close behind me I could feel his breath on my neck. "What would you like?" His low voice so close to my ear felt like hot lava trickling though my head and down my spine.

I'd like to wrap my arms around you and not let go.

I looked at the menu behind the counter and ordered the first thing I saw. Iced mochaccino.

"I'll have the same." Leo placed a ten-dollar bill on the counter.

I felt like Anya's eyes were burning a hole in my back.

After we got our cups I walked as far away from her table as I could and took a seat by a window.

Leo sat across from me. "So, we obviously went to different high schools. Where'd you go?"

"Rising Sun High. How about you?"

"I went to Holy Angels."

I remembered the Catholic school several miles from where I grew up. What an ironic name.

Leo took a sip of his drink, then looked into my face. His eyes were different from Mike's. They were a deep grayish-blue. But they seemed to gaze into my soul. "What brings you to U of D?"

"I've always wanted to play volleyball here. I never thought I'd actually be recruited, but I was. Are you here on a soccer scholarship?"

"Yes. I was shocked to be selected since I went to a pretty small school."

I wanted to find a way to ask him if he was a Christian. Just because he went to Catholic school didn't mean he was a born-again believer. "Did you go to the Catholic church in town?"

"No. Community Bible Church. It's great. My family and I attended every week."

That was good news. At least he didn't only go to church at Christmas and Easter.

"How about you?"

"We went to Pike Valley Methodist."

"Oh, I've heard really great things about your church."

I took a sip of my drink and set it back down on the table in front of me. "So why were you looking at a book about angels?"

"I'm fascinated with them." Leo glanced sideways as if he was uncomfortable about answering in any more detail. "You want to take a walk across campus with me?"

I glanced at Anya. She returned another cold stare. "Sure." Any opportunity to get away from her sounded good to me.

We strolled until the sun went down, chatting the whole time. We had many things in common and knew a lot of the same people. I found it easy to talk to him after just meeting. Far more so than with any other boy I'd ever met.

This has to be the guy Mike referred to.

As the sky darkened into a pinkish blue, I noticed a black figure dash behind a bush along the walkway. I averted my gaze, knowing it was a demon and not wanting Leo to see me staring at something he couldn't see. But Leo's eyes looked in the same direction.

Does he see it too? If he's intrigued by angels, maybe he can see them— every kind.

When we stopped beside the parking lot near Memorial Hall, Leo looked at the sky. His eyes darted in every direction.

I looked up, too, and saw myriad angels streaming across the sky. There were so many I could hardly see the stars behind them. They made a cloud of sparkling white that went on as far as my eyes could see.

"Can you—?" I began.

"Yes, I can."

We had the same gift! Could I ask for anything more? Thank You, God!
Our eyes drifted to the adjacent parking lot, where an enormous
dark cloud hovered. It stretched over the entire concrete area, with a
trail streaming toward Academy Street. I'd never seen such a gigantic
force of evil spirits congregated in one location. Not even at the music
festival. I grabbed Leo's hand. I also felt a familiar invisible hand on my
shoulder. Mike.

Leo squeezed my fingers. "Whatever happens, we're in this together."

I had no idea what we might be getting into. But I knew I wanted to
go there with Leo. Between him, God, and my guardian angel, I had
nothing to fear.

ABOUT THE AUTHOR

DONNA STANLEY LIVES in the beautiful Endless Mountains of northeastern Pennsylvania with her husband, Jonathan, and their teenage daughter, Olivia. She attended Philadelphia Biblical University, Moody Bible Institute, and Mansfield University, where she studied angelology, demonology, and the anthropology of religion. She was a youth leader for ten years and a pastor's wife for sixteen years. She now serves as a young-adult mentor and leader in her local church. Donna has been writing articles for Christian retailing magazines, training manuals for start-up companies, and short stories for twenty years.

CONTACT THE AUTHOR

bestinshow@emlabradors.com

www.donnastanley.com

or

Visit "New Wings" on Facebook:

www.facebook.com/newwingsbook

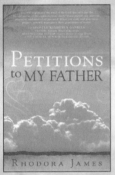

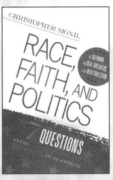